Panic Button

KYLIE LOGAN

BERKLEY PRIME CRIME, NEW YORK

THE BERKLEY PUBLISHING GROUP
Published by the Penguin Group
Penguin Group (USA) Inc.
375 Hudson Street, New York, New York 10014, USA

Penguin Group (Canada), 90 Eglinton Avenue East, Suite 700, Toronto, Ontario M4P 2Y3, Canada
(a division of Pearson Penguin Canada Inc.) • Penguin Books Ltd., 80 Strand, London WC2R 0RL,
England • Penguin Ireland, 25 St. Stephen's Green, Dublin 2, Ireland (a division of Penguin
Books Ltd.) • Penguin Group (Australia), 707 Collins Street, Melbourne, Victoria 3008, Australia
(a division of Pearson Australia Group Pty. Ltd.) • Penguin Books India Pvt. Ltd., 11 Community
Centre, Panchsheel Park, New Delhi—110 017, India • Penguin Group (NZ), 67 Apollo Drive,
Rosedale, Auckland 0632, New Zealand (a division of Pearson New Zealand Ltd.) • Penguin Books
Rosebank Office Park, 181 Jan Smuts Avenue, Parktown North 2193, South Africa • Penguin China,
B7 Jiaming Center, 27 East Third Ring Road North, Chaoyang District, Beijing 100020, China

Penguin Books Ltd., Registered Offices: 80 Strand, London WC2R 0RL, England

This is a work of fiction. Names, characters, places, and incidents either are the product of the author's
imagination or are used fictitiously, and any resemblance to actual persons, living or dead, business
establishments, events, or locales is entirely coincidental. The publisher does not have any control over
and does not assume any responsibility for author or third-party websites or their content.

PANIC BUTTON

A Berkley Prime Crime Book / published by arrangement with the author

PUBLISHING HISTORY
Berkley Prime Crime mass-market edition / January 2013

Copyright © 2012 by Connie Laux.
Excerpt from *Mayhem at the Orient Express* by Kylie Logan copyright © 2012 by Connie Laux.
Cover illustration by Jennifer Taylor.
Cover design by Annette Fiore Defex.
Interior text design by Kristin del Rosario.

ISBN: 978-0-425-25183-6

BERKLEY® PRIME CRIME
Berkley Prime Crime Books are published by The Berkley Publishing Group,
a division of Penguin Group (USA) Inc.,
375 Hudson Street, New York, New York 10014.
BERKLEY® PRIME CRIME and the PRIME CRIME logo are trademarks of
Penguin Group (USA) Inc.

PRINTED IN THE UNITED STATES OF AMERICA

10 9 8 7 6 5 4 3 2 1

ALWAYS LEARNING   **PEARSON**

More praise for

Button Holed

"Kylie Logan's *Button Holed* is absolutely terrific! I love it, and can't wait for the next installment in the series."

—Diane Mott Davidson,
New York Times bestselling author

"This is the opening act of an engaging amateur-sleuth mystery series, and if this book is any indication, readers have a special and original new series to enjoy. The protagonist is independent and resolute . . . She enlists a quirky crew to assist her on her quest. Kylie Logan overcomes the subgenre flaw of why the heroine must investigate with an entertaining plot and a strong cast led by a woman who refuses to be Button Holed." —*The Mystery Gazette*

"[A] unique and fun adventure . . . Fast-paced . . . A very different and very fun cozy series." —AnnArbor.com

"Lots of action and humor thrown together. First rate writing and plotting." —*Once Upon a Romance*

"This mystery was fun to read while still educating me about buttons. I also enjoyed Josie's character—she's fun, funny, and sharp . . . It was also nice to see someone embrace their 'button nerd' side." —*Fresh Fiction*

"I loved it. The writing is superb . . . The characters were interesting, the pace was fast, and there were plenty of clues planted." —*The Mystery Bookshelf*

"That's right, buttons. Who would have thought? . . . [*Button Holed*] was a very enjoyable mystery . . . [Josie is] a very entertaining narrator . . . And the plot unfolds in expert fashion . . . I know I'll never look at a button the same way again." —*CA Reviews*

For Kathleen Morrish,
goddaughter and friend

ACKNOWLEDGMENTS

Every author gets asked the question: Where do you get your ideas?

I have to say that for me, the answer to that question is different for every book I write. Sometimes, an idea comes from a bit of conversation I overhear. Sometimes, it can result from something I see online or in a newspaper. For *Panic Button*, the idea started to form the moment I read about charm strings.

What a wonderful, old-fashioned bit of Americana! Imagine young girls collecting buttons, trading them, getting them as gifts—all so those buttons could be strung and saved. There's bound to be folklore to accompany a hobby that charming, and of course, with the button strings there is. Collect one thousand buttons and your Prince Charming will come along. What writer could resist a legend that delicious!

There are other legends, too, involved in *Panic Button*, specifically, the legend of Lake Michigan pirate, Thunderin' Ben Moran. Thunderin' Ben is based on a real Great Lakes pirate, Roaring Dan Seavey, who was notorious in the early twentieth century.

ACKNOWLEDGMENTS

As always, my thanks go out to the button collecting community which has welcomed me—and the Button Box Mysteries—with open arms, to my writing friends who are always there with support and encouragement, and to my family who put up with the button magazines that come in the mail and the button museums and exhibits we visit.

Chapter One

"Do you believe in curses?"

I was so intent on studying the glorious buttons on the worktable in front of me, I only half heard Angela Morningside's question. So who can blame me! Naturally, I blinked, looked up, forced the pleasant whirr of button daydreams out of my head so I could focus on my customer, and said, "Huh?"

Angela did not seem to hold my inability to concentrate against me. Then again, we'd been working together on this particular project for about six weeks. No doubt, she already knew that antique buttons are to me what Hershey bars are to a chocoholic.

When she repeated herself, her expression wasn't exactly as kind as it was patient. And a little pained, too. "I asked you, Josie, do you believe in curses?"

Anyone who's ever met me knows that I am infinitely practical. Which means my first inclination was to laugh. I controlled myself. After all, Angela was the one who'd canceled each of our first three appointments and made no apology about the reason—her horoscope, she told me, informed her that making the one-hour trip south from Ardent Lake to Chicago on those days was not a good idea.

If she took horoscopes that seriously, it wasn't much of a stretch to think curses might not be far behind.

I flicked off the high-intensity lamp I'd had trained on the string of buttons spread over my worktable and slid off the stool where I'd been perched, the better to walk around to the front of the table and look Angela in the eye. This was not exactly as simple as it sounds since Angela was a full eight inches taller than my bit over five feet and broader by a mile. Still, I am all about making a valiant effort. I lifted my chin, the better to meet her question head-on. "You're serious?"

Angela's shoulders dropped. Her chin quivered.

Hey, I might be practical, but I am not heartless. I grabbed her elbow, piloted her to the nearest stool, and eased her onto it.

"You are serious." Understatement. I knew that as soon as Angela was seated and I got a good look at her eyes—and the fear that shimmered in them, as razor-sharp as sunlight sparking off ice. "Angela, tell me what's going on."

"I will. At least, I'll try." We were in the back room of my shop, the Button Box, and Angela's gaze jumped from the antique buttons on the charm string to the floor and stayed there. "No doubt you think I'm nothing but a crazy old lady. Post-menopausal delusions. That's what some of my friends have told me." Her gaze snapped to mine. "As if my age has anything to do with it. I'm not imagining any of this, Josie. And I'm not making it up."

In the six weeks since Angela had first called and told me about the charm string she'd inherited from her great-aunt, I'd come to learn that she was usually as serious as a heart attack and as levelheaded about her successful medical transcription firm back in Ardent Lake as I was about my shop, where I sold antique and collectible buttons to dealers, hobbyists, and discerning sewers and crafters. Sure, the woman not only read her horoscope each day, but actually remembered it and acted on its advice. That didn't mean she was crazy, did it? Out of the ordinary. Sure, I'd go along with that. But ruddy-cheeked, well-dressed, understated Angela never struck me as crazy.

"Of course you're not making any of it up," I said, because really, a woman like me found it impossible to even imagine that a woman like her could. "You're obviously upset. What's going on, Angela? And what does it have to do with the charm string?"

She tried for a smile, but it wavered around the edges. "I'm not surprised you figured out it's all about those damned buttons. I heard you were smart. That's one of the reasons I chose you when I looked for someone to put a value on that . . . thing."

Again, her gaze landed on the charm string. But only for a second. Angela might be trying to put on a brave face, but her body language spoke volumes. She sat up a little straighter and angled back her spine, putting as much distance as possible between herself, my worktable, and the charm string on it. A skitter shook her shoulders. "You knew, and I didn't even have to tell you. Can you feel the psychic vibrations, too?" Her palm flat, she put a hand over the buttons that, many years ago, her great-great-grandmother had painstakingly slipped onto a heavy piece of string the way so many girls had in the late-nineteenth and early-twentieth centuries. Making charm strings had been something of a fad back then. Girls collected and strung buttons, and the tradition was that each button had to be different. Buttons were traded, given as gifts, and brought back as souvenirs from places like Niagara Falls and New York City, and legend said that when button number one thousand came into a girl's life, so would her Prince Charming.

I can't say if that last bit about happily-ever-after held true for every charm string maker, but I do know that strings with all one thousand buttons on them are rare enough to make any button collector salivate.

Angela's charm string had exactly one thousand buttons on it, and I had been salivating over it since the day she called and asked me to take a look at the photos she'd taken of the buttons so that I could value the charm string for tax purposes before she donated it to her local historical society. Of course, I'd been trying to get her to sell it to me since that day, too.

So far, no dice.

Which, to me, was my own version of a curse.

I snapped out of the thought to find Angela still with

her hand poised over the buttons. "I can practically feel the bad luck bubbling off this thing," she said.

This was the point at which I seriously began reassessing my opinion of Angela.

Not that I could let on. I wasn't about to honk off a customer who was willing to pay for an appraisal just because she was a little . . . er . . . eccentric. Especially not when six weeks after she'd sent my button mania into overdrive by sending me the photos, she'd finally brought me the genuine article to study, admire, and yes, covet anew.

I scraped my palms against the black pants I was wearing with a spring green cotton sweater. "You keep looking at the buttons as if they're going to ignite and take the whole shop with them."

Angela glanced from side to side before she leaned forward and lowered her voice. "I wouldn't be surprised."

"So you really do think the buttons are going to bring you bad luck?"

"No, no, Josie. They're not *going* to bring me bad luck. They *have* brought me bad luck. Ever since the day I inherited them. And funny you should mention fire. I had a fire at home. Not two weeks after I brought these buttons into my house."

Before I followed my dream and opened the Button Box, I'd once worked as an administrative assistant at an insurance agency. I knew the statistics. "Home fires are not all that uncommon," I said, and believe me, I tried to put a kind spin on it. "As a matter of fact, every year—"

"Yes, yes. I know all that." Angela hopped off the

stool and paced the length of my workroom, from the counter where I have one of those mini-refrigerators, a microwave, and a coffeemaker, to the far wall, and back again. "Don't think other people haven't tried to tell me things like that. It was an accident, Angela. It was unfortunate. It happens all the time." Her voice singsonged over the false comfort the way I'm sure her friends' had when they offered it. "But don't you see, Josie, this is different!" She pulled to a stop directly in front of me and, fists on hips, looked down her long, slim nose.

"The fire came after the attempted break-in. And the attempted break-in just so happened to come the day after I got the charm string out of Aunt Evelyn's safety-deposit box and brought it home. That . . ." She stopped here like she expected me to interrupt and, with a glance, dared me to even think about it. "That was the same day the brakes went on my car. While I was on the freeway." The way her voice trembled said volumes about how terrifying the incident must have been.

"As far as that fire," she went on, "maybe the whole thing won't sound like just another statistic when I tell you that not four months earlier, there was a fire at my great-aunt's house, too."

"Aunt Evelyn? You mean the one who—"

"The one who left me the charm string in her will. Yes, that's the one." Angela's smile was *gotcha!* sleek. But only for a heartbeat. The next second, she was right back to looking upset. And pacing again.

"Don't you see, Josie, when Aunt Evelyn was still alive and was the one who owned the charm string, there was a fire in her kitchen, and nobody, not even the Ardent Lake Fire Department, has been able to figure out how it started. Luckily, I just happened to stop in that afternoon to drop off some cookies I'd baked for Evelyn. Good gracious, the woman was eighty-three. If she'd been there alone . . ." Angela didn't finish the thought. She didn't have to. The way her shoulders shook told me she knew exactly what would have happened to Aunt Evelyn if she hadn't shown up.

"And the fire at your house?" I asked.

"Same scenario." As if she'd been over it a thousand times and was no closer to finding an answer now than she had been all those other times, Angela shook her head. She had a head of curls that were far too dark for a woman her age, and they gleamed. "A fire in the middle of the kitchen table? Come on, that doesn't just happen. I certainly didn't leave a pile of newspapers there, and that's what caught on fire. And no one else was in the house. I live alone. I can't even sleep at night, thinking about how bad things might have gotten. At Aunt Evelyn's, you see, I jumped right into action as if I'd been trained. I grabbed a pitcher of water and put that fire right out. At my own house . . ." Though we'd only just met, I knew instinctively that Angela was not the kind of person who liked admitting to weakness. No woman who wore a crisp navy business suit and starched white blouse to what was, essentially, a casual meeting, could possibly be. She glanced away. "I smelled the smoke, I raced into the kitchen, and then . . . I froze." Her shrug told me she still didn't understand. "I stood there like a zombie watching my kitchen go up in smoke and I couldn't move a muscle. Things would have gotten really ugly if not for Larry."

For the first time since Angela had mentioned the curse, the lines of worry on her face smoothed out, and in the light of the overhead fluorescents, her eyes sparkled. "In fact, Larry is the only good thing that's happened to me since those buttons came into my life."

I'm a smart enough businesswoman to know that dealing with a happy customer is far easier than trying to talk one down who's convinced herself that her life is ruled by button bad luck. I knew this was one safe subject and I decided to stick to it.

"Tell me about him," I urged.

"Oh, Larry." Angela shook her shoulders in a way designed to make me think he was no big deal, but the little smile that tugged at the corners of her mouth said otherwise. "He owns the hardware store in Ardent Lake. Has for years. It's not a very big town, so of course, I've always seen him around and bumped into him now and then. His wife died a few years ago, and after that, he kept to himself for a long time. But now . . ."

Because she wouldn't say it, I figured I would. "He's your boyfriend."

Her cheeks turned the color of a Chicago sunset. "That sounds so silly, doesn't it? Like we're in high school or something. Larry and I, we're . . . friends. Well, I guess we're more than friends at this point. And you know, Josie, it's really wonderful. It's nice to have someone to go to the movies with and to cook dinner for. What with Aunt Evelyn dying and all I've had to do to settle her estate, Larry's been a real rock." Her cheeks still flaming, she glanced at me out of the corner of her eye. "He's cute, too."

It was impossible not to smile. Then again, I'd always been a believer when it came to happily-ever-afters. That was the only thing that could possibly explain how I'd been suckered by Kaz, my ex, into thinking that true love is as unalienable a right as life, liberty, and the pursuit of happiness.

But I digress. Thinking of how my marriage had gone sour wasn't exactly appropriate, what with Angela glowing like the spring sunshine outside the Button Box's front display window.

"I'm glad," I told her, and it was true. "But doesn't the fact that you've met Larry tell you something? You've got the charm string and it's got one thousand buttons on it. Prince Charming has come into your life!"

She twinkled like a beauty queen. "Don't think I haven't thought of that. It's one of the reasons I want to get this charm string out of my life as soon as possible. I can't take the chance that anything will go wrong. Not when it comes to Larry."

Talk about the perfect opening!

I whispered a prayer at the same time I said, "You could profit very nicely from the charm string, Angela. If you're interested in selling it rather than donating it—"

"Absolutely not." Her words were as firm as the way she held her jaw. "I don't mean to be difficult, but you've got to understand, Josie. This charm string is most definitely cursed. That means any money I made from selling it would bring bad luck, too. No. The only thing I can do is donate the charm string to the Ardent Lake Historical Society. Everything's arranged. I'll pick up the charm string from you tomorrow, and the next day, the historical society is having a tea in my honor. That's when I'll present them the charm string. They've got the display all ready and they're going to set the charm string into it in front of everyone at the tea." She brushed her hands together. "That will get it out of my life, once and for all."

"Of course, that's up to you." Big points for me, I managed to say this without weeping. "But before you make your final decision, there are a couple things you should know." I went over to the worktable and turned on the high-intensity lamp. "Most of the buttons on your charm string aren't all that remarkable," I told Angela. "They're all very old, which makes sense since the string was made by your great-great-grandmother. But old doesn't always mean valuable. Most of these were fairly common buttons at the time she made the charm string. There are some mother of pearl shirt buttons . . ." I found one and pointed it out, and Angela looked all right, but she refused to get too close. "There are brass buttons." I showed her some of those, too. "There are lots of black glass buttons. Individually, at a button show, most of these buttons wouldn't sell for more than a couple dollars each. But . . ." I swept a hand over the entire length of the charm string. "It's rare to even find partial charm strings these days. To find one that's complete . . . well, honestly, it's enough to take a button collector's breath away!"

Angela clutched her hands at her waist. "All the more

reason to get the thing displayed at the historical society. Then lots of people can see it and admire it."

"That's true. But there are collectors—and not just me, Angela, so don't think I'm saying this for my own selfish purposes—there are collectors who would pay you a bundle for this charm string."

Her chin came up a fraction of an inch. "I told you. I don't want the money. I don't care how much we're talking about."

"And you should also know . . ." I looked down the length of the string, and the button I was looking for wasn't hard to find. I tilted the light so that it glimmered against the button's enameled surface. "Like I said, most of the buttons here are common, but this one . . ." Every time I looked at this particular button, my breath caught in my throat. "It was made in China," I told Angela. "Sometime around 1850. It's enameled and the details are exquisite." The button was about an inch across and right in the center of it was a shimmering red fish set on a background that featured green aquatic plants and turquoise water. "I know collectors who would pay thousands for this button," I told her. I controlled myself; I didn't add that I was one of them.

Angela's lips clamped tight. "Don't care," she mumbled. "Don't want the money."

"That's fine." It wasn't. Not to me. To me, the charm string was the embodiment of every button fantasy I'd ever had. At least I was lucky enough to have it to myself for a while so I could compare the actual buttons to the photos Angela had sent and make my final decisions regarding values. I took comfort (not much) in the thought. "I figured it was only fair to tell you."

"And I appreciate it." Angela backed toward the door. "I hope you can appreciate how I feel about the whole thing."

I did. Even if I didn't understand it.

It was clear Angela was anxious to get out of the Button Box and away from the charm string, and I didn't try to stop her. After all, the sooner she left, the sooner I could immerse myself in studying the buttons. Two days weren't nearly enough, but they were all I had, and I was anxious to get to work.

"You'll be back tomorrow evening?" I walked to the front of the shop with Angela. "I'm usually open until six, but I can stay late if that works better for you." I prayed it did. That meant extra hours with the charm string.

"I'll call," Angela assured me, pulling open the front door of the shop and stepping out into the bustle of my Old Town neighborhood. When she looked down at the sidewalk, there was a hitch in her step, and she hopped on one foot, then turned around and gave me a sheepish smile. "Step on a crack," she said, pointing down at the fracture in the sidewalk, "and break your mother's back."

I smiled, too, like I knew she was kidding. Even though I was pretty sure she wasn't.

"I'll talk to you tomorrow," I'd already said, when I realized Angela wasn't listening. Her gaze was riveted to a park bench a few storefronts down where a whole bunch of crows were digging into what looked to be the last of a hamburger and an order of fries that had been left on the sidewalk.

I grimaced. "Sorry," I said, "not exactly the ambiance the merchants around here want. I bet somebody left it for LaSalle. He's a stray dog we've all sort of adopted," I explained, looking up and down the street. "I'm surprised he hasn't been by for his breakfast. He usually is by now. It's tacky leaving food around, I know. We're not really a garbage dump, and the crows, they're not usually anywhere around here. They must have come over from one of the parks near the lake."

"Crows." Angela's face was as pale as ashes. "Don't you know what it means, Josie? Haven't you counted them? Don't you know the old saying about crows?"

I didn't have to ask what she was talking about, because Angela filled me in. "One's bad," she said. "Two's luck. Three's health. Four's wealth. Five's sickness. And six . . ." Her lips moving, she counted wordlessly, then swallowed hard. "Six is death."

Chapter Two

BY THE TIME EIGHT O'CLOCK THAT EVENING ROLLED around, I was all but ready to throw in the towel and admit that I believed in Angela's curse.

After all, the more time I spent with the charm string, the more I realized the curse applied to me. I was cursed to have only a few more hours with the fabulous buttons, cursed to be lured in by their beauty and their history and the amazing fact that the charm string had remained intact all these years—only to have to surrender it the next day when Angela showed up.

If that wasn't a button lover's curse, I didn't know what was.

The thought swirling in my head, I sighed and told myself to get a grip.

"OK, yeah, so you're cursed," I mumbled, snapping a

picture of a hard rubber button embossed with a geo-metrical pattern. "But you're blessed, too, and don't you forget it." I angled the button so that I could get a photo of the backmark on the underside that said it was a "Goodyear."

"You've got a few more hours tomorrow to play with these buttons until your heart's content," I reminded myself, and that cheered me right up. Still smiling, I slid the charm string a few inches farther down the table and trained the light on the last of the buttons I had to photograph. Technically, I had begun photographing from the wrong end, starting with the buttons that had been strung last and working my way to those Angela's great-great-grandmother had used to begin her charm string.

How did I know?

There was no mystery there.

Each girl who made a charm string started with what was called a "touch button," one button that was a little larger than the others. This touch button, curiously, was just about the same size as the hard rubber Goodyear button, and at the same time I wondered why Angela's great-great-grandmother had started her string with two buttons that were so similar in size, I told myself it really didn't matter. Like the beautiful enameled button with the red fish on it, these two buttons had probably been gifts, or just too interesting for her to resist. In a way, the fact that she was willing to flaunt traditional charm string convention told me a lot about Angela's great-great-grandmother.

And that only made me even fonder of her buttons.

As I had done with all the other buttons, I took

measurements and made notes about this last button. It was metal and there was a picture on it that showed a small, squat building on the left and another, taller brick building behind it. I grabbed my magnifying glass and took a closer look. A schoolhouse, complete with a chunky tower and a bell. Quaint. Not very valuable. And all the more charming because of it.

Satisfied I'd done all I could for the moment, I turned off the light and rolled my neck, banishing the kinks that had settled between my shoulder blades in the hours I'd been busy. There were still a couple buttons I wanted to know more about, but my research would have to wait until morning. I'd promised to meet Nevin Riley for a drink at eight thirty at a new place that had just opened down the street, and I still had to close up the shop and tally the day's sales. Two picky knitters looking for the perfect buttons for the sweaters they were making, a collector from Des Moines who had heard good things about the shop (hurray!) and made a special trip to Chicago to visit, a local artist who wasn't as interested in the history of buttons as he was in the shapes, a mother and daughter working on scrapbooks. And the charm string.

All things considered, it had been a really good day at the Button Box.

And on top of all that, it would be just a little while and I'd get to see Nev.

Were we a couple?

Interesting question, and honestly, I'm not sure I knew the answer, at least not at that moment. Nev and I had been seeing each other semisteadily since that fateful day I opened the Button Box and found burglars, then a murder victim, inside. Over the last few months, we'd discovered we liked lots of the same things: quiet dinners, walks along the lakeshore, Cubs baseball. Nev was smart, and he was cute. He was sweet and considerate, and though he had a sort of teddy-bear exterior that hid it well, he was one heck of a tough cop.

I liked him.

He liked me.

And at this point, neither one of us was anxious or ready for the relationship to go any further.

All in all, what I had with Nev was ideal.

And so unlike everything I'd had with Kaz (which was more like grand opera than a Hallmark Channel movie), that I thanked my lucky stars every single day.

In spite of the hours I'd spent hunched over my worktable, there was a spring to my step when I zipped to the front of the store to lock the door, collected the day's receipts from the rosewood desk where my computer sat next to an array of button research books, and finished the day's paperwork in the back room.

I gave the charm string one last look before I turned out the workroom lights and grabbed my purse and jacket, and yes, I admit it, I mumbled a quick "goodnight" to it, too. Blame it on the buttons. Any button collector would understand.

I slipped on my jacket and headed outside. I hadn't even finished locking the shop door when I felt a wet nose nuzzle my hand.

"Hey, LaSalle!" I took my key out of the lock of the robin's egg blue front door of the brownstone and dropped my key ring in my purse before I turned to give the dog a pat on the head. LaSalle was what would charitably be termed a "mix." In other words, he was a little of this, a little of that, and a lot of things that didn't exactly match each other. He had the floppy ears of a hound, the broad muzzle and big nose of a terrier, and the short legs of a corgi. As for color, well, it was already after dark and the streetlight a couple shops down needed to be replaced, but that hardly mattered. I'd known LaSalle since he first showed up in the neighborhood a month or so earlier, and I knew he was a mottled mixture of white, black, and brown. Classic mutt, and as lovable as any dog I'd ever met. So lovable, in fact, that a couple of the local merchants (yes, including me) had actually thought about taking him home.

LaSalle would have none of it. He was a scrapper, a street dog, as happy to patrol our Old Town neighborhood as he was to greet us as we came and went. Between those of us who fed him, and the florist across the street who'd taken him in to the nearest vet to be neutered, we made sure he was safe and warm.

"You missed out on your breakfast." At the same time I took a look down the street to where the crows had polished off the burger and fries, I bent to scratch a hand over LaSalle's head. I was rewarded by a thumping tail and a sound from deep in LaSalle's throat not unlike the one I make when a particularly interesting button catches my eye. "Not to worry. I knew you'd be by eventually."

I'd tucked a bit of the turkey sandwich I'd brought for dinner into my jacket pocket, and I set my purse down on the sidewalk to fish it out.

That's when it happened.

No sooner had purse touched pavement than, like a shot, a person raced out of the alley between my brownstone and the one next door. Man or woman, I couldn't tell. I registered only a few quick details: dark pants, a hoodie pulled over his (or her) head and down low over her (or his) brow.

Before I could do anything more than flinch and step back, that person snatched my purse off the sidewalk and kept on running.

"Hey!" Not exactly the greatest deterrent to purse snatching, but the only thing I could think to say at the moment.

Have no fear. Turns out, LaSalle did my talking for me.

Before the thief had gone three steps, the dog had him by the back of the pant leg.

Startled, the thief yelped and dropped my purse, and once he did, the dog let go. LaSalle actually might have gone back for a real bite if the thief didn't dart into the street directly in front of a tour bus.

I screeched, clapped my hands over my mouth, and held my breath. That is, until the tour bus rolled by, and when it was gone, I saw my attacker safe, sound, and unsquished on the other side of the street. He took one look in my direction, and since LaSalle was sitting at my side, growling louder than any dog his size should have been able to, the thief apparently decided my purse wasn't worth the effort. He scurried around the corner and disappeared.

"Thanks, buddy. If it wasn't for you . . ." I didn't want to think about it, so I just scratched one hand behind the dog's ears. It was the first I realized I was shaking.

Apparently, LaSalle didn't hold that against me. He licked my hand and I rewarded him with the turkey sandwich, picked up my purse, and headed off to meet Nev.

Was I thinking about curses at the time?

Maybe I should have been. Then everything that happened the next day wouldn't have surprised me.

IT STARTED BRIGHT and early the next morning when I went to put the pictures of the buttons onto my computer and realized the download mojo wasn't working.

Not the best way to start a Wednesday, but hey, as far as curses went, this one wasn't so bad. I'd gotten to the Button Box just as the sun was coming up somewhere behind an elephant gray layer of dark storm clouds (the better to have more time with the charm string) so I wasn't feeling pressured. Plus, the folks in India were still awake and answering the camera company's service calls. It took a couple tries, and a second pot of coffee, but by the time nine o'clock rolled around and I was ready to turn around the sign in the window and declare the shop open, the pictures were downloaded and I was filling in the information on each button in the computer database I'd established for the charm string.

I had a couple more buttons to research, a couple more calls to make to ask friends their opinions about history and value, but other than that, I'd be ready whenever Angela showed up.

It was shallow of me, but I hoped her horoscope would tell her to keep close to home that day. Sure, I was nearly done with the research I had to do on her behalf, but

I wouldn't have minded a couple more days alone with the wonderful charm string.

"Well, you're probably not going to get it, so you better use the time you have," I reminded myself, and went into the back workroom to do just that.

The rest of the morning went by in blessed, curse-free peace and quiet. Well, except for a couple grumbles of thunder. The mail arrived and, along with it, my monthly royalty check for the costumes I'd once designed for a movie that had recently become a campy cult classic. Royalty checks, I reminded myself with a grin, are just the opposite of curses. In fact, this one arriving when it had was a spot of good luck. I'd been thinking about getting another glass-topped display case for the shop and had recently seen one that was just the right size at an antique shop near my apartment. I'd stop on the way home, first at the bank to deposit the check, then to buy the display case, and I made a quick phone call to the nice folks at the antique store to tell them to have the case ready for me.

That's when I was told someone had just come into the shop out of nowhere, didn't quibble about price the way I'd planned to, and walked out with the display case.

Cursed?

I didn't think so.

I was, however, willing to admit to being disappointed. The display case would have been perfect, and I'd already picked out a spot for it near the front window so that when I filled it with glass buttons, they'd catch the light—and customers'—eyes. But have no fear, I eased my dashed hopes by concentrating on the charm string. In fact, I didn't even realize a couple hours had passed until I heard the chink of the small brass bell that hung just inside the front door.

My first thought was "customer," and grateful as I always am for people who appreciate buttons as much as I do, I turned off the high-intensity lamp and scooted to the other side of the worktable.

That is, until a second thought hit.

"Kaz." I grumbled the name at the same time I stopped long enough to look over at the pile of mail and that royalty check that was right on top of it.

When it came to money—namely, money I had and he wanted—Kaz had radar.

"Well, not this time," I told myself, and lifting my chin and squaring my shoulders, I quickly rehearsed all the things I would tell him—about how he couldn't depend on me to get him out of whatever financial mess he found himself in—before I told him to get lost.

The words died on my lips and the tight little knot of aggravation in my gut loosened when I stepped out of the back room.

"Stan!"

Stan Marzcak and I lived across the hall from each other, but he was more than just a neighbor. Stan was a friend, he was family, and he smiled and waved a hello from the door, shaking raindrops off the shoulders of his navy blue Windbreaker. "You look like you were expecting someone else," he said.

There was no use lying. Not to Stan. He'd figure out the truth sooner or later, anyway, and besides, he knew the routine. "Royalty day," I said. "I figured Kaz had the date circled in red on his calendar and was here to tell me that some friend or relative or acquaintance of an old friend's brother's cousin's mother-in-law was in some kind of terrible trouble and only an infusion of cash from me could help. Come to think of it . . ." I guess I hadn't thought of it. Not until that moment. That would explain why a chill like icy fingers traced a pattern up my spine. "You know, I haven't heard from Kaz in a while. That's kind of strange."

"I figured you were going to say something more like *refreshing*."

Stan was right. I jiggled my shoulders to get rid of the odd feeling that had settled there, and laughed. "Maybe Kaz is finally growing up," I suggested.

"And learning to be self-sufficient," Stan countered.

"And taking responsibility for his own life." It was such an odd thought, it left me speechless for a moment. "Now that," I pointed out when I recovered, "would be refreshing."

Stan laughed and took a couple more steps into the store. He was carrying a white deli bag and he held it up for me to see. "Brought lunch," he said. "Figured you'd be so busy with those buttons you've been telling me about, you wouldn't have time to get anything for yourself."

Nice of him, and I told him so. It was also a little out of character. Not that Stan isn't considerate. And generous. And helpful. But he doesn't usually show up without calling first, and Stan doesn't usually call unless something is up.

If instincts can bristle, mine were suddenly at full

attention. Especially when I realized that now that the small talk was over, Stan was shifting uncomfortably from foot to foot, and he refused to meet my eyes. "So you just happened to stop by, huh?"

"Sure." It would have been easier to believe him if Stan didn't ignore me completely and march through the Button Box with more energy than any seventy-something-year-old guy should have. He plunked down the lunch bag on my desk. "I didn't have anything else to do today."

I'd like to think I could take a friend's word at face value. Call me suspicious. When Stan and I last talked, I clearly remembered him saying he was heading up to Evanston to see his new great-grandson that day.

I cocked my head and gave him the kind of look I imagined he'd once used on the bad guys who'd had the misfortune to cross his path back when he was a Chicago homicide detective. Just so he knew he wasn't pulling the wool over my eyes, I crossed my arms over my chest, too, and stepped back, my weight against one foot.

"Uh-huh," was all I said.

So much for trying to make an impression; Stan barely spared me a look. Instead, he made a big show out of opening the deli bag, reaching inside, and pulling out a sandwich. "You want this in the back room?" he asked. "I know you don't like to eat out here and take the chance that your buttons will get something spilled on them."

"I don't like people who are shady, either," I reminded him, though I shouldn't have had to.

Like the *shady* comment couldn't possibly have been meant for him, he dropped the sandwich back where it came from, lifted the bag, and held it close to his chest, the picture of innocence. "What are you talking about, Josie?" he asked.

Rather than screech my frustration, I led the way into the workroom and coiled up the charm string so that I could tuck it onto a nearby shelf. At the same time I pulled a second stool over to the table, I tossed a look over my shoulder at Stan. "I'm talking about you," I said, patting the table to show him where to put the bag. "You didn't just stop in, and don't pretend you did. You talked to Nev, didn't you? I mean, since I saw him last night."

His lips pursed, Stan looked up at the ceiling. It's a nice ceiling. Original to the brownstone, which means late Victorian. It's tin and is embossed with a beautiful small floral pattern and painted a bright white to make the most of the light in the windowless workroom.

But to a man who'd seen it dozens of times, I was pretty certain it wasn't interesting enough to warrant such a close inspection.

"If you say 'Nev who?' I'm going to bonk you with this sandwich bag," I growled.

Stan grimaced and gave up on the ceiling, peeling out of his jacket. "Well, what do you expect the guy to do?" he asked. "First of all, he's a cop so of course he's going to be concerned. Second of all, the guy's crazy about you. He cares what happens to you, and he worries about you, too. So you meet him for a drink last night and you tell him somebody tried to steal your purse and—"

"And so he sent you over to babysit me?" I may have been annoyed, but I was also famished. I peeked in the bag, made the important decision between pastrami and corned beef, extracted the sandwich I wanted, and pushed the bag toward Stan. "I'll tell you exactly what I told Nev. It was random. And it was my fault. As soon as I set my purse down, that creep saw his opportunity. And when he realized he was up against the mighty LaSalle, he disappeared. What do they call that, Stan? A crime of opportunity? Well, that's exactly what it would have been if not for the dog. Which means it's not like the scumbag is going to waltz in here and stick up the place." My laugh was anything but funny. "He'd be plenty surprised if he did. I've got thirty dollars in the cash drawer and another seventeen in my purse. That's all he would have gotten last night if he'd made off with it. Seventeen dollars. Hardly seems worth it."

"Our perp didn't know that." While I was busy lecturing him (yeah, like that was going to get me anywhere), Stan had retrieved the corned beef sandwich. He added mustard and a dollop of horseradish. "And I don't want to worry you, Josie, but you don't know it was random. He might have been staking out the place."

"A button shop?" I asked, only since my mouth was full, it came out sounding more like, "Abhtnshp?" I chewed and swallowed. "You and Nev must have been comparing notes. That's exactly what he said."

"We didn't need to compare notes. We attended the same police academy." Stan made sure he paused here, just to be sure I got the message. "You can't be too careful, kiddo. You should know that what with that actress getting killed here, then everything that happened at that button convention of yours."

He didn't need to remind me. The fact that Josie Giancola, button purveyor, would ever find herself mixed up with murder was as far-fetched as thinking that LaSalle would turn detective.

I opened one of those little plastic packs of mustard with my teeth and coated my sandwich. "Maybe you and Nev would rest easier if you knew the whole story. Then you'd know that guy wasn't staking out the store. He just appeared—poof! You know, because of the curse."

I was going for funny, but Stan wasn't laughing. He narrowed his eyes and gave me a look designed to get the whole truth and nothing but.

I gave it to him. At least as much as I could remember. The bit about Angela and how superstitious she was, and how she actually thought that the wonderful buttons on the wonderful charm string had some crazy power to bring bad luck.

"See?" I asked when I was finished with the details. "Your theory about someone watching me and just waiting for me to set down my purse in a public place is as silly as Angela's theory that bad luck follows the charm string. There's no such thing as bad luck, I know you believe that, Stan. You're too logical not to. And there's no such thing as curses, either. Absolutely, positively not."

Brave words.

They would have been far more effective if, at that very moment, every light in the shop didn't go out.

Chapter Three

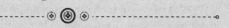

"Don't move an inch."

Honestly, I didn't need Stan to tell me. Any other day, the lack of light wouldn't have mattered nearly as much, but that particular afternoon, with thunder rumbling overhead and Chicago blanketed in a thick layer of black clouds, the shop was plunged into darkness.

"I'll go into the basement and . . . ow!" I heard the bang before Stan's grunt, and I knew he'd run into the corner shelves near the back door. "I'll check the fuse box in the basement," he said once he'd grumbled a couple unrepeatable words, and I pictured his teeth clenched and his upper lip stiff. "If you have a flashlight."

"Of course I have a flashlight." I felt my way along the worktable, took the three steps I knew separated the table from the shelves where Stan was standing, and stuck out a hand toward the shelf at nose level. My fingers closed around the cool cylinder of a small metal flashlight. "Here." I poked it through the dark toward where I knew Stan was, and when he reached for it and I assumed he had a hold of it, it plunked to the floor.

"Don't move an inch," he said again when I was just about to, but then, I guess he didn't want to get stepped on while he scrambled around on his hands and knees. When he stood up again, he was huffing and puffing.

I heard the click of the flashlight's *on* button. Nothing happened. Another click. A third. "What's that you said about a curse?" he grumbled. "Maybe that lady with those old buttons was right. These batteries are dead."

"You're kidding me, right?" It wasn't like I didn't trust him, but I groped through the darkness to pry the flashlight out of Stan's hands. I tried to turn it on, and when nothing happened, I shook the flashlight, tried the button again, and groaned. "I replaced the batteries in this thing not two weeks ago. I know I did."

"Not to worry." Stan's face suddenly glowed an eerie blue in the light of his cell phone screen. "I can find my way using this."

He did, and less than a couple minutes later, the lights were back on.

When Stan came back upstairs and into the workroom, his snowy brows were low over his eyes. "Breaker wasn't tripped," he said. "Not like there was an overload or anything."

"The power must have been out to the whole neighborhood," I said.

He shook his head. Once. When Stan does that, it's a sure sign he's convinced he's right. "I don't think so, Josie." His polite way of saying he knew so. "Looked more like someone turned off the breaker."

"Emilie, I bet." I glanced toward the tin ceiling Stan had been eying such a short time before. The travel agent who worked upstairs from me had a tendency to try and fix things she should never touch. "I bet there's something wrong with her computer. She's convinced that every time it hiccups, it's because something's wrong with the electricity in the building."

Stan pursed his lips. "Maybe. But if that was the case, when all the lights went kerflooey, you'd think I would have seen her down in the basement. And when I came in a while ago, her car wasn't out on the street where she usually parks."

I did not dispute this last bit of information. Retired or not, cops have a gift for remembering such things.

"Then how . . ." I bit off the question because I knew what Stan was going to say, and I didn't need to get teased about Angela's curse. "Well, it's fixed now," I said instead. "And I can get back to work."

"And I'm going to go to Walgreens and pick up some batteries for you." Stan headed to the front of the store. "You should always have a working flashlight."

He was right, and I didn't argue. I finally had the shop to myself again, and I got right down to work. I had the phone in my hand and was about to make a call to a fellow collector in Cleveland about a couple of the charm string buttons when the bell above the front door clanged.

Customer, I hoped.

At the same time I knew my luck wouldn't hold.

"Kaz," I told myself, and in a twist of fate designed to make me believe in déjà vu if not in curses, I stepped out of the back room only to find Stan standing at the front door.

"Forgot my wallet," he muttered, his lips thin with disgust. "I never forget my wallet. It's not like I'm an old man or anything." Still mumbling, he retrieved not only his wallet but his Windbreaker, too, and went on his way.

This time he was gone for a while.

A really long while.

I wrapped up the first phone call and another to a collector in Baltimore who answered the questions my Cleveland friend couldn't. I finished the last of my pastrami sandwich. Because I couldn't resist it, I took a few more pictures of the beautiful enameled fish button, and I even waited on a particularly picky customer who was looking for buttons for a baby's christening gown.

No Stan.

I actually had the phone in my hands and was all set to call Walgreens before I came to my senses. I'd told Stan I didn't appreciate having a babysitter, and I imagined he wouldn't, either.

Still . . .

Stan was no spring chicken, and anything could happen between the shop and Walgreens. If he wasn't back in ten minutes . . .

When the bell above the front door rang, I breathed a sigh of relief and swore I wouldn't let him know how worried I'd been.

That resolve lasted about ten seconds when I walked

out front and realized Stan wasn't the only one who'd stepped into the Button Box. There was a uniformed Chicago cop there, too.

"What happened? Are you all right? Was anybody hurt?"

The way the questions poured out of me and the fact that my heart was suddenly beating double time and making my blood whoosh in my ears, I wouldn't have heard even if I did give either of them a chance to answer. I raced the entire length of the shop and looked Stan over. He didn't seem to be hurt, and if anything had happened to him, health-wise, he wouldn't have been there, right? They would have taken him to the hospital in an ambulance.

"So?" My throat suddenly tight, my gaze darted between Stan and the cop.

Stan stomped past me. "That's the last time I go to that store," he grumbled. "There was this kid behind the counter, see, and she saw me looking at the batteries, and I guess . . . well, I don't guess anything. I know she must have been high or something. Imagine her thinking that I could possibly steal anything!"

"Shoplifting? You?" Honestly, it was so out of the realm of possibility, I almost laughed. Except for the cop still standing near my door.

I spun to face him. "You don't really think—"

"We got it all straightened out, ma'am," the cop said. He was young, fresh-faced, and he held his hat in his hands. "There was a little mix-up and—"

"You call that a mix-up?" Stan's cheeks were maroon. "Back in my day—"

"You're right, sir." I could tell this cop would go far in the department. He had a soothing voice, and he knew how to use it to say all the right things. "And believe me, I understand how you feel. I'm sure Detective Riley did, too."

My turn to interrupt. "Nevin got involved? How? He's working the afternoon shift. He shouldn't even be at the station yet."

"Not exactly involved." Stan had never finished his corned beef sandwich, and he went into the back room to retrieve it and took a chomp. "I had the store manager call him at home. You know, to tell them who I was and how that crazy girl must have been mistaken. And Nev . . ." Stan chewed and swallowed. "Well, she knows he's a nice guy," he explained to the officer in a classic example of too much information. "They're dating, you see. Nev . . ." Stan looked my way. "He vouched for me, and explained everything to Officer Ramirez here."

I looked over my shoulder at the officer. "Thanks," I said.

"No problem, ma'am." He set his hat back on his head. "Funny thing is, after I had another talk with that clerk at the store, she said she didn't think Mr. Marzcak really took those batteries in the first place. Said she didn't know what she was thinking when she said she did. It was like the whole situation was . . . I dunno . . . all confused or something, and then Mr. Marzcak, he told me about those old buttons of yours and the curse, and I remember what my *abuela* used to say about bad luck and—"

I opened the door and stepped back so Officer

Ramirez could leave. Don't worry, I was polite. After all, I didn't point out that he and his *abuela* were both nuts if they thought I put any stock in superstition.

I didn't mention it to Stan, either, after the cop was gone. I didn't need to. By the time I was heading back into the workroom, he was wiping a dab of mustard off his chin.

"I dunno, Josie," was all he said. "You know I don't believe in curses, either, but it's pretty hard to ignore facts."

Somehow, I managed.

"Hey, listen to this."

Stan was sitting across my desk from me, reading the newspaper, and when he spoke, I looked up from the book I'd been paging through. It was nearly six that evening, and though I'd completed all the real research I had to do in regards to the charm string buttons, that didn't stop me. I was happily perusing button book after button book, looking for examples of buttons that were similar to the ones on the string and making notes. Button collecting, see, isn't all about the thrill of the hunt, though that's certainly part of the mania. I always feel a rush of adrenaline when I walk into the vendor room of a button show or through the front door of an antique shop because I never know what treasure I'll find—that little button that's been ignored for years, or even decades, and is just what I need to complete one of my collections or cater to a customer.

But there's a research component to button collecting,

too, and I'll be the first to admit that I love it. Looking through books, sketching timelines, digging into history . . . thanks to a hobby that had turned into a life's work, I often felt as if I was the luckiest woman in the world.

Well, except for the couple murders that had dogged me in the last year.

I shrugged away the uncomfortable feeling that snaked over my shoulders, concentrating instead on the positives. Like the fact that Angela had yet to call so I had some extra time with the charm string. And Stan had (finally!) calmed down. While I'd taken a few more pictures and consulted a few more reference books, making the last of my notations on the spreadsheet I'd print out for Angela, he'd been looking through the day's *Tribune*.

Yes, he could just as easily have read the newspaper at home.

No, I couldn't convince him I didn't need a bodyguard and he could leave. At this point, it was so late in the evening, he had announced that the only proper thing for us to do was to have dinner together. Remember what Angela said about me being smart? I was smart enough not to be fooled; Stan didn't want me to leave the shop alone, just in case that purse thief was lurking somewhere in the ever-deepening shadows outside.

"They're draining an entire reservoir in some little town north of here to do repairs on it," Stan said, scanning the newspaper and interrupting my thoughts. "They flooded over the old town when the reservoir was built. Ardent, it was called."

"Hmmm." I stopped to consider. "Angela lives in Ardent Lake. I wonder if they're close to each other."

Stan read some more. "Doesn't say," he finally commented. "But it does say that they're anxious to see what's left of the old town. Been under water since back in the seventies. And then there's this article." He ran a finger the length of the page and poked it against a photo of a man in a dark suit and top hat. "There's this guy over in Elmhurst who thinks he's the reincarnation of Harry Houdini. Even says he can do magic tricks and he's never taken a lesson."

Stan was obviously reading the odd news of the day.

I gave him a quick smile before I set aside my book and got up to walk over to one of the glass display cases near the wall. "Maybe that magician can explain how curses work."

Stan crossed his arms over his chest and plunked back in the chair. "I never said I believed any of that stuff about the curse, Josie. I just said it's best to keep the facts in mind. You can't dispute facts. As a detective, you know that."

"Except I'm not. A detective, that is." There was a feather duster nearby and I grabbed it and whooshed it over the top of the case, then moved from there to the case closer to the front window. "All I want to do is sell buttons," I told Stan and reminded myself.

"Maybe, but you've solved a couple murders, and that's one of those facts that can't be denied. Don't worry." He got up from his chair and stretched. "I'm not going to talk you into admitting that bad luck exists. In my experience, bad luck happens because people make it happen to other people. The stars or the planets or those buttons of yours, they don't really have anything to do with it."

"Exactly." I kept on dusting, working my way around the perimeter of the shop to the front door, and when I got there, I flipped over the sign in the window to tell those passing by that the store was now officially closed. I did not, though, turn off the lights as I usually did that time of night. When she showed up, I didn't want Angela to think I'd forgotten about her.

"Except she said she'd call when she was leaving home," I mumbled to myself, strolling back toward my desk. "Don't you think it's odd? She definitely needs the charm string back today. That tea at the historical society is tomorrow afternoon."

Stan shrugged. "You need to look at the problem from all the angles," he said. "Maybe her cell phone ran out of juice. Or maybe she forgot she was supposed to call."

"Angela doesn't strike me as the type of woman who forgets anything."

Stan narrowed his eyes the way he always does when he's thinking. "An organized, methodical woman, and yet she believes in curses."

Obviously, the only answer I had to that was a shrug. "Angela's very matter of fact. Very even keel. I mean, except for the stuff about the curses. In fact, if it wasn't for that and her reading her horoscope every day, I'd say Angela was the most levelheaded person I've ever met."

I stand by this description of Angela. At least I did until I heard a furious pounding on the front door and hurried over there to find Angela on the other side of the display window, her hair standing up as if she'd been pulling on it and her face puffy. She was wearing green sweatpants, a hot pink T-shirt, no socks, and a pair of Crocs that looked like they'd last been worn in a muddy garden.

I unlocked the door and pulled it open, looking in wonder at the woman who had been so well put together the last time I saw her. "Angela! I've been waiting for your call. What happened?"

She pushed past me and into the Button Box. "Just get me those damned buttons," she growled. "Now. I can't wait to get them out of my life forever."

It didn't take any magical powers to know something had gone haywire in Angela's life, or that whatever it was, she was bound to blame it on the charm string. If her wardrobe wasn't a giveaway, the dark smudges under Angela's eyes were. So was her red nose. "Are you all right?"

Her jaw stiff, she sniffled. "I'm fine. It's just . . . allergies. My miserable allergies. I need to get home and take some medication and get to bed. I feel miserable, and I don't want to feel miserable and look miserable tomorrow at the tea. I need my rest. That means I don't have time to stand here and chitchat."

I got the message and went into the back room for the floral hatbox Angela had used to bring me the charm string. I'm not saying I was a convert to the believe-in-curses camp, but I do admit to peeking inside the box, just to make sure the charm string was in there where I'd put it along with a copy of the spreadsheet I'd prepared.

"You know, Angela," I said, walking back to the front

of the shop, my hands tight around the box that contained the precious cargo, "it's not too late to change your mind. I'm still interested in buying."

Her shoulders shot back. Her chins quivered. "No. I like you, Josie. I can't let anything happen to you. Besides . . ." She was as reluctant to take the box out of my hands as I was to let it go, but after a couple seconds of awkward tug-of-war, I relinquished my hold. "Maybe once this thing is safely in the museum, I can break the curse. Once and for all. Maybe I can even . . ." Her voice clogged. "Maybe there's a way to reverse some of the bad things that have already happened. Do you think so?" Her eyes snapped to mine, suddenly so full of desperate hope, I couldn't help feeling sorry for her.

My voice was wistful when I looked at the hatbox. "I guess the only way to find out is to give away the charm string."

"Yes." Angela was convinced. She held the hatbox close to her chest. "That's exactly what I'm going to do. Hear that, Universe?" Like she actually expected some unseen force to answer, she looked up and all around, and when the only response she heard was silence, her shoulders fell.

"I've got to get home," she said. "Back to Ardent Lake. One more night to have this wretched thing in my possession. Then . . ." Angela breathed in deep and let the breath out slowly. "Then maybe I'll have some peace."

"I hope that's true." It was a noncommittal sort of thing to say, but I was sincere enough. For all her quirks, Angela seemed a nice enough person. If donating the charm string eased her mind, so be it.

Even if it did just about kill me to think of how I'd cherish the charm string if it were ever mine.

I walked her to the front door.

"Oh, here." Before she walked outside, she reached into her pocket and pulled out a check made out to me. It was for a sum considerably larger than the one we'd agreed on for the appraisal. "Not a word of complaint," she said, when I opened my mouth to do just that. "You did a lot of work, and you did it in record time. I'm going to get a chunk of money off my taxes when I donate this thing, and I wouldn't have known its real value if it wasn't for you. The least I can do is share the wealth."

I thanked her, and opened the door.

We were just in time to hear a dog bark.

"LaSalle," I explained even though I was pretty sure Angela didn't care. She turned to head off down the street to the right and stopped in her tracks when the dog's bark turned into a long, mournful howl.

Angela swallowed hard. "Dog howling in the dark of night," she whispered, "howl for death before daylight."

And with that, she walked away.

I didn't wait to watch her go. Instead, I went into the shop, turned off the lights, and told Stan it was time to get a move on.

"Let's go get Swiss steak at that diner I like so much," he suggested when we stepped out of the shop and headed to the left. "It's Wednesday. They've got rice pudding for dessert on Wednesdays."

I like rice pudding.

And no one tried to steal my purse once we were outside.

All in all, things were looking up.

Maybe Angela was right about the charm string all along. Now that it was out of my life, maybe my bad luck would evaporate.

As if.

Chapter Four

THE NEXT MORNING DAWNED BRIGHT AND SUNNY, AND I was grateful. I'd had enough thinking about doom and gloom and bad luck. With the help of a little sunshine, I could forget about curses and get my life back to the way it was supposed to be—calm and button-filled.

I was humming a little tune when I got off the El, made my way to the shop, and stuck my key in the door.

The song evaporated when I noticed a button lying on the sidewalk.

Remember what I said about the thrill of the button hunt? My head knew this was probably nothing more than just a plastic button that had fallen off someone's raincoat, and still, my button-loving heart couldn't resist. My fingers suddenly itching the way they always did when I was closing in on a new button discovery, I picked up the button and turned it over.

The button was what we in the button biz call a small, that is, between three-eighths and three-quarters of an inch in diameter, and it was made of black glass. There was a flower pattern etched into the glass and it was accented with gold paint.

These kinds of button were common enough back in the days when Queen Victoria was mourning her Prince Albert. She wore buttons made out of jet, an organic mineral that was expensive even back then, and the masses, eager to follow her fashion, copied her by making buttons out of black glass. The glass was far less expensive than jet and some would say just as pretty, though as a purist, I wasn't convinced.

There had been a number of these small black glass buttons on Angela's charm string.

Weird, and the weird got weirder when I realized there was another button lying on the pavement not far away.

This one was a man's shirt button and it wasn't plastic, but mother of pearl. I knew this for a fact because I automatically held the button to my cheek and it felt cool in a way plastic never does. That meant the button was old, and an old button lying on the sidewalk outside my shop—

I would like to say I stayed calm, but let's face it, my life's work—and my life—was contained within the walls of the Button Box. I flashed back to the break-in I'd had soon after I opened the shop and how the goons who'd engineered it had left my inventory in shambles. All those happy thoughts I'd had earlier vanished and my stomach soured. I raced to the door, tried the handle, and—

Locked.

My heartbeat ratcheted back, my breathing slowed.

"Security system," I reminded myself. "You installed a security system after the last break-in. Everything inside is safe and sound. Your buttons are fine."

But that, of course, didn't explain the old buttons on the sidewalk.

My eyes narrowed against the morning sunlight, I scanned the area in front of the shop. Old Town is a popular tourist destination and usually bustling, but it was early, and the other merchants who were my neighbors had yet to open for business. There was no foot traffic, either, not yet, anyway, and I was grateful. That meant I could be pretty sure that nothing had been disturbed. The black glass button had been on the sidewalk to my left at about nine o'clock, the mother of pearl button had been in the twelve o'clock position. Now, I realized there was a button at one o'clock, too, and one at two, and another at three.

I hurried over to pick up those three buttons—two more mother of pearls and a brass button with an eagle on it—glancing around as I did and realizing with a jolt to my midsection that a trail of buttons caught the morning sunlight, a trail that led to the alley that ran between my brownstone and the one next door.

Black glass, clear glass, steel, bone . . .

As much as I was tempted to bring order to the chaos and rescue the buttons from the pavement, at this point, I didn't bother to stop. I was too busy following the brick walkway and the buttons scattered on it that led into the courtyard we local merchants maintained as our private spot to have lunch and take a breather. There was a park bench in the middle of the tiny courtyard, and in a few more weeks when the days were longer and the temperatures were a little warmer, each of us would contribute a potted plant and our little oasis would be complete with color and greenery.

Of course, we'd have to get rid of the body first.

The thought struck like so many out-of-the-blue revelations do, but then, it was a scenario no sane person expects to encounter first thing in the morning, or any other time of the day.

I froze in my tracks, doing as quick and thorough an inventory of the scene as I was able before the panic and horror set in as I knew they would.

Muddy Crocs.

Green sweatpants.

Pink tee. Even before I'd scanned my way from the feet of the still form up to the head, I knew I was looking at Angela. I suppose it was a good thing I recognized the clothes she'd worn the night before, because her face was so blue and bloated, I might not have known it was her otherwise.

Then again, I never would have mistaken the charm string. Or at least what was left of it.

A good portion of the string was still wound like a python around Angela's neck, tight enough to leave bruised impressions of the buttons on her skin, snap the old string, scatter buttons all around, and choke Angela to death.

I swallowed down the sudden sour taste in my mouth and reached for my cell phone, another revelation pounding its way through the fog of horror in my brain.

It looked like Angela was right about the bad luck after all.

"You knew the victim."

I'd been so busy staring into the depths of the glass of water a uniformed cop had given me as soon as he walked me into the workroom of the Button Box and sat me down, I didn't even realize anyone had come to stand next to me.

When I looked up and saw it was Nev, I couldn't have been more relieved. I resisted the urge to jump up and throw myself into his arms.

Partly because that uniformed cop was still there, and I didn't need to start a host of rumors running rampant through the department.

Mostly because we weren't at the throw-myself-into-his-arms stage of what we had of a relationship.

Nev was the consummate professional, and something of a Type A personality. I did not hold this against him. When it came to my work, I was a Type A, too.

"I thought you were working afternoons." While that cop standing in the doorway between the workroom and the shop made a phone call, I took the chance and touched a hand to Nev's. His smile was warm when he briefly closed his fingers over mine.

"I am," he said. "But when the desk sergeant heard where the body was found, she remembered that I'd worked the case here when that actress was murdered, and she gave me a call."

"I'm glad." The cop was done with his call, and I

dropped my hand into my lap and Nev backed away. I wished he didn't have to. There was something about his calm, reassuring presence that helped thaw the ice in my veins. "She was . . ." I couldn't see the courtyard from there, even if my back door was open, but I looked that way, anyway, closing my eyes against the memory of Angela's swollen face. "She was a customer of mine," I told Nev. "The one with the . . ." My words choked against the painful ball of emotion in my throat. "She's the one who brought me the charm string."

"The lady you told me about the other night." Nev pulled another stool up to my worktable and perched on the edge of it. He was a tad over six feet tall, and even seated on the tool, his feet touched the floor. Not mine. Mine dangled. "I remember what you said when we had that drink the other night. You said Ms. Morningside, she was the one who believed in—"

"Curses. Yeah." It didn't seem so funny now. In fact, just thinking about Angela's fear and the warnings she'd seen in the crows and the howling dog made a shiver skitter up my back. I wrapped my arms around myself and the gold cardigan I'd worn that day with blue jeans. "Angela came in last night to pick up the charm string. There was supposed to be a tea today at the Ardent Lake Historical Society. Oh, really, someone needs to call and tell them," I added and I suppose, in some way, thinking about the tea satisfied the need in me to concentrate on the mundane, even in the face of murder. "They're going to make tea and bake cookies and before they do all that—"

"Not to worry." Without even checking to see if the

other cop was watching, Nev patted my hand. "We'll take care of the phone calls."

The reassurance satisfied my need for structure, even in a situation that was all about chaos. "Angela . . ." I sniffled. "She was so excited about presenting them the charm string, and so happy to be getting it out of her life."

I hadn't even realized I'd started to cry until Nev handed me a white cotton handkerchief. I dabbed it to my eyes. "She showed up here a little after six last night," I told him because I knew he was bound to ask sooner or later and I figured we might as well get it over with just in case I fell to pieces. "She picked up the charm string and left. She went . . ." I thought back to all I remembered about the night before. "When she left the store, she turned to her right, in the direction of the alleyway. Stan and I left just a couple minutes later, and we went to our left. If we'd gone the other way . . ."

There was no way I wanted to think about how things might have been different. If I did, I'd only feel worse.

Nev understood. "It's not your fault," he said.

I shrugged. "I know. It's just that—"

"That it's not your fault."

He was right, and I admitted it with a fleeting smile. It was the first I'd smiled since I walked into the courtyard and found Angela's body, and the muscles in my face felt stiff and uncomfortable, but even that felt better than the painful knot wedged between my heart and my stomach.

Maybe Nev realized how close I was to falling to pieces. That would explain why he kept things professional and to the point. I didn't hold it against him. But then, I knew what he knew: if he was going to find out who murdered Angela, he had to get on the trail of the killer, and fast. At this point in his investigation, I was the one best able to help.

"Did she say anything to you?" he asked. "About anyone following her? Or about anyone who might have been angry at her? Anyone she might have been afraid of? Did she act peculiar in any way?"

I'd already shaken my head before I stopped to reconsider. "She didn't call to tell me she was on her way here, and the day before, she told me she would. I know that seems like a small thing, but I don't think Angela was the type who made promises she didn't intend to keep. And then when she did get to the shop last night . . . well, it was pretty obvious that she was upset," I told Nev. "Her eyes were swollen like she'd been crying, but when I asked her about it, she said it was because of her allergies. She was a mess, too. It's hard to believe seeing her the way she's dressed now, but the first time I met Angela, she looked like the poster girl for how women should dress for success. Something was definitely wrong."

"But she didn't say what."

Another shake of my head. "She didn't strike me as the kind of woman who would easily share, especially with a stranger."

"And with friends?"

"I hardly knew her." My throat felt as if there were a hand around it. So not a pretty thought considering the way Angela had been killed. Hoping to wash away the uncomfortable thought, I took a sip of water, and when it hurt to swallow, I made a face.

Nev excused himself long enough to go over to the counter and put on a fresh pot of coffee. "When that's done brewing," he said to the cop nearby, "how about pouring a cup for Ms. Giancola."

The cop nodded and dutifully went over to watch the pot drip, and Nev came back to sit next to me. "Did she say anything about her life back in Ardent Lake?"

"She said she had a boyfriend." I thought about the way Angela had worded it, that they were more than friends, and my voice clogged with tears. "She was so happy about Larry. She said he was the one good thing that had happened to her since she inherited the charm string. He owns the hardware store in Ardent Lake. That's what Angela told me." I remembered how Angela's eyes had gleamed when she talked about Larry, and I thought about how he was going to feel when he heard the news. "The poor man," I said, automatically reaching for my cell though I didn't have a clue what Larry's number, or even his last name, was. "Someone needs to tell him."

"That's my job." Nev made a note of this in the little leather-bound notebook he pulled out of the breast pocket of his gray suit. "I'll get in touch with the Ardent Lake police and have someone there tell Larry what happened, after we check for next of kin. Then I'll go up there and have a talk with Larry. He's bound to know more about Ms. Morningside's personal life."

"And what about all that other stuff?" Normally, I would have shrugged it off without another thought, but murder is serious business and Angela's felt strangely personal. Maybe that was because I'd grown so close to those buttons of hers. The ones she'd now never have a chance to donate to the historical society.

"I know you're going to tell me I'm crazy, Nev, but she was convinced the charm string was cursed and now—"

"You, of all people? You're not going to tell me you believe any of that hooey, are you?"

"No." I didn't. Honest. "I mean, I know inanimate objects don't have a will of their own, so they can't bring bad luck to anyone. And even if they could . . . I mean, buttons? Buttons are so wonderful and so interesting and so—" It wasn't that Nev didn't already understand how my life and buttons were intertwined, it was just that I figured I didn't need to remind him. Sometimes, it was hard enough for a cop and a button nerd to find things to talk about. There was no use pointing out the obvious differences between us.

"I think what's important," I said, "isn't if buttons can really bring bad luck but that Angela believed they could. It's almost like she brought the bad luck on herself, because she saw it everywhere she looked, and she believed it could happen."

"I've seen weirder things." Still, Nev dismissed my theory with a shake of his head that sent his shaggy, sandy-colored hair dipping into his eyes. He pushed it back with one hand. "But I think we'll find there's a very human element behind this crime."

"I didn't see anyone hanging around when Angela walked out of here," I said.

"Not even that guy who tried to snatch your purse the other night?"

This was a connection I'd never even considered, and I sucked in a breath. "You don't think—"

"You know me better than that. I don't think anything until I have all the facts, and right now, facts are mighty slim around here. I do know that this is usually a pretty safe neighborhood. If it wasn't, I'd help you pack your buttons and get you out of here."

The uniformed cop chose that particular moment to deliver a mug of steaming coffee. "Cream or sugar?" he asked, and before I could answer, Nev suggested sugar and lots of it. "It will help with the shock," he promised.

Half a cup of coffee later, I couldn't say if that was true, but I could say that some of the tension inside me had eased. I wrapped my hands tighter around the red mug with "I ♥ Buttons" in white lettering on it, savoring the warmth as it seeped into my fingers and spread into my hands.

"Seems funny, don't you think," Nev said, and call me cynical, but I think he'd waited until this very moment to bring up this theory, until he knew I was a little more relaxed and likely to be caught off guard. "An almost crime one night, and a real crime the next."

A cha-cha started up inside my chest. "Then you do think the two are related?"

"I didn't say that. But I do want you to be careful. I could come by in the evening when it's time for you to lock up."

I shouldn't have had to give him a pointed look, just like I shouldn't have had to say, "You've got a job, remember? And you can't spend your evenings looking after me."

Fortunately, he didn't get the opportunity to argue.

Before he could say a word, a crime-scene technician came into the shop and headed for the back room, her arms stacked with small plastic evidence bags that were perched on top of a crumpled floral hatbox. She set everything down on the table and I saw that each bag contained a charm string button.

The woman looked at the pile of evidence bags and shook her head in wonder. "There are an awful lot of buttons lying around out there," she grumbled.

"One thousand, to be exact." I wasn't trying to show off, but I figured it was important.

"One . . . thousand." I swear, the woman's face went a little green.

Nev grinned. "Looks like you've got a busy day ahead of you, Kovach," he said.

She rolled her eyes. And went back outside.

"So . . ." Nev fingered the nearest evidence bag. "What do you think, Josie? Do these buttons have anything to do with Angela Morningside's murder?"

"I wish I knew." I looked through the bags of buttons, too, carefully setting each one aside as I did. If this was where the techs wanted to stage their evidence, they'd need a whole lot more room.

"You took pictures of the buttons, right?" Nev looked at the individually packaged buttons, too. "That's what you said the other night. You said you photographed each of the charm string buttons."

I nodded. "You're welcome to look through the pictures if you like."

Nev's smile was sheepish. "I was kind of hoping you'd do that for me."

I felt the familiar protest ride in my throat. "I'm not—" I was going to say *a detective,* but I swallowed the words. I might not be a trained crime fighter like Nev, but I was a button expert. And when it came to buttons, Nev needed all the help he could get.

Chapter Five

"Nine hundred and ninety-five, nine hundred and ninety-six, nine hundred and ninety-seven."

It was the second time I'd counted—out loud—all the evidence bags and the buttons in them, and my mouth felt as if it were filled with sand. I ducked into the workroom to grab a bottle of water out of the fridge and took a long drink before I walked back into the shop and dared a look in Nev's direction. He was standing near my desk, and just as I feared, he didn't look any happier at the end of this count than he had the last time I finished counting.

"I told you, Nev . . ." I drained the last of the water out of the bottle. "There are three buttons missing."

"You're sure?"

I bit my lower lip. It was the best way I could remind

myself that it had been a long day. For both of us. It was after dark, and while the crime-scene techs had been busy working out in the courtyard, Nev had left to do whatever it is homicide detectives do when they're newly assigned to a case. Now he was back from doing that whatever he'd been doing, and his white shirt was crumpled. His shirt collar was unbuttoned. He hadn't bothered to take off his trench coat when he walked into the shop nearly an hour earlier, and the belt on it hung cockeyed. That little vee between those blue eyes of his told me he thought he'd hear better news after this count than he'd heard the first time around.

As a way of reminding him that my day hadn't been any easier, I waved a hand around the shop, silently indicating the folding tables the crime-scene techs had arranged against the walls. Even before they asked (nicely) if I would help out, I'd already decided this was the only way to make sense of the sea of buttons they'd rescued from the courtyard. Yeah, it was a little anal. OK, so it was a lot anal. But it made sense. And right about then—with images of Angela's dead body etched in my mind and memories of how, just twenty-four hours earlier, she'd stood right there in my shop talking to me— bringing order to a world that was suddenly upside down calmed me and helped me feel useful.

Under the watchful eye of a crime-scene tech named Jason, who was still at the shop to assure what he called "the chain of evidence," I'd carefully arranged each evidence bag on top of a copy of the picture I'd taken the day before of the button inside it. Little plastic bags gleamed all around us and I looked over them all before I turned to Nev. "You want to count them?"

"Of course not. I'm sorry. I didn't mean to second-guess you." He ran a hand over a tie that was a shade of blue too green to look good with his gray suit. "I'm just wondering what we do next."

Had he not been so tired, I'm sure he would have thought of this himself, but for now, I had the chance to work a little button magic and I wasn't above gloating about it. I whisked three photos off my desk. "We have nine hundred and ninety-seven buttons. Plus"—I waved the photos in his direction—"we know which buttons are missing."

Nev's expression brightened. It wasn't so much a smile as it was an acknowledgment that there might be at least a glimmer of light at the end of the investigative tunnel. "Of course! And if we know which ones are missing—"

He expected me to supply the logical rest of the statement, but honestly, I couldn't. "I'm not sure what it tells us," I admitted. "But it's a start."

He was hoping for more. He settled for what he got, leaning over to take a look at the pictures that I laid out one by one on my desk.

"This is a sort of greenish button," he said, picking up the first photo and giving it a careful once-over. "Looks like glass."

"You're learning." I leaned over his shoulder so I could tap a finger against the button in the photo. "This button is made out of uranium glass, or what some modern collectors call Vaseline glass. And this one . . ." I put the first picture back on the desk and handed him the second.

Nev looked at it for a moment, and maybe I was tired and, thus, being fanciful, but I liked to think that he was trying to call up any little bit of button knowledge he'd learned from me in the past months. It was sweet of him, really. Even when he finally pursed his lips and gave up. "It's a button with a picture of a red fish on it. Honest to gosh . . ." Shaking his head, he set the picture back where it came from. "Before I met you, I never even imagined there were buttons as fancy as that. I mean, who even thinks about buttons?"

He knew the answer to that question, which explains why he cringed as soon as the words left his mouth. When he bent to retrieve the last photo, the tips of Nev's ears were pink. "And one more photo of a button with a picture of a . . ." He squinted for a clearer look. "It looks like a metal button with a building or something on it."

"Check, check, and check." I laid out the pictures side by side. "Now, either these buttons are still outside and the techs just never found them . . ." He was sitting in the wing chair in the far corner of the shop reading a magazine and not paying the least bit of attention to me, but I offered an apologetic look in Jason's direction anyway. "Or—"

"Or the techs couldn't find the buttons because they're not out there." Head cocked, Nev thought this over. "Are any of these buttons worth stealing?"

"Stealing? Well, yeah. I suppose so. I don't know a button collector anywhere who hasn't seen that one, perfect button they need to complete a competition tray and not thought about making off with it. Even if they'd never actually do it. Killing for a button, that's another matter."

Rather than think about what sort of warped person might actually murder a fellow human being for the sake of a button, I concentrated on the facts. I tapped a finger against the photos, first of the uranium glass button, then of the metal button. "These, not so much. But this one . . ." I moved on to the picture of the beautifully enameled button with the fish at the center of it. "This one's old, and valuable."

"Valuable enough to kill for?"

I made a face. "Is anything that valuable?"

"What you think and what I think don't really matter. You know that, Josie. It's what a killer thinks that counts. If we knew if these three buttons were really missing . . ."

I'd been waiting for the opening. Yeah, it was kind of shallow of me, showing off like this, but let's face it, I wasn't about to miss the opportunity to impress Nev. Besides, I had a very real skill I could offer at this point in the investigation and I could guarantee that neither Nev nor Jason could hold a candle to it. It would have been careless of me not to step forward and use my expertise.

I ducked into the back room, got a special keychain from the drawer in the worktable, and breezed back into the shop. "Come with me," I said, including both Nev and Jason in the invitation, and together, the three of us stepped outside.

There's always something happening on Thursday night in Old Town, and that night was no exception. The music was cranked at the bar down the street, its deep bass line punctuating our steps and vibrating my bones. Lights sparkled from the display window of the interior design studio that had opened almost directly across from the Button Box only a couple weeks earlier, and tourists scrambled all around us, heading for nearby clubs and restaurants. The scene was just as lively and interesting as our merchants and residents association promised tourists it would be on our website and in our e-mail newsletter.

When we stepped under the yellow crime-scene tape that was draped across the entrance to the alleyway and on to the brick walkway that led back to the courtyard, though, it was as if we were entering another world.

There, the music was muted and it was nearly pitch dark. Still, when we stepped from between my brownstone and the one next door and into the courtyard, and Nev felt along the back wall of my brownstone for the switch that would turn on the faux gaslight near the park bench, I stopped him.

"We'll have to look for the enamel button and the metal button once it's light," I told him. "But if we're going to find that uranium glass button, this is the ideal time to do it. We need to do it in the dark."

I pulled out my keychain and switched on the light at the end of it.

"Hey, it's a black light." Jason was young, but perceptive enough.

He couldn't see me nod, so I explained. "Uranium glass really does have uranium in it. It was added to the glass prior to melting, before the melted glass was pressed into the button molds. And when a UV light is shined on an object with uranium in it—"

"Cool!" Jason was obviously a science nerd. "It glows.

Hey," he added for Nev's benefit, "when it comes to buttons, she really knows her stuff."

Jason was right.

But only if I found the uranium glass button.

Keeping the thought in mind, I swept the light over the ground near our feet, and when I didn't see a thing, I moved a couple steps and began the sweep all over again. As I mentioned before, the courtyard wasn't big, but looking through it inch by careful inch still took time. The minutes ticked by with me, Nev, and Jason walking side by side, scanning the ground, and after a while, we were nearly to the center of the courtyard.

Nearly at the spot where I'd found Angela's body.

Darn it, I tried my best to act like it was no big deal, but before I could control the reaction, my spine stiffened and my breath caught.

He didn't say a word, Nev just slipped his arm through mine.

I didn't thank him. For one thing, Jason was standing on Nev's left, and for all I knew, he hadn't noticed Nev's gallant gesture. For another . . . well, I was afraid if I tried to speak, my voice would crack and the raw emotions I was hiding would come tumbling out.

This wasn't the time for that.

Though it was most definitely the place.

I skimmed the black light over the pavement where, hours before, Angela had been sprawled on her back, her eyes staring up into a clear morning sky she couldn't see, her mouth gaping in an expression that was at once a sign that she'd been gasping for air and an indication of how surprised she'd been by the attack.

Now, of course, the body had been removed, and nothing remained to show the horror that had happened at the spot the night before, nothing more than the chalk outline of Angela's body.

"No . . ." My words were tight in my throat, and I coughed. "No sign of the button here," I said, and I kept on looking.

Jason wasn't convinced. Not that I could say for certain, of course, since it was nearly impossible to see his face in the dark, but I heard the little click of his tongue that told me that while he might be impressed by the mumbo-jumbo of the black light as a way to locate the uranium button, he wasn't one hundred percent certain it was going to work.

"If there were still buttons here, we would have found them," he said. Jason might be enthusiastic when it came to the theories of science, but obviously he wasn't all that thrilled about the grunt work. He was bored, and when Nev and I stepped forward, beyond the park bench and into the back part of the courtyard, he hung back. "A glass button. Isn't that what you said it was?" Jason asked. "It was sunny this afternoon, remember. If there was a glass button out here, we would have seen it shining in the light."

"Not if there wasn't much of it left to shine." I guess Jason heard the very real relief that washed through my voice because he hurried over to stand at my side and sucked in a breath of wonder when he looked at the ground where the light was trained.

The brick there was coated with what looked to be a dusting of particles that glowed an eerie green in the black light.

"It got stepped on and broken!" Jason almost made this sound like a good thing, as if the fact that the button wasn't whole—and whole buttons were what his team was looking for—actually made a difference.

"It's still evidence," Nev reminded him, and though it took a couple seconds for the fact to register, the kid finally got the message. He dashed inside for another evidence bag, and the brushes and such he would need to make sure he picked up all the specks of the smashed button.

"That . . ." Nev waited until Jason was gone before he put his hands on my shoulders and turned me to face him. "That was amazing."

I didn't try to hide my smile. "It was pretty cool, wasn't it?"

"Nobody else would have known about the button glowing in the black light. Nobody!" Even through the gloom, I saw the wink of Nev's smile. "You're—"

"The world's greatest button expert?" I hitched my hands around his waist.

"I was going to say . . . well, you know. But if you'd rather be known as the world's greatest button expert . . ."

"How about the world's greatest fabulous button expert?"

"Done." He leaned a hairsbreadth nearer and I thought he might kiss me, but the sounds of Jason scrambling his way back down the alleyway put an end to that. I dropped my hands, and Nev backed away.

"Can I use the black light?" Jason asked, his voice high with excitement. He swallowed down what apparently sounded even to him like too much of an unprofessional reaction. Jason cleared his throat and forced his voice down an octave. "I mean, of course, it will be easier for me to retrieve the shards of glass if I can use the UV light to find them."

"Of course." I handed him the keychain and we left him to his work.

Back inside, Nev walked right over to the desk, retrieved the photo of the uranium glass button, and plunked it down in an empty spot on the nearest table. "When Jason brings what's left of that button in, we're ready for it," he said.

He was right. "I only wish . . ." I strolled over to the nearest table, automatically letting my gaze roam over bag after bag after bag of buttons. "I wish we could figure out if it means anything."

"You mean the buttons that are missing?"

"I mean the charm string being used as a weapon in the first place." The thought creeped me out, and I shivered. "Who would do such a thing?"

"Professional opinion?" Nev almost perched himself on the edge of my rosewood desk, but he stopped and reconsidered. It was a delicate antique, and he knew better than to press his luck. "My guess is the murderer didn't come here to kill Angela. If he had—and I'm only saying *he* in a general sort of way, not because we know anything about the killer—if he had, he would have brought a weapon with him."

"So it could have been random."

Thinking, Nev scrunched up his nose. "Weird random. He obviously lured her into the alleyway, and what woman in her right mind would allow something like that to happen?"

"Except Angela wasn't in her right mind. Not last night. I told you, she was really upset."

"Nobody's so upset they completely forget about safety."

"So what you're saying is that you think she knew her killer."

"I think . . ." Nev pressed a hand to his stomach. "I think I didn't have time to eat lunch today and I'm starving. After Jason gets these buttons packed and out of here, let's get a burger."

I wasn't about to argue. Now that I thought about it, I hadn't eaten lunch, either. At first, I was too upset. Then, I was just plain too busy printing out all those photos and helping the techs match them to the proper buttons. Hungry or not, though, I wasn't done wondering. "Could it have been robbery?"

Nev shrugged and I knew how much he hated to do that in answer to a question about a case. "There was no purse found with the body."

I closed my eyes, thinking back to the night before. "I don't think she had one with her."

"And that seems odd, doesn't it?"

It did, and I tried again to picture everything that had happened when Angela came for the charm string. "She had her car keys in her hand," I said.

Nev nodded. "We found those under the body."

"And when I handed her the hatbox that she'd brought the charm string to me in . . ." I walked through the motions of all I remembered, stepping back toward the workroom, then out again into the shop, my hands out as if I were carrying the box. "I handed her the hatbox, and it wasn't like she had to hoist her purse up on her shoulder to take it from me. Or move it from one hand to the other. She just grabbed the hatbox and got out of here. I'm pretty sure I'm right. She wasn't carrying a purse."

"Which, unfortunately, doesn't prove much of anything. Maybe Angela's money is what our killer was after, and when he realized she didn't have any, he got angry. Or maybe he thought there was something of some real value . . . OK, I'm sorry!" He rolled his eyes and groaned. "I know you think the buttons are valuable, but a street thug sure wouldn't think that. He might have seen Angela carrying the hatbox, figured there must have been something worth stealing in it, and gotten mad when he realized there was nothing inside but buttons."

I shivered. "That takes a special sort of cold person, doesn't it?"

"Unfortunately, there are plenty of them out in the world."

That uncomfortable thought was interrupted by Jason arriving with the newest evidence bag. "I've got them all cataloged," he said, reaching for the clipboard and the list numbered from one to nine hundred ninety-seven that he'd worked on as I matched buttons with photos. He added the uranium button to the list. "Now all I have to do is put these boxes in my truck and get them downtown." He looked from me to Nev. "I don't suppose you two—"

"We'd love to help." I was smiling when I sidled past Nev and got to work. Helping Jason with the buttons gave me one last chance to look at them, and besides, there was a burger in my future. The sooner we finished, the sooner we could eat.

We helped Jason pack the boxes and load them into his truck, and once we were done, Nev and I returned to the Button Box to turn out the lights and lock up.

I grabbed my purse out of the back room. "It's been a really long day."

"You got that right. And if I don't come up with some answers about this case soon, it's only going to be the first of many. What do you think, Josie?" We already had most of the lights in the shop off, but when he stopped at my desk and picked up the two remaining photos, I looked at them, too. "If we don't find these two buttons, does that mean someone took them?"

I wished I had the answer to that one, and I told him that right before I added, "The metal button, no. There's no reason anyone would want it. You saw the charm string buttons laid out on the tables. There must have been at least two hundred metal buttons. Buttons with eagles on them. Buttons with animals on them. All of them—including this one that's missing—are pretty common late-nineteenth-century buttons. There's nothing special about them. In fact, the artwork on the one that's missing isn't even particularly good. See . . ." Yeah, the light was bad, but I leaned over and pointed at the details on the picture as best as I was able. "It's a town of some sort, and a building of some sort. Very uninspired, and not something a collector would find especially appealing."

"But the other one . . ."

"Ah, the other one." I looked at that photo, too, and I

swear, even in the dim light, that enameled button just about jumped off the page and shouted its beauty to all the world. "If someone brought that button in here, I'd pay plenty for it, and I'd be glad to do it."

"But not everyone would know that."

It seemed a no-brainer. At least to me. "Anyone who saw it would know it's beautiful."

Was that a pointed look I got from Nev? I used the dark as an excuse to pretend I didn't notice. "Come on, admit it, Josie. Pretty or not pretty, ninety-nine out of a hundred people would walk by that button and not give it a second look. It's just a button. And that's just what they'd think. It's just a button."

"So what you're saying is that a common thief—"

"Wouldn't bother with the button, no matter how pretty it was. I mean, OK, even if our killer knew that buttons could be sold to collectors, wouldn't he have grabbed more of them? Why would just these two be missing? And here's my prediction, we'll find that metal one tomorrow. It probably just rolled under something and the techs missed it the first time through. They were pretty overwhelmed by all those buttons."

I'm not exactly sure when I realized where this conversation was heading. At least I wasn't until goose bumps prickled up my arms. I started for the door. "No," I said.

"I haven't asked you to do anything."

"The answer's still no."

"But you're good at this, Josie."

"I make a great pasta sauce, too, but you don't see me opening a restaurant."

Nev chuckled. "I'm not asking you to open a restaurant. I'm just asking you to help me out." I guess he realized I was going to protest, because he sailed right on so I couldn't get a word in edgewise.

"You can't deny the facts," he said, "and the first fact is that there is one valuable button missing. If that's true—and for now, we're going to say it is, because we don't have anything to prove otherwise—that leads to fact number two: our killer knew that one button was valuable. Fact number three, then, is that our killer must know something about buttons. What's that you said outside? That you're the world's greatest fabulous button expert?" I had just turned out the last of the lights and reached for the door handle. That didn't keep me from seeing the gleam in Nev's eyes.

"Our murderer knows something about buttons," he reminded me. "Or at least about buttons that are valuable. Josie, that means I really need your help."

Chapter Six

MY DEFINITION OF HELPING DID NOT NECESSARILY MESH with Nev's.

Ever practical, I suggested spending the next couple days in the shop, calling button dealers throughout the country who might be approached by a person looking to sell an unusually beautiful enameled button.

Nev, while admitting that there were benefits to this strategy, had other plans. He was sure that the only way to root out suspects—and find out which of them knew what about buttons—was to get to know the people Angela knew. There was no better way for me to do that, he insisted, than for me to attend her wake and funeral.

This would look completely natural, he insisted, because I'd recently done business with Angela. No one would suspect that I was really trying to dig up information. No one would imagine that I had any other motive beside offering my condolences.

No one would think I was a mole.

Me? I wasn't convinced. For one thing, I wasn't sure I could blend in as completely or as inconspicuously with the other mourners as Nev assumed I would. For another . . . well, I admit it, attending the wake and funeral of a person I hardly knew made me feel ghoulish.

Then again, Nev knew I felt a little responsible for what had happened to Angela and that I spent the weekend playing the ugly game of *What If.*

What if I'd taken her more seriously when she talked about the curse?

What if I'd walked her to her car that fateful night?

Maybe aside from a little information, Nev was hoping that my involvement in the investigation would absolve my guilt.

Maybe I was hoping for the same thing.

The Monday after the murder, I changed my voice mail so customers who called would know it might take me a day or two to get back to them. I put up a blog post on my website and a note on the front door of the Button Box: I'd be open for business again in a couple days. Those details taken care of, I headed north out of Chicago.

"You really didn't have to do this." We had just passed a sign that said we were four miles from the town of Ardent Lake, and I glanced toward the passenger seat of my car. "You're going to miss your poker game tonight," I reminded Stan.

He shrugged away the comment as being of no

consequence. "I can play poker any Monday night. But investigating a murder . . ." A smile on his face, he rubbed his hands together. "It's like the old days! I can't wait to get started."

"You do remember what Nev said?"

"About being subtle? Yeah, yeah, not to worry. I've played this game before, remember. Besides, for all anybody knows, you're just the button lady who was doing business with Angela, and I'm just the old friend who came along for the ride."

All well and good, but talk about guilt! "It's Marty's turn to host the poker game tonight, isn't it? You're going to miss his wife's berry cobbler. It's your favorite."

"Cobbler, shmobbler. I can get a piece of cobbler anytime. What I can't get is a chance to do some official investigating."

"Unofficial investigating," I reminded him. "All we're supposed to do is talk to people and get some initial impressions."

"I know, I know." Stan shifted in his seat, winced, and pressed a hand to the small of his back. We'd been in the car a little over an hour, and he wasn't used to sitting still for so long. "Nev's already been here interviewing people, but he knows what I know: they're not going to open up. Not to a cop. But when we shake 'em down—"

I laughed. "We're not trying to shake anybody down. We're just here to talk about buttons."

"Well, sure." Stan's smile sparkled in the spring sunshine. "I won't forget. And I do appreciate it, Josie. I mean, you inviting me along. You could have asked Kaz."

I rolled my eyes. Which would have had a bit more of a dramatic effect if I hadn't been making a left-hand turn at the same time. "If we're talking subtle, you know Kaz would be the wrong choice. Kaz is about as subtle as a tsunami. Besides . . ." We were at an intersection, and the traffic light turned red. I slowed to a stop and drummed my fingers against the steering wheel, debating the wisdom of saying any more. On one hand, if I told Stan what I'd been thinking, it would look like it mattered. On the other, if I didn't say a word and it turned out that it actually did matter . . .

I grumbled under my breath, and when the light turned green, I eased the car forward. "He's not answering his phone," I said.

"You mean Kaz?" Stan scratched one finger along the side of his nose. "When did you call?"

"Thursday, and Friday." I made a face, and as if it wouldn't actually make me look pathetic—or worse, like some kind of stalker—I added quickly, "And Saturday and Sunday. It's not like I care what he's up to or anything—"

"I get it, no need to make excuses. You're just curious."

I would have been happy to settle for curious, but while it was the truth, it wasn't the whole truth. If I didn't admit it now, Stan would only figure it out himself eventually. And then the way I was behaving would look more suspicious than ever.

"I'm worried," I said.

"About Kaz?"

OK, admitting that I cared enough to even think about

Kaz was an odd thing to confess, but Stan didn't have to make it sound like I was some sort of deviant.

"He hasn't called," I said. "He hasn't stopped to see me."

"I thought we decided that was a good thing."

"It is. Except it's weird. And unusual. And now he's not answering his phone and . . . oh my goodness!"

These last words rushed out of me at the end of a breath of pure astonishment.

But then, we'd just driven past a gorgeous wooden sign painted blue with the town's name highlighted in gold, and I'd just gotten my first look at Ardent Lake, Illinois.

Wide streets lined with trees that were just beginning to sprout and added touches of fresh green to the landscape.

Redbrick sidewalks.

Houses set beyond neatly trimmed lawns and bordered with bright swaths of spring flowers.

Daffodils in front of the first house.

Crocuses (in gorgeous shades of purple and yellow) in front of the next.

Early tulips—pink and white—bordering the front walk of the third.

In fact, everywhere I looked, there were bushes springing to life, and flowers poking their heads out of the earth and Victorian homes the likes of which I'd never seen anywhere.

"It's like something out of a storybook! Look at the gingerbread on that house, Stan." I let go of the steering wheel just long enough to point. "And the wraparound porch on the one next door. Honest to goodness . . . isn't it amazing?"

"Humph." Stan crossed his arms over his chest just as we drove past an ice cream parlor with a brightly colored red and white striped awning and one of those old-fashioned popcorn carts outside the front door. "All this Victorian bric-a-brac. Seems awful fussy, don't you think?"

"Awfully wonderful." My GPS told me to turn right, and I did, onto a street lined with houses that looked like they'd come out of the pages of an architectural magazine. Turrets, porches, more gingerbread . . . I am not usually one for frills, but it was all done so tastefully. And it was color-coordinated, too.

"You suppose they had some big town meeting and all went out and bought paint together?" Stan was thinking what I was thinking and he must have been looking where I was looking, too, at perfectly tended house after perfectly tended house, each painted a soft pastel color that coordinated—perfectly, of course—with the one next door to it. Soft gray accented with taupe and grape. Blush pink touched with white and steel. Lilac made to look all the more delicious with eaves painted pewter and a mauve gazebo out back.

"What amazes me is the way it's all preserved and maintained," I said. "Imagine every Victorian building in town restored to perfection. No wonder the historical society was so interested in Angela's button string. It was made for a place like this, and it would obviously be appreciated by the folks here. The whole town is simply amazing. And you . . ." Again, I darted a look in Stan's direction. "You're not impressed."

"Haven't you learned anything about police work?" He shook his head sadly. "Never trust anyone or anything that's perfect."

Perfect.

Ardent Lake certainly was.

In a Stepford kind of way.

The thought hit just as I spotted the sign for Foder's Funeral Chapel and a feeling like cold fingers on my neck sent a chill down my spine. I didn't have time to indulge the fantasy, and maybe that was a good thing. Though the wake had started only a short while earlier, the parking lot next to the funeral home was crowded, and I waited for a car to leave so I could park, then took a good look at the building.

Foder's was a sturdy building with a wide front porch and a roof that was topped with a cupola. Unlike the pastel colors we'd seen on so many of the homes we passed, the building was painted a deep, dusty blue, its somber hue in keeping with its purpose.

I tilted the visor so I could put on a fresh coat of lipstick, ran a brush through my hair to tame my shoulder-length brown curls, and when I got out of the car, I tugged the black suit jacket I'd worn with a knee-length black skirt and taupe-colored camisole into place.

Inside the building, Stan excused himself to find a men's room (and to do a little sleuthing, too, I'd bet), and I stepped into my role as mole.

There was a sign hanging outside a room down the corridor and to my left: "Angela Morningside, Services Tomorrow, 10 A.M., First United Methodist Church of Ardent Lake." And a long line waiting outside the door.

I wasn't surprised. Angela was middle-aged, which to me, meant she was probably still active and had a circle of friends. Plus, she owned a successful business. It stood to reason that she knew a lot of people. I took a quick look at the sober expressions of the people waiting in line ahead of me, wondering as I did which, if any, of them might be the murderer.

There was only one way to find out.

When the woman in line directly in front of me made eye contact, I pounced. In as polite and non-mole-like a way as possible, of course.

I introduced myself, and made sure I mentioned my button connection to Angela.

The woman, older than me by ten years or so and neatly dressed in a short-sleeved black dress decorated with tasteful pink and blue flowers, lit up like a Christmas tree and stuck out a hand to pump mine.

"Susan O'Hara, and isn't this a piece of good luck. I didn't expect you to be here, of course. But I was hoping." It seemed Susan was good at reading blank expressions, because she took one look at mine and laughed in the uncomfortable way people do when they realize they may have committed a social gaffe. "I'm sorry, I'm not making a whole lot of sense. But then, I haven't been thinking clearly. I mean, not since I heard the terrible news about Angela. It's hard . . ." Her voice broke, and she turned toward the window to our right, and in the light that filtered through the lace curtains, I realized I'd been wrong about Susan.

Not in her forties. She was fifty at least. There was a network of crow's-feet at the corners of her eyes, and her ashen hair was streaked with more silver than I'd noticed at first. Her lips were pinched and dry and her fingernails were chewed to the quick.

She pulled a tissue out of her purse and touched it to her eyes. "You'll have to excuse me, I've never been to the wake of a person who was . . ." Her voice dipped even lower as if she knew something no one else there at Foder's knew. "You know, someone who was murdered. It's all too horrible to even think about."

I was about to say something noncommittal in agreement when, behind us, the front door opened and spanked shut and a group of women walked in.

Susan's eyes were green, and not the least bit attractive when she shot a look over my shoulder. It was such a change from the cordial way she'd been looking at me, I couldn't help wondering what was up.

Reminding myself I needed to be as inconspicuous as possible, I turned around to look where Susan was looking at.

The three newcomers were all younger than Susan and more stylishly dressed. The one in the middle, a petite woman with spiky red hair and wearing tall stilettos and big jewelry, made such an effort to keep her eyes on her companions and not look at the line ahead of her, I had no doubt she was the one Susan wasn't happy to see.

Apparently, the feeling was mutual.

Interesting, I told myself, turning back around and keeping my expression blank.

Interesting, and probably completely irrelevant.

Susan wadded her tissue into a ball and shoved it in her purse.

"You were the one who was doing the appraisal for Angela, right?" she asked. "In Chicago? I wonder . . . Do you think . . . I mean, do you have any idea if they'll still let us have it?"

Oh, how I hate it when I feel I'm out of the loop! Right about then, I not only was out of it, I wasn't even sure where the loop was.

Apparently Susan realized it because after we inched forward and closer to the door to the room where Angela's coffin was displayed, she offered a small smile.

"I mean the police, of course," she explained. "Do you think they'll still let us have the charm string?"

"I can't say what the police might do." I congratulated myself, spoken in true mole fashion. "But why—"

"I'm being such an airhead!" Susan riffled through her purse, then handed me a business card. "I'm the curator," she explained before I'd even had a chance to read the ecru card tastefully printed with sepia ink. "Of the Ardent Lake Historical Museum."

Now it all made sense! I tucked the card in my own purse for future reference, and considered what I could— and couldn't—tell Susan. I decided to start with the basics. That is, the information that had been included in all the newspaper and TV accounts of Angela's murder in the first place.

"I'm afraid the charm string was seriously damaged when Angela was attacked," I said.

Susan gulped. "Then it's true? What I heard on TV? About Angela being . . . choked . . . with it?"

"I'm afraid so."

She slid me a look. "And the buttons?"

"I can just imagine how anxious you were to put the charm string on display." How's that for a slick way to sidestep a direct question? "Angela said so many wonderful things about your museum, I'm hoping I have a chance to stop there before I have to get back to Chicago. What other kinds of buttons do you have on display?"

"Buttons?" Top lip curled ever so slightly, Susan backed up and gave me a look. "As a matter of fact, we don't have any. I know buttons are your business, but the fact is, our visitors aren't exactly interested in things like buttons. Or in much of anything else of historical value for that matter. My goodness, I don't think there would be a museum here in Ardent Lake at all if it wasn't for Ben."

I don't think I was making much of an impression. I mean, what with looking confused all the time. Lucky for me, Susan was a kind woman. She didn't hold it against me. Or if she did, at least she didn't let on.

In fact, she laughed, then realized it wasn't an appropriate sound in a place like that, and pressed her fingers to her lips.

We inched forward in line before we stopped to wait some more. "Thunderin' Ben Moran," she explained. "I should have remembered you're not from around here so you might not know. Why, Ben's the closest thing we have to a celebrity in these parts. But then, pirates have that whole wild and crazy persona going for them."

I had never associated northern Illinois—or any other part of the state—with pirates, and I told Susan so.

"Well, you're just going to have to stop by the museum and see. We'll change your mind, and your ideas about Great Lakes history."

We moved forward again. We were getting closer to paying our last respects to Angela, and here, we could hear the hushed organ music being piped in through the sound system.

I made sure I kept my voice even lower when I got the conversation back on track. "The police have recovered the buttons from the charm string."

"All of them?" Susan seemed honestly surprised. Was it because she knew there were so many buttons to begin with? Or did she know two of them were missing?

Ridiculous.

I answered my own question. As far as I knew, Susan was just a museum curator who had nothing to gain from Angela's death. In fact, she had something to lose.

The charm string.

"You said you didn't have any buttons in your museum." I pretended to think this over. "Your patrons must have really been looking forward to having the charm string on display."

Again, Susan's gaze flickered over my shoulder and a small smile eased her expression. "Well, it was something of a coup," she confided. "Angela wasn't the easiest person in the world to work with. But then, you probably already know that."

I didn't, but I didn't let on. Instead, I nodded. "You're talking about her belief in the supernatural."

"Oh, that!" I had a feeling if we were anyplace else, Susan would have thrown back her head and laughed. The way it was, she kept her cool and simply smirked. "That was one thing, of course, and let's face it, we're logical, intelligent women. We both know how pathetic it is for anyone to believe that kind of hogwash. Imagine a woman basing her life on horoscopes and psychic predictions! That's just another thing that proves how unstable she was."

"And the other thing?"

Susan shifted her purse from one shoulder to the other and bent her head closer to mine. "Well, I just assumed that, working with Angela, you knew how flighty she was. Honestly, I'm not at all surprised by what happened to Angela. Not that I'm saying she deserved it or anything. Don't get me wrong. But facts are facts, and the facts about Angela are impossible to ignore."

We were at the threshold of the room bathed in a soft glow of pink light. Against the far wall there was a veritable sea of white and pink flowers surrounding a white coffin. Thankfully, it was closed.

Susan glanced at the coffin and at the short, chubby guy who stood near it, quietly chatting with each visitor. In just a moment, it would be her turn to offer her condolences.

"Angela's cousin," she said, indicating the short man in the brown suit. "Charles. The only family she had."

"And the one who inherits."

Susan's sharp look reminded me this wasn't exactly the time—or the place—for comments like that. At least if you're just supposed to be a button dealer who is definitely not investigating a murder.

I smiled by way of apology. "Sorry. I've been watching too many old movies."

"You're not too far off base." We moved forward again. Susan would be the next person to speak to Charles. "Well, you didn't hear it from me," Susan said, "but I always thought he was jealous. You know, of everything Angela got when their great-aunt died."

"And how did Angela feel about all that?"

The man in line in front of Susan finished talking to Charles and she moved up to take his place, but not before she whispered, "Angela? The woman was a certified nutcase."

Chapter Seven

IF STAN HAD BEEN BACK IN CHICAGO PLAYING POKER, he would have gladly stayed up until what he considered the wee hours. That is, ten or eleven. The way it was, by eight, we'd finished dinner at a small but charming (naturally) restaurant in the heart of Ardent Lake's small but charming (naturally) downtown, and he grabbed a book and headed for the communal library/coffee room at the B and B where we were staying. (I'm not even going to bother to mention how charming the B and B was; suffice it to say that it was called The Victoria Inn, and lived up to its regal moniker.)

As it turned out, that reservoir draining project Stan had read about in the newspaper back in Chicago was happening not far away, and one of the engineers working on it was also a guest at the B and B that night. Stan was interested, and I had a feeling he wasn't planning on reading as much as he was hoping to bump into the engineer and ask a lot of questions.

The night was mild, and in the distance, I heard the first of the spring peepers croaking out their love songs. I told Stan I'd see him in the morning, grabbed a jacket, and went for a walk.

I have to make something perfectly clear here. I love Chicago just as much as I love buttons. The city is in my blood. I swear, my heart beats to the sounds of traffic on Michigan Avenue.

But I have to confess something else, too.

Though the peace and quiet of Ardent Lake weren't nearly as thrilling as the buzz of the big city, after a block of strolling, I found myself breathing easier. After two, I realized I had more spring in my step than I'd had since that morning I found Angela's body in the courtyard.

Energized at the same time I was relaxed, I headed toward downtown—a whole three blocks from the B and B—and window-shopped at the antiques store, a women's boutique, and a bakery. There wasn't much on display in the bakery window aside from some cookies shaped like tulips, but what I saw looked so scrumptious, I promised myself a trip back the next day. I ambled through the neatly tended park smack in the center of town, and when I realized there was a canopy of stars overhead the likes of which we never see in Chicago, I sat on the steps of a white gazebo, tipped back my head, and decided right then and there that there was a lot to be said for small town living and the kind of peace and quiet broken only by the occasional swoosh of a car passing the park.

That, and the noise of a twig snapping now and again as someone slipped through the darkness.

Suddenly alert, I sat up like a shot. There were showy Victorian lampposts up and down the walkway, and if I leaned forward and squinched up my eyes, in their dim light, I could just make out a figure scooting from shadow to shadow.

Fight or flight?

In a place as idyllic as Ardent Lake, both options seemed silly to the point of impossibility, and just to prove it to myself, I stayed right where I was. That doesn't mean I'm anybody's fool. Just in case, I reached in my pocket for my B and B room key. If I needed a weapon, it wouldn't be much of one, but hey, I can poke and jab with the best of 'em.

Thus armed, I bent my head to listen more closely and strained to try and get a clear look at the figure.

As the person drew nearer, some of the details came into focus.

Small. Tiny, in fact, except for the odd, lumpy blob at chest level. Dark sweatshirt. Dark pants. Sneakers. One second, the figure was lost in shadows and I'd convinced myself I was imagining things. The next, the light of the nearest lamp gleamed on spiky red hair.

It was the woman who'd been behind me in line at the wake that afternoon, the one Susan O'Hara hadn't been happy to see.

More curious now than I was afraid, I sat up, and waited for the right moment. When the woman was no more than twenty feet away, I called out a greeting.

She slowed to a trot and I wondered if she was going to

pretend she hadn't heard me. Apparently, the fact that I stood up and moved into a halo of light changed her mind.

"Oh, hi." Keeping her place, she shifted from foot to foot. "I didn't see you there."

"Beautiful evening, isn't it?"

The woman's shoulders were so slim, I barely noticed when she shrugged. She took a step closer and I saw that the funny lump that made her look so misshapen in the dark was actually a paper shopping bag she had clutched to her chest. "My husband thinks I'm out jogging," she said with a quick smile and a look that darted all around, as if she wanted to make sure we were really alone. "That's what I tell him, anyway. You know, when I want to go out at night and catch a smoke." She took a couple steps back. "He thinks I quit at the first of the year."

From the odor of cigarettes I caught even at this distance, I doubt he was fooled. Not that I cared a whole bunch. I do admit, though, to being more than a tad curious about who would claim they went jogging carrying a shopping bag.

As casually as possible so she didn't notice and think I was paranoid, or worse, some kind of danger to her, I slipped my room key back in my pocket, and when I moved forward, the soft glow of the nearest lamp lit my face. The woman took a good look at me.

"Hey, you're that Josie from Chicago who was at Angela's wake."

Not to worry, I wasn't about to join Angela in the league of paranormal believers.

I nodded. "Let me guess, Ardent Lake is a small place. And everyone here knows everyone else."

"You got that right." The woman set down the shopping bag and I heard the clink of glass. When I took a step closer to her, she nudged the bag farther into the shadows near her feet. "And everyone knows everybody else's business, too. Believe me, everyone was talking about you before you were out of Foder's parking lot. They said you were that button lady who was appraising the charm string for Angela."

"That's right." Though she already knew my name, I officially introduced myself.

"Marci Steiner," she said in return. She took a pack of cigarettes out of one pocket and a pink plastic lighter from another. "Angela, she was killed right outside your shop, wasn't she?"

The very thought still made my throat clutch. I cleared away the uncomfortable sensation with a cough, and even though I knew I had nothing to get defensive about, it was kind of hard to control the reaction. My back stiffened. "It's not like she was killed on the sidewalk right on the other side of the display window," I told Marci. "It was actually down an alley and back in a courtyard. But close enough." Speaking the truth took some of the starch out of my spine. "That's why I made the trip to Ardent Lake. Angela had just left my shop before she was killed. I felt . . . I feel like the least I can do is pay my respects."

"That's not what people are saying. I mean, some people. I heard them talking this afternoon. They said they remember seeing your name in the paper when that What's-Her-Name, that famous actress, got killed. They said you're here to find out who murdered Angela."

It wasn't a question so, technically, I didn't owe Marci an answer. Morally, I felt obliged. Oh, not to give Marci the truth. To keep my word to Nev and cover for what I was doing.

"Boy, if they needed my help, the cops would be really hard up!" I laughed. "Honest, I'm here because I feel . . . I don't know . . . I guess I feel I owe it to Angela. She seemed like a nice lady."

Marci barked out a laugh. "You think so? Then you didn't know her very well, did you?"

"Did you?" I asked her.

She dropped her cigarette on the ground and snuffed it out with the toe of one sneaker, then picked up the shopping bag and took a step back. "I guess I'll see you at the funeral tomorrow," she said.

What was it Nev had said—subtle? Doing my subtle best, I stepped forward, and when Marci started walking, I fell into step beside her.

"So, did you know Angela well?" I asked.

She threw me a sidelong glance that might have meant she was surprised at the question. Or maybe she was sending the signal that she wasn't happy I'd tagged along. "You're asking awfully personal questions for someone who's just here to pay her respects."

For a short woman, she sure had a long stride. I did my best to keep up with Marci. "Well, you have to admit, the whole thing is pretty interesting. I mean, in a sad way. What happened to Angela is a mystery, and I only know what everyone else knows, what I've read in the newspapers. Naturally, it's got me wondering . . . Do you think there's any chance that someone here in Ardent Lake might know more about what really happened?"

She barked out a laugh. "I can't speak for anyone but myself, and all I know is that the woman made me nuts. What with her crazy talk about astrology and spells and whatnot. I didn't like her. There. That's the honest truth. If that makes me a suspect, then a whole bunch of other people here are suspects, too."

We got to the broad sidewalk that ringed the park and a cross street, and I hoped Marci didn't decide to cross against the light. I was already scrambling to keep up with her, and I didn't want to look like a stalker.

She glanced over her shoulder, back the way we came. "I'll bet anything you're staying at the Victoria. It's one of the few places to stay in town and I know for a fact that other B and B is booked solid with a group of antiquers. The Victoria is back that way."

I shrugged like it was no big deal. "It's a beautiful night. I don't mind walking some more. Besides, if your husband asks, you can tell him we bumped into each other, and that's what delayed you."

"Yeah. Sure. Thanks."

The light changed and we crossed the street.

"So you were saying . . ." She wasn't, but I was hoping she wouldn't come right out and call me a liar. "About people who didn't like Angela."

She darted me a look and took a moment to make up her mind. "Well, if you don't hear it from me, you'll only hear it from somebody else," she finally said. "There's that bitch Susan O'Hara, for one. I saw you talking to her at the funeral home. I'll tell you what, the moment I heard that Angela had been murdered, I prayed Susan was the one who did it. Damn, that would be perfect! Miss High and Mighty O'Hara, led away in handcuffs."

Oh yeah, I was tempted to pounce on this nugget. Like a pigeon on a bread crumb. I controlled myself, playing it cool far better than any theater major who'd never been much of an actor should have been able to. "I never met Susan until this afternoon. She doesn't exactly seem like a murderer."

"Yeah, that's what they always say, isn't it?" We came to another cross street, and since there was no sign of traffic, Marci hurried across and I followed along. "From what I've read in the papers, the cops say robbery wasn't the motive in Angela's murder. Is that true?" she asked.

"I only know what I've read in the papers, too."

"Well, if it's true about robbery not being a motive, it's got to make you wonder, doesn't it? We're not exactly country bumpkins here in Ardent Lake. I mean, we watch *CSI* and all the other cop shows. We know what's what. And I know the first thing the cops are going to ask is who had a reason to kill ol' Angela."

"And you think Susan did?"

She stopped in front of a sweet little Victorian cottage with a white picket fence out front and an arbor that spanned the walk that led to the front door. I pictured it in the summer, with roses growing all around.

Marci put her hand on the gate inside the arbor and pushed it open. "I don't think it," she said. "I know it."

I had played it cool long enough. Even a button nerd who truly was in town just to offer her condolences wouldn't pass up an opportunity for hot gossip like that, right?

Eager not to look . . . well, too eager, I schooled my voice when I asked, "Why would Susan want to kill Angela?"

Marci slid me a look. "So you are working with the cops."

"Please!" I made sure my laugh was light and airy. "A person doesn't have to be connected with the police to be curious. And you've got to admit, what you said about Susan was bound to make me wonder what's really going on and how much you know about it. It's like some really good book. Or a movie. I can't help but want to know more."

Behind the lace curtains in a front window, there was a light on, and Marci threw a glance that way.

I was going to lose her, and this opportunity to learn what I could from her.

The thought pounded through my brain, and I folded my fingers into the palms of my hands and wondered where I'd gone wrong at the same time I decided that there was nothing like a little upping the ante on the gossip to keep the conversation going.

As if sharing a secret, I lowered my voice. "Susan told me—"

"What?" Marci flinched as if she'd been slapped. "Because if that bitch said one word about me—"

"Your name never came up. But she did say that she thought Angela was a nutcase."

"No big news flash there." Marci shifted the shopping bag from one hand to the other, and again, I heard the rattle of glass. Whatever she was carrying, it was bigger than a drinking glass, smaller than a pitcher. "But of course, Susan would say that. She'd do anything to make Angela look bad."

This didn't make sense to me. "But Angela was donating the charm string to her museum," I blurted out, thinking out loud. "And Susan was grateful. In fact, she asked me if I thought she might still get the charm string. If she was so appreciative, why would Susan want to discredit Angela?"

Marci let go of the gate and it slapped closed. "Did you see the guy at the wake? The one with the silvery hair?"

I had a vague recollection of a man at the back of the room who looked sadder than the rest of the folks gathered there. "Larry?" I asked.

Marci nodded, confirming my suspicion.

"He's obviously pretty broken up."

Another nod sent her spiky hair twitching. "Larry's a nice guy. Kind of quiet, you know?"

"And he and Angela were dating."

"She told you, huh?"

"She mentioned it when she came to the shop. She said Larry was the only good thing that had happened in her life lately."

"Yeah." Marci chuckled. "On account of the curse! God, maybe for the first time in her life, Susan is actually right. Maybe Angela really was a nutcase."

"But that's not exactly a reason Susan would want to kill her."

Oh yes, I was fishing. For all I was worth.

Marci glanced around. We were the only ones out there on the street, but she stepped nearer, anyway. "Larry's the reason."

"The reason Angela believed in curses? I don't think so. She said—"

"Not the reason she believed in curses. The reason Susan hated Angela."

I am not usually slow, but this took some thinking. "You're implying—"

"Implying!" Marci punched open the gate and stepped onto the walk that led to the front door. "I'm not implying anything, I'm telling you flat out. Susan and Larry used to be a couple. That's why Susan hated Angela so much. Angela stole him away from her."

I WASN'T SURE how well Marci was connected to the Ardent Lake gossip grapevine, but I did know this much: at the funeral the next day, Larry looked positively inconsolable. He was a tall, handsome guy and as we stood around the coffin at the cemetery, I made sure I positioned myself directly across from him and watched his face twist with pain as the minister read the last of the prayers.

"I'll need to talk to him," I said to Stan after we walked away from the service. "But I'm thinking this would be a bad time."

"There's a luncheon." Stan pointed to the line in the church program that invited everyone attending back to the home of Angela's cousin, Charles.

"You hungry?" I asked him.

"After that fabulous breakfast we had back at the B and B? Heck no. But I'm thinking if we want to talk to suspects . . ."

I knew just what Stan was talking about. I'd had two cranberry muffins back at the B and B, as well as a gorgeous fruit compote and a bowl of yogurt drizzled with honey from the hives in the back garden.

We went to the funeral luncheon, anyway.

COUSIN CHARLES LIVED in a modest house in a development called Vista View Hills about two miles outside of town. I didn't see any hills, or anything that even began to qualify as a vista, either, for that matter. In fact, as we pulled down the street and parked, the only thing I saw were more cookie-cutter versions of Charles's split-level. The only thing I could think when we got inside was that it was a very good thing the house wasn't in town. His seventies throwback shag carpeting and avocado appliances would never pass muster within Ardent Lake city limits.

There was a buffet table set up in the dining room, and it was heaped with food. I suspect it was homemade by the women who were running back and forth into the kitchen to make sure everything was hot and restocked. Angela's garden club members, I heard someone say. They were working hard, and their expressions were sad. I didn't need anyone to tell me they were also Angela's friends. Stan volunteered to talk to them, and since many of them were close to his age and would, no doubt, appreciate some masculine attention and maybe talk a little more freely because of it, I left him to it and took a turn through the rest of the house.

There was quite a crowd, but I was disappointed when I realized Larry was a no-show. And though he was officially hosting, Cousin Charles was obviously nobody's idea of the life of the party. Even an after-funeral party.

He was a plump guy with fiery cheeks and thinning dark hair. Still dressed in the dull olive suit he'd worn at the funeral, Charles sat on a folding chair in front of the fireplace in the family room, a plate of rigatoni and salad on his lap. He glanced up at his fellow mourners as they walked by, and looked away again before there was any chance they could make eye contact.

"It's so nice of you to host everyone at your home," I said, settling myself in the empty chair next to him.

His gaze fluttered in my direction. "That's me, Mr. Nice Guy."

I wasn't sure how he expected me to respond, so I took a bite of tasty chicken Marsala. "You're . . ." I gave him a chance to look my way, and when he didn't, I pressed on. "You're Angela's cousin, right?"

He gave me another fleeting glance. I'd introduced myself to Charles at the wake the day before so I wasn't surprised when he said, "And you're that button lady."

I gave him a smile I was sure he didn't notice. But then, he'd dropped his gaze to his pasta. "There are so many people here. Angela must have been very well liked."

"I suppose some people liked her." Charles's top lip curled when one of the garden club ladies walked by. He poked his fork around in his salad. "You appraised the charm string."

There was no use denying it. Aside from the fact that it was true, everyone in town seemed to have the inside track on my business.

"How much?" Charles asked.

I happened to be taking another bite of chicken when he said this. That was a good thing because it gave me the opportunity to think of a politically correct answer while I pointed to my mouth, chewed, and swallowed. "I'm not at liberty to discuss Angela's business. I'm sure you understand."

"Of course I do." He didn't so much set his plate on the hearth as he dropped it. Good thing lunch was being served off plastic. "Charles always understands." His voice was singsong. "Charles is Mr. Nice Guy."

I wondered what I'd gotten myself into and glanced around, hoping there would be someone nearby who I could draw into what was quickly turning into an uncomfortable conversation. No such luck. Apparently, there were reasons Charles was sitting there alone. Just as apparently, I was the only one in town who did not know those reasons. At least until now. That would explain why I'd gotten enmeshed in trying to chat with a man who could have been taught a thing or two about congeniality by Ebenezer Scrooge.

But then, his cousin had just been murdered.

The thought touched a chord, and I decided my initial impression of Charles may have been rash. He was grieving, poor man. I owed it to Angela's memory to be patient.

"You and Angela," I said, making the attempt, "you must have been close."

"Well, that's one thing that would explain why I

forked out the bucks for this little shindig. Oh sure, the garden club helped out. But do you have any idea how much a couple cases of beer costs? And all this plastic-ware? Not to mention the cost of the funeral itself. Kind of funny, don't you think, when we both know that if I was the one who'd been whacked, Angela wouldn't have opened a package of Oreos and passed them around the funeral home in my honor."

"But you did what you did because you're Mr. Nice Guy."

I was going for funny.

Charles didn't laugh.

I, too, set aside my plate. If ever there was a moment to get down to business, this was it. "What you're telling me is that Angela wasn't very generous."

Charles grunted. "That's putting it mildly. All that stuff Aunt Evelyn left her? I guess that's all the proof anyone needs."

"You mean the charm string."

Charles leaned to his right, closer to me. "Aunt Evelyn was loaded. And not just with money. The old girl had been collecting antiques for years."

"And Angela—"

"Got it all."

"But you were her nephew, just like Angela was her niece."

One corner of Charles's mouth pulled into what was almost a smile. "I knew I liked you," he said.

I wasn't sure I took that as a compliment.

"So you can see why I'm curious, right? About the charm string?" Charles gave me a wink.

I didn't like that, either.

"If I could get a hold of some of those buttons and pawn 'em off to some collector, at least I could recoup some of my losses. And before you think you can get away with anything . . ." This time, he looked me right in the eye. "I've done my homework. I know the black glass and the mother of pearl aren't worth all that much. But that enameled button, the one with the fish on it, that ought to bring in a pretty penny."

It was a good thing I stopped eating. I would have choked on my lunch. "You know something about buttons?"

"I make it my business to know about things that can affect my bottom line."

I tried to sound casual when I asked, "How much of a bottom line are we talking?"

"For the charm string? You tell me. I do know that last week on eBay, a button almost just like that fish button sold for nearly four hundred dollars."

I watched the auctions, and I'd seen that button. I didn't have the heart to tell him it was nowhere near the quality, or that in my experience, there were few buttons like the enameled one on Angela's charm string. I also didn't bother to mention that if I was selling the buttons off the charm string—or buying it for that matter—four hundred wouldn't even come close. Not for the enameled button.

"I've already called the cops in Chicago," Charles added. "I've informed them that I'm Angela's only living relative. I've told them when they're ready to release those buttons, I'm the one who gets them. Hey, you could put in a good word for me."

I was about to tell him I didn't have that kind of influence with the police or with anyone else.

Charles didn't give me a chance.

He scooted his chair a little closer. "I knew you'd understand," he said. "I could tell yesterday. Right when we met. I knew you weren't like these mindless morons who were fooled by Angela's act. All that crazy talk about curses and astro-signs. All she wanted was for people to think that she was this harmless, scatterbrained lady."

"When she was really . . ."

"Conniving," Charles said, and nodded to emphasize the point. "Selfish and conniving. You want proof?"

I did, though I didn't expect him to offer it right then and there.

Charles popped out of his chair, and reaching for my hand, he pulled me up to stand beside him.

"We'll go over to Angela's," he said, quietly enough so no one else heard. "And I'll show you."

I'm a big girl. A professional. A business owner.

And I'd already investigated a couple murders on my own.

Of course I knew it wasn't wise to up and leave with a man I barely knew, especially when he'd just come right out and told me that he was jealous of the favoritism ol' Aunt Evelyn had shown Angela, and angry that Angela never shared the wealth.

Charles had motive.

And that meant one of two things:

Either he was as innocent as the driven snow and, thus, didn't care about revealing his true feelings about Angela.

Or he was one devious—and deviously clever— murderer.

Chapter Eight

Angela lived in the heart of Ardent Lake, just a block from the park where I'd met Marci Steiner the night before. Her house was one of the big Victorians, this one painted white with touches of purple, gold, and flamingo pink that livened up the curlicue woodwork on the front porch, the gables, and the framing around the tall, pointed windows.

The inside of the house was surprisingly modern.

And incredibly cluttered.

"Wow." Charles and I stepped in the front door and I got my first look at the avocado green shag carpet, the sleek leather oxblood-colored couch, the oak end tables, and what looked to be a lifetime's worth of . . .

Stuff.

Afraid to move and not sure where I'd go if I did, I tried to take it all in.

There were dozens of paintings in all shapes and sizes leaning against the couch, and hundreds of pieces of glassware—from pink Depression glass serving platters to elaborate china vases—on every flat surface.

"Wow." I couldn't help myself. It seemed the only reasonable response.

"See? It's just like I said." Charles carefully picked his way down a foot-wide path between a pile of antique quilts and a life-size marble statue of some Greek god with a harp in one hand and an apple in the other and very little in the way of clothing. "I told you Angela got it all."

"You mean . . ." Panic flashed through me when I watched Charles turn a corner and pictured losing him in the maze and never finding my way outside again. I hurried after him, sidling between the statue and a curio cabinet filled to bursting with Royal Doulton figurines. "This all once belonged to Aunt Evelyn?"

Charles nodded. At least I think he nodded. It was kind of hard to tell because he was on the other side of a mahogany buffet heaped with Limoges. Yes, buttons are my first love. But that doesn't mean I don't appreciate other beautiful old things. I took a closer look at a fabulous china punch bowl beautifully hand-painted with bunches of red and purple grapes.

"This stuff is amazing," I said. "Aunt Evelyn had good taste."

I heard Charles tsk. "Except when it came to her niece."

I had no time for family drama. There was too much to see. My attention was caught by the colored glass balls hanging in each of the room's three windows.

Charles had been there before and had apparently developed the talent of seeing over and through the heaps of antiques. "Witch balls," he said, looking where I was looking. After he looked at me from between two gigantic Limoges urns, that is. "And they're not antique. Angela bought them new, another one every few months. You'll see them hanging in all the windows. They have something to do with some old New England fishing tradition. I don't remember the details though, believe me, Angela told me plenty of times. What it comes down to is that a witch ball is supposed to trap any evil that tries to get into your home. There's other weird stuff around here, too."

From behind the mountain of porcelain, I saw Charles point to the French doors that separated the living room from the dining room. There was a fabric bag hanging from the knob of each door.

"Some kind of herbs," he said, wrinkling his nose. "They're supposed to ward off evil. At least that's what Angela always said. All I know is that when she got fresh ones, they smelled terrible."

"Too bad none of these good luck charms worked in her case." I carefully made my way over to where he was standing. Through the French doors, I could see into the dining room, and the kitchen beyond that. Every bit of space in the house was crammed with more stuff.

There was a life-size wooden cigar store Indian standing next to the dining room table and the table itself was jam-packed with antique clocks. There were old hatboxes stacked on the floor, and in the kitchen, all but one square foot of counter space was piled with more glassware. In fact, the only thing that was perfectly clear in there was the table, and that had a singe mark the color of ebony piano keys in the center of it, a remnant of that fire Angela told me about.

"How could she live like this?" I asked no one in particular. "And why would she want to? Angela seemed so organized, so together."

"Well, she was. Or at least she used to be." Charles crossed his arms over his chest. "Until all this stuff got delivered from Aunt Evelyn's."

"And Angela never put it away? Never gave it away?"

I might have known this last question would have elicited a sour look from Charles. "She never had much of a chance. Aunt Evelyn died only four months ago. At first, Angela bragged that she'd have everything under control and organized lickety-split, but when she realized there was so much . . . well, it just goes to show, she wasn't as perfect as she thought she was. Not even Angela could decide what to do with Evelyn's collections. Of course, she could have shared a little with me."

Rather than deal with his bitterness, I glanced around. "Have the cops been here?" I asked Charles.

He grunted an affirmative.

"Then if we looked around a little more . . ." I was already doing that; I had my hand on one of the French doors.

Charles shrugged. "I can't imagine it would hurt anything. And hey, poetic justice—it will all be mine one of these days, including the house, I imagine."

"It's not what I expected," I admitted, referring to the house, not Angela's will and what might, or might not, be coming to Charles. "I mean, the house is so over-the-top Victorian on the outside and in here . . ."

We were both in the dining room now, and there was a very un-Victorian-like sleek ceiling fan above the glass and chrome table, more shag carpeting, more clutter. "Not so much. You'd think with all the time and effort everyone here in Ardent Lake puts into restoring their homes—"

"You're kidding me, right?" Shaking his head—I wasn't sure if it was because he felt sorry for me or if he was just disgusted—Charles led the way around the corner. Between the dining room and the kitchen was a stairway that led to the second floor. "If you want to know more about Angela, her bedroom is upstairs. While you're up there looking around, maybe you could start to get a handle on what you think all this stuff might be worth. Obviously, I don't have room for it all, and even if I did, I wouldn't want to keep half of it. I'm going to unload this junk and cash in, fast."

I didn't tell him I was qualified to appraise absolutely nothing except for buttons. Why take a chance? No way was I going to miss out on the golden opportunity to get a look into Angela's private life.

I took the steps two at a time. Not the best plan since I was wearing black pumps. My calves screaming in pain, I paused on the landing at the top of the steps. Angela's bedroom was straight ahead at the end of the hallway, and I promised myself I'd have a good look around in there after I checked out the room directly to my left, one she obviously used as an office.

There was no clutter up here, thank goodness, and I imagined it was because Angela knew she could never work crowded by the flotsam and jetsam of Aunt Evelyn's life. The glass and metal computer desk was spotless except for a couple small piles of paper. No date book, and that's what I'd hoped to find. Then again, I knew Nev had been there before me, and he was a thorough sort of guy. I glanced through the papers, notes about work, one about calling a repairman to look at the air conditioner and another reminding herself to get her best suit from the dry cleaners for the ceremony at the historical museum. There was a small pile of receipts, too, and when I shuffled through them, Charles waved in my direction.

"Just take the garbage," he said. "The cops didn't think any of it was important, and I can't imagine it is, either, but hey, if you get rid of some of the junk, it will mean one less thing for me to clean out once I get the all-clear from Angela's attorney and the place is officially mine."

I tucked the receipts in my purse, and moved on to the table next to the desk. It was covered with books, and since Angela owned a medical transcription service, I wasn't surprised to see that many of them had to do with specialized medical terminology. Those books were neatly arranged between a set of stainless bookends. In front of them, scattered over the table, were maps.

"Ardent Lake," I said, picking up the top map and looking it over. "And . . ." I reached for the map below it. This map showed a wider view of the area, with the town marked by a star at the very center. Along with the maps, there were more books on the table. Absently, I picked up one called *Early Illinois*, and set it back where it came from next to another slim volume titled *Ardent, The Lost Town*.

With as little respect as Angela had for the charm string, I was surprised she was interested in history. And speaking of the charm string—

My hand froze over the table.

Next to the pile of history books was another pile, photos of the charm string buttons, much like the ones I'd taken, only not nearly as meticulous. I had taken photos of each button individually. Angela had taken pictures of sections of the charm string, and she'd done it right here in her office; the charm string was laid out on the desk. Through the glass top I saw the champagne-colored carpeting at my feet.

I studied the picture on top of the pile. This particular section of charm string included black glass buttons, a couple metal buttons, and a particularly sweet little one in white china decorated with a blue floral pattern, what's called a calico button. Angela had circled each of the black glass buttons and in the photo's margin, she had scrawled . . .

I squinted and tipped the photo toward the window, trying to bring Angela's cramped handwriting into focus.

" 'A dime a dozen.' "

I was so intent on looking at the picture, I jumped when Charles read the words from over my shoulder. "I've seen Angela's handwriting before," he said without bothering to apologize for nearly causing me apoplexy. "I know it's next to impossible to read. 'A dime a dozen.' That's what she's written on the photo."

The next photo was similar. This one had arrows drawn on it, each one pointing to one of the metal buttons.

" 'Fifty cents at the local thrift shop.' " Charles supplied the translation of the tight script before I could even begin to decipher it, and pointed to the words, too, just in case I missed them.

"She was doing her homework." I set the photos down. "Just like you did."

"Then I bet she found out the same things I found out. Those buttons weren't worth much. All that talk about curses. I think Angela was just blowing smoke. She probably decided to donate the charm string to the museum because if she sold the buttons, she'd get next to nothing, but if she took the cost of the charm string as a tax deduction . . . well, you know all about that. How many thousands of dollars was she going to tell the government that charm string was worth?"

He was trying an end run around the question he'd asked earlier about the value of the charm string, and I wasn't biting.

Fishing, though, was another matter.

"You're right about one thing, she'd get next to nothing for most of the buttons," I reminded Charles. "Except the red enameled one, of course."

I'd hoped to get something more out of him than simply a grunt, and when that didn't happen, I left the room and went into Angela's bedroom.

It was a pleasant enough room, though hardly dramatic or inspired. The walls were painted an icy blue that matched the embroidery on the white bedspread. The furniture was utilitarian and unremarkable. There was a flat-screen TV on a stand across from the bed, and more witch balls—a cobalt blue one in the left window that looked out over the front of the house and a yellow one in the right window. Like the office, the bedroom was free of clutter, and I was grateful. If we'd had to pick our way through Aunt Evelyn's antiques, I never would have seen the photographs that were piled on the dresser.

Unlike the ones in Angela's office, these had nothing to do with buttons.

"Angela and Larry." I knew Charles was hovering at my shoulder, so when I picked up the first framed photograph, I tipped it so he could see. Even though she was huddled in a down coat and looked like her teeth were chattering, Angela was all smiles. She was standing near a picnic table and behind her was a long, narrow lake, its waters icy, its shoreline frosted with snow. His smile as wide as hers, Larry stood at her side. He was a tall man with vivid blue eyes. His arm was around Angela's shoulders.

From what I'd seen of him, I wasn't sure Charles would know happiness if it came up and bit him, but I offered my opinion. "They were a nice couple. They look good together."

Charles's shrug told me he didn't know and he didn't care. "She talked about him ad nauseam. Larry did this and Larry did that. Larry said this and Larry said that. Honestly, you'd think a woman her age—"

"It doesn't matter how old Angela was. She was still entitled to happiness. And a little romance in her life."

I set the photograph down and threw out a line.

"So . . ." I leaned back against the dresser, my arms crossed over my chest. "Larry and Angela, they look pretty happy together. Like the perfect couple. But I heard—"

"What?" Charles's head snapped up.

I eased into the subject, the better to make it look like it was no big deal. "Well, I don't put a lot of stock in gossip. But I heard that Larry used to date Susan O'Hara. You know, the curator of the historical museum."

Charles rolled his eyes. "Ardent Lake! The Peyton Place of Illinois." He glanced my way, then looked away again quickly, his cheeks fiery. "You don't seem to be the kind of woman who'd listen to rumors."

"Is that what it was, a rumor? Larry and Susan never dated?"

His answer was begrudging. "I saw them around together a few times. At some of the restaurants in town. And last summer at the big band concert."

"So they were dating?"

Charles shrugged. "If that's what you'd call it, I guess so."

"And then Angela caught Larry's eye."

Charles was certainly shy, but I'd never assumed he was stupid and he proved it when his eyes popped wide. "You think Susan was angry. That she killed Angela!"

I stood up straight, my arms at my sides. "I didn't say that. But it's only natural to wonder who might not have liked Angela." I didn't add *besides you*. If Charles couldn't see how guilty he was making himself look with all this talk of how he couldn't wait to get his hands on Angela's possessions and what he saw as Angela's fortune, I wasn't about to point it out. Not when I was alone with him, anyway. "And if Angela stole Larry from Susan, then maybe Susan had her reasons for disliking your cousin."

I was hoping Charles would fill in the blanks, Ardent Lake gossip–wise, but instead, he cocked his head, screwed up his mouth, and did some serious thinking. "Except if Susan was angry, it didn't stop her from accepting the donation of the charm string."

He was right.

"Unless Susan swallowed her pride for the sake of the museum," I suggested. "Or maybe once Larry was gone, she realized she didn't miss him all that much."

Charles grunted.

I pounced. "She did miss him."

He threw me a sidelong glance. "I heard she was pretty broken up."

"And angry at Angela?"

He shrugged.

End of the gossip party. I knew it as surely as if Charles had hung out a sign: "Not saying another thing."

I bided my time, turning back to the framed photographs and promising myself Charles and I would revisit the topic at another time. The next picture in the stack was an eight-by-ten in a frame that was studded with colorful rhinestones and faux pearls. A special frame for a special picture, and it apparently showed a special occasion—Angela and Larry were dressed in formal clothes and posed in front of a sparkling Christmas tree.

"Her company Christmas party." Charles supplied the details. "Angela just loved to play Lady Bountiful for her employees."

"And that's a bad thing?"

"It is when you're just doing it to show off," he said, his words ringing with conviction. "Angela didn't really care if anyone had a good time or a bad time at that party of hers every year. She just wanted to show everyone that she could afford to throw a bash. And just for the record, she never invited me."

I actually felt a momentary stab of sympathy for Charles. Which is saying a lot. "Oh, I'm sorry. I didn't realize you worked for Angela."

"I didn't." He walked away and poked through a pile of magazines on the nightstand next to the bed, taking each one out and flipping through the pages as if he expected to find a treasure trove's worth of tens and twenties tucked inside. "I wouldn't have worked for Angela even if she asked me. Which she never did. And you'd think it was the least she could have done since we only had each other, family-wise."

Rather than question his convoluted reasoning, I went right on looking through the photographs. Each one showed Angela and Larry, always smiling, always happy.

Cradling one photo of them dressed for Halloween (she was Wilma and he was Fred), I glanced around the room, wondering where all the pictures had come from and why they'd been piled on the dresser. Something on a nearby wall caught my eye, and I walked over there for a closer look. "There's an empty picture hanger here. And here." I moved to the next wall. "And more over here. It's like she had the photos hanging, then took them all down."

"She was probably getting ready to redecorate. As if

the rest of us common folks have that luxury. Then again, Angela was rolling in dough, she could afford it."

"That would certainly explain why the pictures were taken off the wall. She wouldn't have wanted anything to happen to them. But . . ." I glanced around again. Having just redone my own apartment, I knew a thing or two about redecorating. No, Angela and I did not have the same taste. But something told me she wasn't a woman who changed things just for the sake of change. And the bedroom . . .

I ran a hand over the wall.

"It's as clean as a whistle, and it looks like it was painted not that long ago," I told Charles.

He was paging through an issue of *National Geographic* and didn't respond.

Left on my own, I shuffled through the rest of the photographs on the dresser. I got to the last one and turned around to show it to Charles. "This photograph . . ." He closed the magazine and tossed it back on the pile it came from. "This is Larry again, but this sure isn't Angela." I took a good look at the slim, elderly lady sitting on a park bench next to Larry. She had a cap of silvery curls and she was wearing a pink sweater over a white turtleneck. Like Angela in all those other photos, her smile was a mile wide. "Who is she?" I asked Charles.

"That's Evelyn." Charles walked around the bed to stand in front of me and tapped a finger against his great-aunt's nose. "Taken in town, it looks like. In the park. See." He pointed to a building in the background. "There's the historical museum. Look." He latched on to my arm and turned me so I was facing the windows that looked out over Angela's front yard. "From here, if you look across the park, you can see the building."

I peeked around the damask draperies and narrowly avoided getting bonked by the yellow witch ball. From the bedroom, I could see the facade of the square tan-colored stone building on the other side of the park. Even in the sunlight, the front of the building looked dour that day, while in the photograph . . .

I took another look.

The day the picture of Evelyn and Larry was taken, there was some hoopla going on at the museum. There were people all around, and a bright banner hung across the entrance. "Thunderin' Ben . . ."

"Thunderin' Ben Moran," Charles said, which was a good thing, since there was a shadow over the rest of the banner and I wouldn't have been able to read it. "That picture must have been taken when the exhibit about that pirate opened at the museum. Everyone in town made a big deal out of it." The tone of Charles's voice told me he wasn't included in that *everyone*. "I remember there was an ice cream social and historical reenactments. Susan's convinced Moran is Ardent Lake's one and only celebrity, and she's going to make the most of him. You know, to keep people coming to the museum."

"But why were Larry and Evelyn there together? Where's Angela?" I asked.

Charles didn't hesitate. "Angela probably took the picture. See, when Angela and Larry first started dating, that was before Evelyn died. Angela and Larry, they used to invite Evelyn to go all sorts of places with them."

"It's nice they wanted to include her."

His mouth thinned in a way that told me I was stupid if I didn't see the truth. "Angela was sucking up. And it paid off, didn't it?"

Actually, not so much.

Angela was, after all, the one who'd been murdered.

Chapter Nine

THEY SAY NO NEWS IS GOOD NEWS, BUT WHEN THE NO news is no news from anyone in the button community about that beautiful red fish button, the no news turned out to be not so good.

Back in Chicago and behind my desk at the Button Box the day after the funeral, I clicked off my phone call. "That's the last of them," I told Stan, who'd volunteered to come in and do some dusting and vacuuming even though I told him I'd be happy to do it myself. "I've called every button dealer I know. Not one of them has heard from anybody trying to sell that enameled button."

"Bad luck, kiddo." Stan was just coming by with a dust rag and a bottle of beeswax furniture polish and he stopped next to my desk. I knew he understood my frustration. Years on the job, and no doubt, he'd seen more than his share of this sort of dead end.

Which is why I asked, "What do we do now?"

I had hoped for something definitive. Instead, he scratched a hand through his thinning white hair. "We can always move on to Plan B."

"Yeah. If there was a Plan B." Too disappointed to sit there doing nothing, I got up and grabbed the bottle of window cleaner he'd left nearby along with a roll of paper towels. While Stan tackled the nearest old library catalog file drawer where I stored buttons—first applying a liberal coating of polish, then letting it dry, then wiping and buffing—I worked on the nearest glass-front display case.

"There was nothing else on that charm string worth stealing," I said, attacking a fingerprint smudge especially hard, not because it needed it, but because activity helped chase away some of my frustration. "The only other button missing is that metal one with the picture of the building on it, and just to cover all my bases, I asked all the dealers I talked to about that button, too. Not that I needed to bother. Believe me, Stan . . ." I was bent at the waist, running the paper towel over the front of the case, and I looked at him through the glass. "There's no way that button was worth killing for."

"Well, you know buttons better than anybody else, that's for sure. I can't argue with you. So maybe . . ." He stopped the buffing for a moment. "Maybe the person who killed Angela didn't care a bean about buttons. Maybe that person had some other reason to kill Angela."

This was what I'd been thinking, too, and I can't say it cheered me up. After all, greed is an unpleasant and petty motive, but it's not nearly as nasty as hate. "Well, there is Susan," I said, reminding Stan of everything we'd discussed on the drive home from Ardent Lake including about how Susan had once dated Larry. "And Cousin Charles, of course."

"And we never did catch up with Larry," he said.

I finished with one display case and moved on to the next. "Yeah, but Nev did. He told me he talked to Larry the day before the wake."

"And found out nothing helpful."

"You got that right." I sprayed and rubbed and sprayed some more. "Missing, missing, missing," I grumbled. "The two buttons are missing. Information is missing. Kaz is missing."

I grimaced as soon as the words fell out of my mouth, but by that time, it was too late to call them back. All I could do is keep spraying and rubbing and hope Stan didn't make too big a deal out of what was sounding a little too much like obsession, even to me.

"Still no sign of him, huh?" Bless Stan for not making it sound like they were recasting *Misery* and I was first in line for the Kathy Bates role. "He hasn't even left you a voice mail or anything?"

"Aha! See?" I straightened up and pointed a finger in Stan's direction. "It's not so crazy for me to wonder what's going on and why I haven't seen Kaz, and where he is. You think it's odd, too."

Maybe there was too much fire in my eyes. And too much conviction ringing through my words. Maybe that's why Stan looked at me as if I'd just started speaking fluent Martian. "You really are worked up about this," he said.

"Worked up? Me?" I marched over to my desk so I could throw away the used paper towels in the garbage can that I'd once decorated with hundreds of glued-on buttons. "I am not worked up," I insisted, my voice loud because I was, after all, pretty worked up. "I'm just—"

"Grateful?" Stan flashed me a smile that said he wasn't trying to be mean as much as he was trying to get me to see how unreasonable I sounded.

He was right.

I dropped into my desk chair.

"It just doesn't make sense," I said, not trying to assure him as much as I was trying to convince myself. "It doesn't make sense that Kaz has fallen off the face of the earth. And it doesn't make sense that I care."

"Well, sure it does." Stan set down his rag and bottle of polish. "You two have history."

My laugh contained zero amusement. "Not good history."

"Maybe not. But it's not like you hate Kaz or anything. He did bad things, sure, and he did bad things to you, but I know you don't wish anything bad on him in return. You're not that kind of person."

I gulped. "Do you think that's what's happened to Kaz? Something bad?"

"More like something with long legs, blond hair, and big—" Stan swallowed the rest of what he was going to say. "My guess is Kaz is busy. You know, with a woman."

There was a time just thinking something like that would have shaken me to my core. Now it was oddly comforting. I drew in a deep breath and let it out slowly.

"You're right. Kaz is a big boy. He can take care of himself."

As if it would prove I really meant it, I slapped the arms of my desk chair and got to my feet. Good thing I did because it made me look calm and in control when a customer walked in the door.

"Hello, welcome to the Button Box." I moved to the front of the store. The woman was in her sixties with a sleek dark bob and wearing jeans, ankle boots, and a red leather blazer over a neat dark tee. She looked familiar. "You've been here before," I said.

"Well, no." She was carrying one of those reusable shopping totes, and she switched it from one hand to the other. "We've never actually met. I'm Mary Lou Baldwin. I saw you. Yesterday, at the funeral."

My memory jogged, I realized the woman looked familiar because she was one of the people who helped with lunch at Charles's house. I told her how much everyone appreciated the food and all the work Angela's friends had done and asked the inevitable, "What can I do for you?"

"Well, your friend . . ." Mary Lou looked past me to wave at Stan. "He told me how you two were in Ardent Lake because Angela had been one of your customers, and I . . ." As if it might somehow explain, she hoisted the tote bag in both hands. "My mother left me some buttons. I thought you might be interested in looking through them, and maybe buying them if they're worth anything."

I do not need to say how much this cheered me.

Finally, I could get down to business. My real business. Which—just for the record—has nothing to do with murder, and everything to do with buttons. Besides, every button stash brings with it the tantalizing possibility of a newly discovered treasure.

My fingers itching to get started and my blood singing with the endless possibilities of unearthing some gorgeous button that had been ignored for years, I ushered Mary Lou into the back room, and when she refused a cup of coffee, I put on a pot of water for tea and settled her on one of the stools pulled up next to the worktable.

An hour later, we'd been through the buttons and two cups of Red Zinger, and I had a small pile of choice buttons on the table in front of me.

"You're sure about selling?" I asked one last time.

Mary Lou nodded. She was a pleasant woman who'd told me about how she met Angela through the Ardent Lake Garden Club. They weren't close friends, she admitted, but that didn't stop Mary Lou's eyes from filling with tears when Angela's name came up.

I liked Mary Lou.

"I've got enough of my mother's things to remember her by," she said. "It's not like I need those few buttons. Plus . . ." Her shoulders shot back and she sat a little straighter. "I'm saving for a cruise to the Caribbean. It's a surprise for my husband for our fortieth anniversary."

I grimaced. "If you're thinking these buttons—"

"Oh, no!" Mary Lou laughed. "Don't worry. It's not like I think they're worth enough to pay for the entire cruise. But every little bit helps."

"As little as seventy-five dollars?" I asked.

She grinned. "I was sure you were going to say fifty. Sold!"

Truth be told, seventy-five dollars was a tad too generous on my behalf, but that didn't stop me from writing out a check and gladly handing it over to Mary Lou. I hoped knowing she'd made something of a button killing would keep Mary Lou's spirits up.

Especially since I was about to launch into a not-so-pleasant subject.

"So . . ." I sorted through the buttons I'd chosen, making small piles. Clear glass to my left. Fabric buttons on my right. Realistics right in the middle. I have a special place in my heart for realistics, those cute buttons that are made to look like actual objects. I fingered a small yellow squirrel. "You knew her, Mary Lou. What do you think about Angela's death?"

She wasn't expecting the question, and Mary Lou's bottom lip suddenly quivered. I was almost ready to throw in the towel, admit that I was poking my nose where it had no business and apologize for upsetting her, when she said, "I've never known anyone before who was actually . . . you know . . . murdered." She gave that last word all the gravity it deserved.

Mary Lou folded her hands together in her lap. "It's hard to imagine everything that happened to her that night." Apparently, not that hard, because her eyes filled with tears. She glanced away. "I'm sorry. Like I said, Angela and I weren't close, but just thinking about anyone dying that way . . ."

"I absolutely know how you feel." Now that I'd gotten her talking, I didn't want Mary Lou to get any ideas— like about leaving—so I filled the electric kettle again and plugged it in. I got out two fresh teacups and plopped a tea bag in each, and when the water boiled, I poured and carried the cups back to the table. "I saw Angela that night. Just before—"

"Of course! I'm so sorry." Mary Lou put a hand on my arm in sympathy. "Here I am getting all mushy and I hadn't talked to Angela since the Garden Club Christmas luncheon. And you saw her that night. Just before . . ."

Neither of us needed to elaborate.

After an appropriate minute of silence that filled in for all the details neither of us wanted to mention, I fished the bag out of my teacup with a spoon and added some honey. "So what are they saying in Ardent Lake?" I asked. "Any theories?"

"About Angela?" Mary Lou had fixed her own tea moments before and she was in the middle of blowing on it. She paused, the cup at her lips. "You know she thought she was cursed."

"And I think we can both be pretty sure the curse had nothing to do with her murder."

One corner of Mary Lou's mouth pulled into a wry smile. "It would be easier, wouldn't it? I mean, thinking that you're cursed, and that's why bad things happen to you. Or you're somehow blessed and that's why you're successful. If you believed that, then you wouldn't have to accept the fact that there are people who actually choose to do evil things to other people."

"And you think someone chose to do this to Angela?"

Mary Lou's gaze snapped to mine. "Well, obviously. Someone killed her."

"But you don't think it was random. You think it was planned. Why do you think that, Mary Lou?"

She set her cup on the worktable. "Well, I can't say for sure. Believe me, if I could, I'd go right to the police with the information. But it does make you wonder, doesn't it? About what's in people's hearts. About their motives."

"Did anyone you know have a motive to kill Angela?"

Mary Lou lifted her teacup and took a sip. Over the rim of her cup, her gaze flickered my way. "You know there was bad blood between Angela and Susan O'Hara?"

"I heard something about that, yeah."

"Well . . ." Mary Lou set down her cup. "Maybe Susan shouldn't have been so convinced she lost out. You know, where Larry is concerned."

I wasn't sure what Mary Lou was getting at.

Unless . . .

I put down my cup, too, the better to concentrate on my guest. "You're saying that Susan had a chance to get Larry back. Because . . ."

Mary Lou scooted forward on the stool. "Well, I don't know all the details because I could only hear some of it, but . . ." She leaned nearer. "It happened the afternoon Angela was killed. I was in Larry's hardware store picking up a few things. It's a big, old-fashioned sort of store. You know, lots of aisles, lots of inventory. I was the only customer there. Larry was up by the cash register and I was by the plumbing supplies. That's way in the back of the store. I'm sure that's why Angela didn't see me when she came in."

Something that felt very much like hope blossomed in my heart. Oh, I didn't expect Mary Lou to hand me the solution to this case on a silver platter. But—finally—I was about to hear information. Information about the day Angela died.

I didn't want to scare Mary Lou. Or make her think I was some kind of weirdo. I controlled my curiosity, and my voice, when I asked, "She was shopping?"

"More like she was looking to bust heads." Mary Lou gave me a steady look. "Namely, Larry's head."

"Really? But they were—"

"Madly in love? Yeah, that's what everyone in town thought. Including Susan, which is why she's been so upset all these months. She couldn't believe Larry dumped her for Angela. But if Susan had been in the hardware store that day . . ." Mary Lou whistled low under her breath.

And I could only pretend to be semi-interested for so long. I leaned forward, too. "What happened?"

"Well, like I said . . ." Mary Lou settled herself more comfortably. "I was the only person in the store, and Angela didn't see me when she walked in. That would explain why she came in spitting fire."

"You saw her? From where you were at the back of the store?"

"Didn't need to see her. Didn't have to." Mary Lou shook her head. "I heard her."

"And she said?"

Mary Lou laughed. "What didn't she say! The first words I heard after the front door banged shut behind her were something like, 'Larry, we need to talk.' And you have to admit, that doesn't sound like much, except for the way she said it."

As if reliving the moment, Mary Lou got quiet. A second later, a shiver snaked over her shoulders. "There was venom in her voice, that's for sure. That's what got me to sit up and take notice, so to speak."

"So you . . ."

Mary Lou's cheeks got dusky. "I moved up closer to the front of the store, of course. So I didn't miss a word."

"And Angela still didn't see you?"

"She didn't. And honestly, I think Larry forgot all about me being there. But then, I got the impression Angela blindsided him. He greeted her like everything was normal. Asked how she was. Told her she looked pretty that day."

I remembered Angela's outfit—the sweatpants, the T-shirt, the Crocs—and decided right then and there that Larry must have been one special boyfriend. "What did Angela say to that?" I asked.

"She said that Larry should quit it with the bullshit." Mary Lou nodded. "I know, that doesn't sound like much. But if you knew Angela, you'd know she never talked like that. But it's exactly what she said. Bullshit. And when Larry tried to ask what she was talking about . . . well, that's when all proverbial hell broke loose."

"She got mad?"

"That's putting it mildly."

"But did she . . ." I wanted to make sure I got as much information as I could out of Mary Lou, so I phrased my question carefully. "Did she say why she was angry at Larry?"

She shook her head. "He asked. A couple times. And she kept saying the same thing. That he should know what she was talking about. That she couldn't believe it herself, but that she'd been through it over and over and that now she was sure."

"Of what?"

Mary Lou shrugged. "Unfortunately, another customer came in, and Larry ushered Angela into the back office. While they were in there, I rushed out of the store as fast as I could. I couldn't bear the thought of either of them realizing I'd heard what I heard. I mean, it would have been so embarrassing. For both of them!"

Suddenly, those pictures that had been taken down off the wall at Angela's house made a whole lot more sense. "She was angry," I told myself. "Angry enough to rip his pictures off the wall."

Mary Lou confirmed this. "I kind of waited around in the parking lot for a little while after I left the store," she said. "I hoped Angela would come out. I wouldn't have told her I knew what happened in the store, but I thought I could . . . oh, I don't know. I guess I thought if I just tried to pretend we'd just run into each other and be friendly and engage her in conversation, it might help."

"But she didn't come out."

"Not while I was there. That other customer came and went and I figured . . . well, I guess I figured that would give Angela and Larry a chance to talk a little more. I didn't want to go in and interrupt. I figured they'd work things out."

I wondered if they did.

"You never said anything to Larry?" I asked Mary Lou. "Not even at the funeral?"

"Oh, good heavens, how could I?" She fanned her flaming cheeks with one hand. "He was so darned broken up at the wake. And at the funeral, the poor man could barely hold himself together. I knew what that meant. He and Angela had settled their differences. Whatever they were. Otherwise, he wouldn't have looked so terribly unhappy."

She was right, and I told Mary Lou as much. Still . . .

"That explains why Angela looked so terrible when she came here to the Button Box," I said. "And why she never called to say she was on her way, either. The poor woman was too upset. But if she and Larry had already made up . . ."

Mary Lou looked at me hard. "What are you saying? That you don't think they made peace?"

"If they did, Angela would have been happy, and she wouldn't have looked as miserable as she did when she walked in here that evening. And she wouldn't have talked about how she hoped once she gave away the charm string, the bad things in her life might be reversed. She wasn't talking about the attempted break-in at her house. Or that fire in her kitchen. She was talking about breaking up with Larry. She thought it was the fault of the charm string, and once it was out of her life, she thought maybe they could get back together again. She wouldn't have said any of that. Not if she and Larry had already kissed and made up."

"You're right." Mary Lou looked at her watch and slipped off the stool. "And I have to get going. Thanks for taking those buttons off my hands. Maybe I'll see you around Ardent Lake sometime."

Maybe?

I didn't waste a nanosecond considering my answer to that question. As soon as Mary Lou walked out the door, I checked with Stan to see if he could watch the Button Box for me the next day.

I was heading back to Ardent Lake.

It was time I had a serious talk with Larry.

Chapter Ten

It was slow going to Ardent Lake the next day. The main drag into town was filled with giant equipment—cranes and bulldozers and big yellow trucks with wheels taller than my car—coming and going at the reservoir. I was sorry I hadn't invited Stan to join me for the return trip. Aside from the fact that it would have given me someone to talk to while I waited for a really big earthmover to crawl across the road, Stan was interested in the reservoir draining project; I'm sure he would have enjoyed watching all the activity.

I may have been slowed down, but I kept my eyes on the prize. The first thing I did when I (finally!) got into town was go straight to the hardware store.

A bit of a confession here: I love old-fashioned hardware stores.

I know, I know, it sounds a little crazy, especially coming from a woman whose head is usually filled with nothing but buttons. But really, there are so many things in a hardware store that a button nerd can appreciate:

Toolboxes with little compartments that are perfect for sorting buttons.

Awls for punching holes in the heavy mat board collectors use to display their buttons.

Coated wire to attach the buttons to that mat board.

Polish for metal buttons, lemon oil to clean wooden buttons, soft rags to buff the mother of pearl buttons.

With the right attitude and time to kill, a button collector can make a visit to a hardware store a field trip worth remembering.

Unfortunately, I didn't have the time that day. Or for that matter, the inclination. I was there strictly for information, though when I pushed open the front door and got a look at the rough-hewn timbers of the old oak floors, the wooden shelves with their patina of age, and the tin ceiling where fans gently whirred overhead, I nearly forgot the purpose of my mission.

Maybe that was a good thing, because when I drew in a deep breath, let it out slowly, and gushed, "There's nothing like an old hardware store," Larry smiled at me from his place behind the cash register.

I headed to the front counter and set down my purse, gazing up at the ceiling as I did. I love my tin ceiling at the Button Box. It's very pretty, and original to the brownstone, which was built back in the late nineteenth century. But in the world of embossed tin, my shop ceiling is . . . well, it's a ceiling. Larry's was the Sistine Chapel. Each brass square featured a central motif of an ivy wreath, and each wreath was surrounded by exquisitely wrought fleur-de-lis.

"You're new in town," Larry said.

I laughed. "And you know this because people who are new in town always stare at your ceiling in wide-eyed wonder?"

He was a tall, broad guy with even features and a long thin nose, and according to what Nev had told me, Larry was sixty-five years old. Larry's hair was silvery, and though I'd seen him at the funeral, there his eyes had been cast down and swollen from crying. Now, I realized that the pictures I'd seen of him at Angela's didn't do those eyes justice. They weren't just blue, they were a blue so vivid and so lively and intelligent, I suddenly understood why Angela and Susan felt he was worth fighting over.

"What can we do for you?" Larry asked, his question shaking me out of my thoughts.

"Aside from telling me the history of this place?"

"You are new around here." A woman walked up to the counter with a pint of wood stain, and Larry rang up the order. While he was at it, he asked the woman about her husband and how his surgery went, and how her son was doing in the Army. It was the kind of personal and very special customer service big box stores can't possibly offer, and I put another mental tick mark in the column I called "Why I Love Ardent Lake."

Larry finished and the customer left. Let's face it, when it comes to investigations, I'm not a professional.

I mean, not like Nev. But I know a thing or two about easing into my questioning.

"So . . ." My hands flat against the counter, I looked toward Larry. "What can you tell me? When was it built?"

"This building?" A tiny smile played around the corners of his mouth. "That would be 1982."

"You mean 1882."

"I mean 1982. Like the rest of the town."

I do not look especially attractive with my mouth hanging open, but I am hardly vain. I snapped it shut mostly because I didn't want to look stupid.

Larry didn't hold it against me; his laugh was filled with humor. "I'm sorry. I just can't help myself. I love the look on people's faces when they first hear the news."

"But . . . you're telling me . . . that . . ."

"It was built in 1982." He pronounced the date carefully and slowly just to be sure I understood. "There was no Ardent Lake before that."

"But then . . ." I looked over my shoulder toward the front windows of the store and the houses I could see beyond. "The beautiful Victorian homes, they're all . . ."

"Phony baloney. Every single one of them."

I groaned at my own slowness. Of course, it had all been staring me in the face from the moment I first drove in to Ardent Lake. "That explains why all the house colors match. And all the flowers, and why everything looks perfectly—"

"Restored. You got that right. When the hydroelectric company built the reservoir, they flooded Ardent, and we all lost our homes and our property. They gave us this land, but on one condition. City Council and the hydro-electric company's board, they decided on a planned community, and we had to agree to abide by their rules, and the look of the place. What you see is what we got. Ardent Lake."

"It looks perfect because it is perfect. It was planned to be perfect."

"It's home sweet home."

That explained why Angela's house had such a wonderfully Victorian exterior and an inside that was more early Madonna.

"But that doesn't explain . . ." I glanced around Larry's store. "The old wood floor?" I croaked.

He tapped one foot. "Laminate made to look old."

"And the beautiful ceiling?" I was almost afraid to ask.

There was a broom nearby, and Larry lifted it by the bristles and tapped the handle to what I'd thought was antique tin. The broom handle made a dull, thumping sound instead of the metallic ping I expected. "It's called anaglypta," Larry explained. "It's heavy embossed wallpaper, painted to look like tin."

"Well, somebody did an amazing job!" Just to be sure, I looked up at the ceiling again. "The whole town—"

"Is a sham."

Larry said this with good humor, but I have to admit, I was pretty bummed. What I thought was a Garden of Eden was really a stage set.

"Well . . ." I drew in a breath. "I guess we don't have to discuss history then."

"Oh, there was history, but that's all gone now." He

shook his head sadly. "That was lost when the water swallowed Ardent. We're lucky some people around here are trying their best to make sure people don't forget. They teach a whole unit about the old town over at the elementary school, and we've got not one, but two historical museums."

Two?

This was news, and I wondered why no one had ever bothered to mention it before.

"I've seen the museum near the park," I said, though truth be told, I'd only seen a picture of the museum over near the park. A picture that featured Larry and Aunt Evelyn. "There's another one?"

"Over that way." He pointed to his left toward some distant, indistinct place on the other side of town. "The first one—the one you were at—is what we like to call the Big Museum, though obviously, *big* is a relative word. That museum was established first. It's the one the city likes to brag about, the one that gets all the publicity and holds all the fancy fund-raisers and such."

"And the other one?"

Larry pursed his lips, apparently trying to decide if he should toe the line or dish the dirt. "Run by sort of a scatterbrained woman. You know the type, all enthusiastic and wide-eyed, but not exactly sure how to make their big plans work. When the curator of the Big Museum left a few years ago, she applied for that job. She didn't get it, and I suppose that's what made her decide she could do a better job on her own. She bought a house and opened a museum in it. Around here, we call that one the Little Museum. Who does that?" he asked himself more than me. "Who just starts a museum? Not that I'm saying it's a bad little place." I couldn't fault Larry for covering his bases. He didn't know me, and as a business owner, he couldn't afford to alienate anyone.

"It's in a house she bought for a song when the original owner got foreclosed. There isn't much in that Little Museum," he added, "but I hear the collection's growing. If you decide to check it out, tell Marci over there that I sent you."

"Marci Steiner?"

Like anybody could blame me for being surprised? For all her talk about Susan, Marci had never bothered to mention that she was something of a rival, museum-wise. Or that she had once applied for the job Susan ended up getting.

I guess my astonishment showed, because Larry's mouth pursed, and his eyebrows did a slow slide upward. "I see you know Marci."

"We've met." I didn't bother to add the bit about how Marci dissed Susan and gave me the dirt on Susan and Larry. "I'll be sure to stop into the Little Museum," I said instead, and added the visit to my to-do list.

Oh yeah, Marci and I had a few things to talk about. For now . . .

There was a display of palm-sized flashlights on the counter and I picked through the various colors. After our mishap with the fuse box at the store, I knew Stan would be happy to have a few more flashlights around.

I chose a blue one to go in the top drawer of my desk in the shop and a yellow one for the back workroom. I set them on the counter.

"It's too bad when history gets lost," I said, sticking to the subject at the same time I did my best to nudge it in a slightly different direction. "As time passes, so many stories get lost. Or somehow turned around. You know, so that people think one thing is true when it's really not."

Larry was still hanging on to the broom, and he leaned it against the wall behind the counter. "We're not talking about Ardent anymore, are we?"

I smiled in a way that told him he just might be right. "I'm Josie," I explained. "I'm the button dealer from Chicago who—"

"Was helping Angela out with the charm string."

I can honestly say I'd never seen anyone's expression fall quite so quickly or so far. Larry twined his fingers together, his left thumb playing over his right hand. "Have the police found anything?" he asked. "Do they know who . . ." There was a bottle of water sitting nearby and he uncapped it and took a swig. "I'm sorry. It's hard for me to talk about her. Maybe . . . maybe you understand."

"I do. The day Angela dropped off the charm string, she talked about you. I know you two were close."

Larry was wearing a white golf shirt with the words *Larry's Hardware* embroidered over the heart in red, and against the pale color, his skin looked ashy. "I lost my wife four years ago," he said. "And I had pretty much come to grips with the fact that I was going to grow old all by myself. Old and lonely. Then Angela came along."

"But not until after Susan did."

The softness vanished from his expression and he grabbed the broom so fast, I thought he might use it to shoo me out the front door. Instead, he got to work, sweeping behind the counter. "Who told you that? And what do you care about Susan, anyway?" he asked.

"I'm just trying to understand, that's all."

"Why?" Both his hands clutching the broom handle, he sent a laser look across the counter. "You're just the button lady who helped Angela with her charm string. Why? Why do you care what goes on here in Ardent Lake?"

"I suppose I shouldn't. I don't. Not really." There was something about Larry's very blue and very direct gaze that made my knees quiver, and rather than take the chance of letting him know, I strolled over to the nearest display rack. It featured maps of the area, gum and mints, and a free Ardent Lake Chamber of Commerce publication.

I grabbed one of those along with a pack of Juicy Fruit and set them down near the flashlights. "I just wondered . . . you know, if once you left Susan for Angela, if Susan might have been angry enough to—"

"You're kidding me, right?" The tone of Larry's voice had nothing to do with kidding. In fact, it was positively icy. "You think Susan might have killed Angela? You obviously don't know Susan."

"We've met. And she never bothered to mention her relationship with you."

"Maybe that's because it's none of your business."

Technically, he was right.

And I was out of my league.

I thought about the times I'd seen Nev interview people—suspects and victims alike—and I hoped that, like I'd seen him do so many times, I could defuse the anger that would stop Larry from talking.

"Angela was such a nice woman," I said.

"You think by trying to shmooze me, it will make me think you're not being nosy?"

Big points for Larry, he knew how to lay things on the line.

And I knew better than to try and get away with anything.

"You're absolutely right." I unzipped my purse and pulled out my wallet, shoving the few items I'd taken from Larry's shelves closer to him and getting out a ten-dollar bill. "It's none of my business, and I'm being nosy, and you know what? I just can't seem to help myself. I talked to Angela two days in a row, you see, and I knew she was so worried about that curse she believed in. But I didn't take her seriously. And when she left my shop the night of the murder and we heard that dog howling . . ."

"Angela and her superstitions." Larry barked out a laugh. "I hope you're not on some holy mission to find out who murdered her because you feel like you should have done something to help her."

"Of course not." I was getting pretty good at lying, so I barely batted an eye. I wasn't about to bare my soul—and my guilt—to Larry. "I know the curse wasn't real. But I was so close, Larry." Even the best liar can't be completely unemotional. I sucked in a breath. "I feel as if I've got a stake in finding out what happened to Angela. That's why when I heard that you and Susan once dated, I wondered if maybe the fact that you broke up with her had anything to do with Angela's murder. Then I heard . . ." I took the plunge. "Then I heard that maybe it didn't matter that you broke up with Susan to date Angela. Because I heard that you and Angela were finished."

He flinched as if I'd slapped him. "That's crazy."

"But you did have a fight the afternoon Angela was killed."

Larry had been about to take the money out of my hand and he froze. "Who told you that?" he asked.

"Then it's true. What did you fight about?"

He pounded the keys of the cash register, and when it popped open, he snapped the money out of my hand. "Angela should have known better. She'd listened to some gossip she never should have listened to."

"Gossip about . . ."

"The fact that I said it was gossip should make it clear that it's not worth repeating." He counted out my change. "You heard all this from that busybody, Mary Lou, didn't you? She was in here that afternoon. She must have been the one who told you. See what I mean about gossip? Serves no purpose. None at all. And more often than not, it leads people to the wrong conclusions. Just like what's happened to you."

Larry slapped my change into my hand and reached below the counter for a bag. "What Mary Lou didn't hear was the whole part about how Angela and I talked things out, and we realized that the whole thing was nothing more than a misunderstanding. When Angela left here, she was happy, she was smiling, and we were back to where we were to begin with. Angela and I, we were solid."

I thought about the way Angela looked when she arrived at the Button Box the night of the murder. "But she wasn't happy when she came to Chicago that evening."

Larry slammed the cash register drawer shut and scooped my purchases into the bag. "I don't know about that. I can't say. Maybe there was a lot of traffic between here and Chicago. Maybe she got a speeding ticket. Maybe she ate something for lunch that didn't agree with her.

"All I know is that day was the last time I saw Angela. The last . . ." His voice broke. "The last time I talked to her. Ever."

"I'm sorry." I was. Honest. I was sorry I'd upset Larry. I was sorry I wasn't better at this whole investigating thing, because if I was, I wouldn't have simply grabbed the bag Larry handed me and hightailed it out of his store as fast as I did.

I was sorry I'd blown the whole thing and I hadn't been smarter and found out what Larry and Angela were fighting about.

I was sorry Angela was dead.

When I got into the car, locked the doors, and was finally able to take a deep breath, I realized that, really, that was the only thing that mattered.

Angela was dead, and someone had to work to find out who murdered her and bring her justice. Nev was doing that through legitimate means, and he'd asked me to help more casually.

If I upset Larry in the process, maybe it wasn't such a bad thing.

I started up the car and wheeled out of the parking lot, heading in that vague direction where Larry indicated the Little Museum was located and telling myself that the morning hadn't been a total loss.

After all, I knew Larry was lying. I mean, about Angela being happy and them being a couple again after their little tiff.

I knew this because of the way Angela acted when she came to the Button Box to see me that evening. And because of the way she looked. As a woman who'd once been done wrong by the man she loved, I also knew that she wouldn't have taken down his pictures from her wall—and kept them down—if they had made their peace.

I also knew that Marci hadn't told me the whole story about how Susan had gotten the job Marci wanted and how that might affect how she felt—and what she said—about Susan.

I wheeled down a street of attractive homes and realized I knew one more thing, too.

The pristine facade of Ardent Lake was nothing more than fiction, one that hid a whole lot of secrets.

Chapter Eleven

OK, SO MARCI HADN'T EXACTLY LIED TO ME. BUT SHE
had left out a big chunk of the truth.

Don't think I wasn't going to check into it.

I followed my nose, and that gesture Larry used to
indicate the other side of town. Luckily, Ardent Lake
isn't all that big and I didn't have far to drive. Not three
blocks away from Larry's Hardware, I found a pale gray
Victorian with purple trim and a sign out front that
announced that within its walls was a history of Ardent
Lake along with *curiosities and items of local historical
importance.*

The Little Museum.

There were no cars in the tiny parking lot, and from
what I could see when I pressed my nose to the glass on

the front door and knocked, no one was around. I was about to declare my mission a complete and total failure when a black BMW wheeled into the lot and Marci got out.

I guess when you run your own museum, you have the luxury of making your own hours. (And just for the record, this perk does not translate to the button business.)

Marci seemed honestly surprised to see me. Then again, from what Larry said, I guess it was to be expected. It wasn't like the Little Museum was exactly on the hot list of local tourist attractions.

"I'm headed back to Chicago," I told Marci once we'd exchanged all the usual greetings and small talk and I turned away to get a breath of air that wasn't tainted by the pall of cigarette smoke that hung over her. "But I didn't want to leave until I stopped by to see your museum. The other day when we met at the park, you forgot to mention that you had a museum that was in direct competition with Susan's."

She'd been punching in the code on the security system just inside the front door, and Marci's hand froze over the panel. She snapped herself out of her daze just in time to keep the alarm from sounding, touched the rest of the numbers, and closed the door behind us.

"As I recall, we weren't talking about museums." She swung her Coach bag onto a chair behind an oak rolltop desk that sat against the wall in what used to be the parlor of the house. "I'm glad you stopped in," she chirped in what I imagined was her best tour guide voice. "There's a lot to see here. And a lot to learn. More than at that snooty museum across town where everything's treated like it's gold. Here . . ." She gestured to indicate the entire room.

"My museum," she said, emphasizing that first word, "is an exact replica of a home of the late nineteenth century. Authentic down to the last teacup. You can look around. You can sit in the chairs. You can go upstairs to the nursery and play with the kids' dolls and blocks if you like. The whole point of my museum"—there was that emphasis again—"is to give people a genuine appreciation for what life was like in Ardent back then. Not to make them stand behind a velvet rope and look at some exhibit that's behind glass."

"You mean like the exhibits at Susan's museum? The museum where you applied for the curator's job. The job you didn't get."

Marci's hair was especially spiky that day. She tucked one stiff curl behind her ear. "You've been talking to . . . who? Susan?" She brushed off her own question as inconsequential. "Not that it matters. Not that the stupid job over at that other museum mattered. I applied for it, yes. They didn't give it to me. Yes, that's true too. It's also true that it's their loss." She shrugged to emphasize the point. "And it's true that I'm far more qualified than Susan. I once did an internship at the Field Museum in Chicago, you know. Susan . . ." Marci's smile was as stiff as her hair. I waited to hear the crack. "Susan has all the right friends. Like on the museum board. She got the job because she has connections. And you know what? Not getting that job turned out to be the best thing that ever happened to me. It gave me a chance to open this place. I'm plenty busy."

As if it would somehow prove it, she pointed to the calendar on her desk. "I've got school groups scheduled to come in every day this week. Not to shuffle through some stuffy museum and learn absolutely nothing, but to get a genuine feel for what life was like for their great-grandparents. The kids love coming here."

"I can see why." I wasn't trying to shmooze Marci. Honest. I did a quick turn around the parlor and realized there was a lot to like about the Little Museum. If I didn't know that the town was fake, I would have thought I'd been picked up and dropped right into the nineteenth century. Then again, though I knew the house wasn't genuine Victorian, it didn't mean the furnishings weren't.

There was a red velvet fainting couch in one corner that looked incredibly uncomfortable but was as funky as all get-out. There were curio cabinets nearby filled with teacups and teapots. There was a man's top hat and cane in a stand by the door, and even a stuffed pheasant on top of a china cupboard.

Victorian.

Oh, so Victorian.

No buttons, as far as I could see, and that was probably a good thing. I wasn't there to get distracted. I was there to pin Marci down. Was she telling the truth about Susan and Larry? Or had her jealousy led her to concoct a story?

I strolled from the parlor into the dining room and stopped cold.

"That punch bowl." I didn't have to point—after all, the punch bowl in question was in the center of the mahogany table and impossible to miss.

Gorgeous china antique. Exquisitely painted and decorated with red and purple grapes.

My mind flashed to my visit to Angela's, and the punch bowl that had once belonged to Aunt Evelyn.

And then it flashed to the park and the night I'd met Marci.

She was carrying a shopping bag that night, and it kerchunked when she handled it.

Like there was glass inside.

Not the punch bowl, surely. I hadn't seen it at Angela's until the next day. But something Marci didn't want me to see. Something glass.

I scanned the dining room and the gorgeous oyster plates on the sideboard, the fabulous serving platters on the buffet, the cut crystal stemware, glistening in the morning sun that streamed through the window on my left.

And I wondered how much of it might have been pilfered from Angela's stash.

"That punch bowl is so distinctive," I continued, hopefully as if I hadn't been gobsmacked.

Marci smiled. "It's hand-painted. One of a kind. I know it's not exactly historically accurate to portray a house in Ardent as having so many fine things, but I'll tell you what, I come across something like that punch bowl at an antique shop or an auction and I can't help myself. I have to buy it. I have to display it. Beautiful things deserve to be seen and appreciated, not locked away."

"And you bought the punch bowl in . . ."

She brushed aside the question. "Saint Louis, maybe.

Or it might have been last summer when I took a trip up to Milwaukee. I did quite a bit of shopping there."

I didn't dislike Marci. She struck me as being a little flighty, and let's face it, she did admit to lying to her husband about jogging and not smoking, but hey, there were worse crimes. The least I could do was cut her a little slack.

"I suppose," I said, strolling closer to the table and touching a finger to the punch bowl, "you'd have the receipt. You know, to show the cops when I tell them I think this came straight out of Angela's house."

Her jaw went slack. Her face paled. Marci was wearing the same ridiculously high heels she'd worn to Angela's wake, and her knees knocked and her ankles gave way. She plunked down on one of the green velvet-cushioned dining room chairs and I was glad. Yeah, she was a petite woman, but I didn't fancy the thought of hauling her up off the floor.

It seemed she was also a lousy crook. At least if covering her tracks and acting innocent had anything to do with it.

"How do you . . . When did you . . ." Marci's hands shook and a single tear trickled down her cheek. "Are you going to turn me in to the cops?" she asked.

"That depends."

She swallowed hard. "On . . ."

"On if you tell me the truth."

"I have. I always have." Like a bobble-head, Marci nodded. "Well, not about the jogging. And the smoking. But I didn't lie to you about the smoking, I lied to my husband about the smoking. So that doesn't exactly count.

And I didn't lie about Susan. You've got to believe me. She did used to date Larry, and she was as mad as hell when Larry broke up with her to date Angela."

"I believe you." I did. There was no use beating around the bush. Marci was sitting at the head of the table, and I took the seat to her right. "But what about the punch bowl, Marci? Why did you take it? And how much of this other stuff is Angela's?"

"Well, none of it's hers anymore, is it?" Marci's voice was sharp. Until she remembered that she was in over her head. The starch went out of her, and her bottom lip quivered. "Angela inherited so much from Evelyn," she said, her voice bouncing over the words with each unsteady breath she drew. "She never even noticed some of it was missing."

"So you've been doing this for a while? Since before Angela was killed?"

Marci stopped to think, and I could only imagine she was wondering what would make her look guiltier.

I figured I'd help along her thought processes. "If you were stealing from Angela when she was still alive, and she found out about it, she'd have a reason to be really angry. And she might have threatened to go to the police and turn you in. On the other hand, if you didn't take anything until after Angela was already dead, then it's going to make you look like you were taking advantage of a really bad situation. Personally, I'd go with the second option if I were you. The first one gives you a mighty good motive for killing Angela."

"Me?" Marci hopped out of her chair. "I didn't! I couldn't! I'd never . . ." She gulped. "OK, I admit it, I've been sneaking into her house for a couple months and taking some of the stuff Aunt Evelyn left to Angela. But Angela never found out about it. I swear. She never missed a thing. She didn't know. So she couldn't have turned me in to the cops for stealing. She didn't know about me stealing. And stealing . . . You've probably already figured it out. That's what I was doing in the park the night I ran into you. Teapots, that night. I took a couple teapots. But I'd never . . ." There was so much of a green tinge in her complexion, I couldn't help believing her.

"All right, I admit it," she said. "I thought about killing Angela a time or two. But I never did it. I never would. Taking some of her stuff, that was different and there's not a person in Ardent Lake who wouldn't say it was justified. After all, Angela owed me."

First things first. "You thought about killing Angela a time or two? You want to explain that?"

The head bobbing started again. "Because she lied to me. And she owed me. You know that, don't you? You understand? Angela owed me big-time."

"Because . . . ?"

Marci dragged in a breath. "Because of the charm string, of course," she said.

At this point, even a pretty intelligent woman was allowed to be confused. I was plenty intelligent. And plenty confused.

I patted the table to invite Marci to sit back down, and when she did, I spoke slowly and carefully. "Start at the beginning," I suggested.

She flicked the tears from her cheeks. "Yes, that's

what I need to do. I need to start from the beginning, and tell you what happened. Then you'll understand and you won't . . ." Hope gleamed in her eyes along with the tears. "Then you won't have me arrested."

"Talk," I said instead of making any promises I wasn't sure I could keep.

She actually might have if she didn't jump out of her chair, hurry into the parlor, and come back holding that date book I'd seen on her desk. "It started a couple months ago," she explained, flipping back the calendar pages. "That's when . . . that's when Angela came to me." She stabbed her finger against a Monday circled in red on the calendar. "She offered to donate her charm string."

"To this museum?" I didn't mean to make it sound like I was dissing the Little Museum so I scrambled. "What I mean is, that's not what I heard. That's not what happened. Angela was donating the charm string to Susan's museum."

"Yeah. Well, that's how things ended up. Only . . ." For the first time since I'd caught her red-and-purple-grape-handed, Marci's expression brightened. "Only as it turned out, Susan never did get that charm string, did she? Serves the bitch right."

"And gives you another motive."

Her smile vanished. "That's not what I meant. I just meant, well, Angela, she calls me one day out of the blue. Says she's got this authentic and complete charm string and she'd like to see it displayed here. And I admit, I'd never even heard of a charm string so I didn't have any idea what she was talking about. But we agreed to meet and discuss it, and before we did, I did some research. I realized she had something special and I told her I'd be thrilled to accept her donation and display the charm string here."

"Only Angela apparently changed her mind."

"And fast." As if she still couldn't believe it, Marci made a face and tapped her finger against the very next Wednesday on the calendar. "We agreed on the donation on Monday evening, and then on Wednesday, she calls again, says she's changed her mind and she's going to give the buttons to the Big Museum."

"And you were surprised?"

"That's putting it mildly. The night before, I even talked to my volunteers about where we were going to put the charm string. In the parlor." Marci poked a thumb over her shoulder toward that room. "And how we'd host a little party one evening. You know, as a way to let people know about the charm string and to thank Angela for donating it. We even planned a menu! And not twelve hours after all that, she calls me to tell me she changed her mind. Oh yeah, surprised is putting it mildly. We're not a fancy organization, not like over at the Big Museum. But I do have some loyal supporters, mostly the teachers in the local school system. I was so excited about the charm string, I'd already sent out an e-mail to all of them telling them all about it. That Angela . . ." Marci crossed her arms over her chest. "She made me look stupid and incompetent."

Motive.

I didn't say this out loud because, let's face it, alone

with someone who has motive to be a killer isn't the best time to bring up something like that.

And it wouldn't have mattered, anyway. Marci was on a roll. She wasn't listening. "Once Susan made the announcement that the charm string was going to the Big Museum and there was an article about it in the *Ardent Lake Gazette* . . . well, that's when I knew it was official, and that's when I started going over to Angela's and picking up stuff," she explained, as if *picking up stuff* was enough of a euphemism to excuse the stealing. "That charm string must have been worth thousands. The way I figured it, that's what Angela owed me. Thousands. One way or another, I figured I'd get it from her." She darted me a look. "You going to turn me in?"

I pretended to think about it. Just to make her squirm.

"You going to return it all?" I finally asked.

The wistful look Marci gave the punch bowl was all the answer I needed.

So here was the question, at least the question I was asking myself:

Why had Angela offered the charm string to Marci, then changed her mind and promised it to Susan?

As far as I could see, there was only one way to find out.

The last I saw of Marci, she was getting out a roll of brown paper and a stack of boxes to pack all her purloined exhibits. That taken care of, I headed to the Big Museum.

Susan wasn't in her office, so while I waited for a woman wearing a yellow T-shirt that said "Docent" on it to find her, I took a quick stroll around.

Unlike Marci's homey little place, the Historical Society museum was roomy, a broad stone building that, according to a plaque on the wall, had once been a private—and pricey—psychiatric clinic. It had a central entranceway with a marble floor and rooms with tall ceilings that fanned out on either side. The first room to my right featured a display about the "old" Ardent, including some photographs of the town before the reservoir was built.

I confess, it was a bit of a letdown. After seeing the fictionalized version of the town in all its color-coordinated glory, I expected more. More spectacular. More charming. More interesting.

In fact, Ardent wasn't all that different from thousands of other small towns. One picture showed a main street with a pizza place, a gas station, and a convenience store flanking the police station and a firehouse. Another picture showed an old-fashioned railroad. A third must have been taken on the Fourth of July, because there was red, white, and blue bunting on the gazebo in the town square, and flocks of people in summer clothes were eating ice cream cones and listening to a band whose members had shaggy hair and wore leisure suits.

The room beyond that one had a small crowd of senior citizens in it, all of them jockeying for position around a poster with big, thick lettering: "Thunderin' Ben Moran," it said. "Ardent's Own Pirate."

Years of button collecting had taught me never to try and get ahead of a senior citizen in any line. I politely waited my turn, but I had just stepped up to the front of the line for a chance to read the poster when I heard Susan call my name.

In a gray suit and crisp pink blouse, she looked trim and as orderly as her museum.

"I'm glad you stopped by," she said, extending her hand and shaking mine. "I knew you'd enjoy yourself here. There's so much to see."

"And learn." I gestured toward the poster I hadn't had time to read. "You weren't kidding when you told me about the pirate at the wake. There really were pirates. In Illinois!"

Susan laughed. "Well, not too many of them. In fact, we like to think of old Thunderin' Ben as the one and only. That's what makes him so fascinating. He was born in Ardent, you know. Did you have a chance to look at the exhibit?"

I told her I hadn't and she waited until the senior citizens had moved on to the next room and ushered me closer so that I could get a good look at the grainy black-and-white photograph of an old lake schooner, sails unfurled, cutting through the water.

"That was Thunderin' Ben's ship," Susan explained. "The *Annie Darling*. He captained that ship for nearly fifty years, and wreaked havoc up and down the shoreline of Lake Michigan." She smiled. "These days, it all sounds like something out of a screwball comedy, but I suppose back in the early 1920s—that's when Ben was at his thunderin' best—well, it was serious business."

Inside the glass display case in front of the picture was a replica of a buoy bobbing in the southern end of a painted Lake Michigan, and Susan pointed to it. "One of the things Ben was famous for is what's called mooncussing," she said. "Don't ask me where the word comes from! I only know what it means and that was that pirates like Ben would move the buoy markers and that would cause ships to go aground. Then once the crew abandoned ship, Ben and his crew of bandits would board the vessels and steal everything they could. They used to do the same sort of thing with the *Annie Darling*, sneak into a port at night when no one was around, and dock the ship long enough to steal anything that wasn't nailed down."

I couldn't help it. In my own imagination, I wondered if someday there would be a display about Marci Steiner in the Big Museum.

"Of course, what Ben is really famous for around here . . ." Susan snapped me out of the thought with a wave toward a book with a tattered brown cover inside the display case. "His diary," she said, her eyes lighting. "And though I've read it cover to cover and never found a thing, there are supposedly clues inside. You know, about the treasure."

Aha! Now all the interest in Thunderin' Ben was starting to make sense.

"Let me guess," I said, "Caribbean islands, sandy beaches."

"No such thing." Susan laughed. "The legend says that the treasure is buried nearby." Still smiling, she turned from the display. "Every once in a while, someone gets it into their head to try and find it, but so far, no one's had any luck. Personally, I think old Thunderin' Ben made it all up. He was as big a storyteller as he was a pirate."

"You mean no pieces of eight and gold doubloons?"

Susan's shrug said it didn't matter. "Never that," she said. "The story says that on one of those midnight raids of his, Ben ended up with the chest full of money that was headed up to the mining camps along Lake Superior. Thousands and thousands of dollars. Who knows if that's true! All I know is that the more interest there is in Ben and his treasure, the more people come to visit the museum. And really, that's all I care about."

"Which is exactly why you were so happy to get the charm string, right?"

It seemed the most natural question in the world to me, yet something about it must have signaled to Susan that the topic of our conversation had shifted. Just a tad. She gave me a quick, sidelong look. "Would you like to see the spot we had picked out for it?" she asked, and without waiting for me to answer, she led the way.

We crossed the wide entranceway to the other side of the building and a room that reminded me a whole lot of the parlor at the Little Museum. Victorian bric-a-brac, flamboyant furniture, elaborate paintings. Like the Little Museum but not. Susan's palatial to Marci's homespun. If she was trying to compete, I could understand why Marci had turned to a life of crime.

"There." Susan waved her hand toward a wide—and very bare—expanse of wall. "We were going to install it starting there." She swung around to her left, then did a slow arc in the other direction. "All the way to there.

One thousand buttons. The charm string was going to take up a lot of room."

"It would have looked great. And to think, you almost didn't get the charm string at all."

Have I mentioned that I'm getting really good at sounding casual when I'm actually digging for information?

Maybe not as good as I thought, though, because Susan glared at me, her eyes narrowed. "What are you talking about?"

"Angela," I said, still oh so casual. "You know, she originally offered the charm string to Marci."

Susan flinched. "You're kidding me, right?"

"Heard it from Marci."

"Well, consider the source."

"Let's pretend she is telling the truth." I dangled the possibility in front of Susan. "That would leave us with two questions. Number one, why would Angela offer the charm string to Marci in the first place? And number two, why would she change her mind within just a couple days and call you?"

"Is that what happened? Who knows why? I told you before, Angela was crazy."

"That actually might explain it," I conceded, but I didn't add that it wasn't likely. In my experience, there were far more complicated and sinister reasons for murder than simple craziness. "But what if it wasn't because she was crazy? Why would Angela want the charm string to go to the Little Museum?"

"Well, that seems like a no-brainer, doesn't it?" As if

the thought sat uncomfortably, Susan twitched her shoulders. "Angela and I weren't exactly best friends."

"Because of Larry."

I wasn't imagining it—a small smile touched the corners of her mouth.

"But if that's true, why would Angela change her mind?" I ask.

That smile froze in place and Susan's shoulders shot back. "Maybe Angela realized Marci was just as nuts as she was. Imagine, anyone taking that tacky little museum of hers seriously! And the woman is so enamored of herself, she's even had a state-of-the-art security system installed. Honestly, Marci Steiner's ego could float a boat."

"So Angela withdrew her offer because of Marci's ego?"

"Well, Angela had something of an ego of her own, you know. She's the one who insisted we put on that tea party in her honor. You know, as a thank-you to her for donating the buttons. We've never done anything like that for any other donor. But Angela said, no party, no charm string."

"And you caved."

"I cooperated." Susan stepped away from me and I knew what it meant. Marci might be uppity and think more of herself than any museum curator should, but Susan was important and had things to do. "I did what was good for my museum," she pointed out. "In the end, that was all that mattered anyway."

"So you're willing to believe that Angela simply

changed her mind. Kind of like Larry changed his mind when he dumped you for her."

Her chin came up a fraction of an inch, and that tiny smile was back.

"Ancient history," Susan said. "And it doesn't matter now, anyway. Larry realizes he made a mistake. He freely admits it. And in case you don't know what I'm getting at here, Ms. Giancola, let me be perfectly clear: it doesn't matter what Angela did or said. Angela is dead. And Larry and I? We're a couple again."

Chapter Twelve

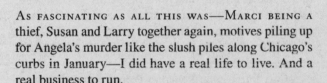

As fascinating as all this was—Marci being a thief, Susan and Larry together again, motives piling up for Angela's murder like the slush piles along Chicago's curbs in January—I did have a real life to live. And a real business to run.

I intended to do both the next day.

As soon as I made one quick stop.

A note here, and it's an important one:

It wasn't like I was missing Kaz. Honest. But when it came to Kaz, something strange was going on, no doubt about that. There had been a major change in the routine he'd followed in all the time we'd been divorced, the one that had Kaz coming around to see me at least once a week to ask for money.

Which, naturally, meant there had been a change in

my routine, too—the one where I roll my eyes when he shows up and firmly tell him no.

I didn't have to be pining for my ex to be curious. And believe me, I wasn't pining for my ex.

But I was plenty curious.

Hence my detour on the way to the Button Box that morning.

After our divorce, when I stayed in the apartment where I'd dreamed we'd have our happily-ever-after and Kaz went on (or so he claimed) to build a new life for himself, he'd rented a place above a storefront in a Chicago neighborhood known as Bucktown, and in spite of my objections, he'd insisted I keep a key. "Just in case," he said.

I was reasonably sure that *just in case* should actually have been *when hell freezes over*, but to shut him up, I took the key. It hung on a hook inside my kitchen door, and it had remained untouched—and pretty much forgotten—for more than a year.

But sometimes life holds surprises, and truth be told, this was one of them.

When I arrived at Pelogia's Perogi Palace and went around to the back entrance reserved for the tenants who lived above the take-away Polish food joint, the rain that pelted down from thick gray clouds was icy cold.

Hell, it seemed, was about to freeze over.

I let myself into the building and climbed the steps to the third floor. From what Kaz had told me, I knew his apartment was up front and to the left.

Yeah, that one.

The one with at least a week's worth of newspapers piled in front of the door like Lincoln Logs.

It's embarrassing to admit, what with me actually being a button seller and all, but I immediately slipped into detective mode.

No sign of forced entry.

No sounds of distress—or anything else—from inside the apartment.

Nothing that indicated anything was wrong.

That didn't keep me from slipping my key in the lock as quietly as I could. Just as carefully, I pushed open the door.

"Kaz?" Well, he was never going to hear me if I sounded like a squeaky little mouse. I told myself not to forget it, and tried again with a little more oomph. "Hey, Kaz. It's Josie. Are you home?"

No answer.

Since it was gloomy outside and gloomier in, I felt along the living room wall for the switch that operated the ceiling fan and overhead light and flicked it on. Kaz's apartment is a lot like Kaz himself. That is, pretty basic. He isn't Mr. Neatnik, but he's not a slob, either, and from the look of the issues of *ESPN, The Magazine* scattered over the coffee table and the beer bottle (empty) on the floor next to the couch, it was impossible to determine when he'd last been in the room.

The kitchen proved no more helpful.

Which only left his bedroom.

I remembered Stan's theory about Kaz shacking up with some buxom blonde and knew (thank goodness!) that if it was happening, it wasn't happening here. There was no sign of a woman's presence, no whiff of perfume, no sound of a throaty, satisfied laugh coming from the bedroom. And no sign of Kaz, either, when I peeked in there and in the bathroom.

I breathed a sigh of relief, and it wasn't because I feared I'd find Kaz with some cutie. That might have been embarrassing—not to mention awkward—but it wouldn't have broken my heart. Kaz had done that long before and for all different reasons.

No, truth be told, I knew there was always the possibility of Kaz getting on someone's bad side. Someone he'd borrowed money from. Someone he'd lost to in a poker game. Someone he'd beat in a poker game (hey, it actually happened once in a while) who was a sore loser. At least I could put that image to rest, the one of Kaz lying by the side of his bed, kneecapped and bloody.

"Very odd," I told myself, plunking down on the couch and taking another look around the room. While I was at it, I wished Kaz had a landline instead of just a cell. That way, at least I might be able to check his messages. I was just about to throw in the towel when I noticed a couple pieces of mail on the coffee table. The postmarks showed they'd been sent nearly two weeks before, and that told me that nearly two weeks ago, Kaz had been home.

Also on the table was a pile of charge receipts and I shuffled through them:

Dinner at the local greasy spoon.

Jeans and sweatshirts from a nearby emporium.

And a receipt from a sporting goods store that showed the purchase of one waterproof tent, a metal detector, and a sleeping bag.

Camping? Not exactly a pastime I'd ever associated with Kaz, and as befuddled as ever, I left the apartment, locking up behind me.

"Camping, huh?" I grumbled once I was outside, huddled in the folds of my raincoat, my shivers keeping tempo with the rain that pinged against the sidewalk. "Well, at least that explains where Kaz is. Maybe."

I'm pretty sure I was still grumbling like this when I got off the El at the stop nearest to the Button Box and approached the shop. I already had the key to my front door in my hand before I noticed the car parked in front of the shop. And the slightly disheveled guy behind the steering wheel watching my every move.

"Hey." Nev, man of many words. He walked around the unmarked police car and joined me on the sidewalk, apparently oblivious to the rain that was soaking his sandy-colored hair and turning it to a shade that reminded me of honey. "I was surprised the shop wasn't open when I got here."

"I had an errand to run." I guess I didn't have all that many words to offer, either. Besides, I was wet and cold and anxious to get inside, and this seemed a simpler explanation than the whole bit about Kaz and how I wasn't missing him.

I opened the shop, discarded my wet coat in the back room, and went through my morning routine, turning on spotlights over the display cases, flicking on my computer and the stained glass lamp that sat atop my desk, putting on a pot of coffee.

"What's up?" I asked Nev when I was done.

He'd slipped off his trench coat and hung it over the back of the chair next to my rosewood desk. "I just wondered what you found out in Ardent Lake yesterday."

Where to begin?

I told him about Marci and made sure to add that she'd promised to return everything to Angela's. That way, it was up to him to decide if the Ardent Lake police should get involved. I also told him Larry and Susan were a couple again, though since he didn't react, I guess he didn't think it was relevant. Maybe he was right.

"What I really don't understand," I admitted, "was why Angela promised the charm string to the Little Museum, then gave it to the Big Museum."

"You think it matters?"

I glanced his way. That morning, Nev was wearing a gray suit, a cream-colored shirt, and a green plaid tie. He hurt my eyes. "Do you think it matters?" I echoed back. "I'm just the button expert here, remember. You're the professional."

"If only that meant I had all the answers!" The aroma of fresh-brewed coffee filled the Button Box, and Nev went into the back room. When he returned, he had a mug in each hand and he set one down on the desk in front of me.

"That Marci, the first museum curator, she might have been mad at Angela for changing her mind about the charm string," he said, falling into professional mode and walking us both through the case. "Or from what you've said about her stealing, she might have been worried that Angela knew what she was up to. That gives her motive, too."

"It does." I took a sip of coffee, enjoying the heat against the back of my throat.

"The second museum curator was jealous that Angela stole her man from her. And now that Angela's out of the way, they're back together. Which pretty much proves that Angela was the one keeping them apart. That looks like pretty good motive for her."

"And the man in question . . ." I was just about to take another drink of coffee and I paused, the cup near my lips and the aroma tickling my nose. "He and Angela had a fight. The afternoon of the day she was killed. He says they were golden again by the time she left the hardware store, but there's no way to prove that. So that might give him motive, too. And all we need to do is figure out which motive is the motive that's the motive for murder."

Big points for Nev, he did not mention how nearly incomprehensible my last comment was. In fact, all he did was shiver. "I can't get warm today," he admitted. "It's like the cold goes right through you out there."

"Which means it would be terrible weather for camping."

Blank stare.

Well, what did I expect?

Fortunately, I didn't have to explain. The phone rang, and I spent a pleasant fifteen minutes talking button gossip with a collector from Saint Louis who was interested in some of the moonglow buttons featured on my website. We came to an agreeable price, she gave me her credit card number, and I promised to ship the buttons that day and send her an e-mail receipt.

"Receipt." I hung up, mumbling the word and drumming my fingers against the phone. "There were receipts," I said, and no, I didn't add *at Kaz's*. Like I said, all that was too complicated to explain to a cop on a rainy morning. "Receipts at Angela's," I said. I dug through my purse to look for them, and when I fished them out, I was sure to mention that Charles had given me permission to take them. Just so Nev didn't get any ideas about me having a felonious side.

When I set them on the desk, he nodded. "They were in her home office. I looked through them when I was there the day after the murder. As far as I remember, there was nothing promising. Or even anything interesting."

Just as a way of having something to do, I looked through them, too. Though there were more of them, Angela's receipts weren't any more interesting than Kaz's.

"Restaurants." I set those receipts on one pile. "Clothing stores." They went in their own little stack. "Hairdresser, nail salon." I started a third stack. "Groceries." These, too, were set aside. It took me only a couple minutes to finish, and when I was done, I was left holding only two receipts. Neither of them fit neatly into any of the categories.

"A fishing charter," I said. "Scheduled on a Monday . . ." I held up first one receipt, then the other. "And canceled on a Wednesday."

"Hmmm . . ." Nev scanned the piles of receipts. "Do you have a pile for recreation?"

Honestly, sometimes even the brightest cop can be dense. I look at him hard when I asked, "Did Angela seem like the kind of woman who would fish for recreation?"

He pursed his lips. "Can't say. I didn't know her. What do you think?"

"I think she wore tailored business suits and got her nails done." I pointed to each appropriate pile in turn. "I think her house was full of expensive antiques, and in the one photo I saw of her and Larry in the great outdoors, I think she looked cold and uncomfortable. Call me crazy . . ." I gave him a chance, but like I said, Nev is pretty bright; he knew better than to take me up on the offer. "Angela on a fishing charter seems odd to me. So does scheduling a boat and then canceling it so soon after. So does . . ."

I took another careful look at the receipts. Something about them jogged a memory, and I tapped my finger against them.

"The dates," I said, thinking back to my meeting with Marci at the Little Museum. "I knew they looked familiar. That Monday, that was the day Angela called Marci and offered the charm string to her."

Nev came around to the other side of the desk and leaned over my shoulder for a look at the receipts. "And the day she canceled the charter?"

"That . . ." Just to be sure I took another gander. "That was the day after she told Marci she'd changed her mind, the day after she offered the charm string to Susan."

Nev didn't say if he thought this was significant or not. Then again, cops are a closemouthed bunch. Especially when it comes to offering an opinion before they have all the facts. What he did instead was slip the receipts off my desk and get out his cell. He made a call, and while he waited for the person on the other end of the phone to answer, he said, "Maybe the weather forecast was bad for the day the boat was scheduled. Maybe that's why she canceled."

I was already one step ahead of him. Except for that day with the rain pelting down and the one morning when I had the charm string in my possession to photograph, it had been a mild and mostly sunny spring, but just to be sure I hadn't forgotten any particularly nasty weather, I looked online and saw that the weather the day of the scheduled fishing excursion had been ideal.

While I pointed to the computer screen, Nev nodded and started talking to the person on the other end of the phone. He identified himself and asked about the receipts in question.

"So was she excited? I mean when she hired the boat in the first place?" Nev asked. "Did she say she was interested in doing a little fishing?"

He paused and listened, then thanked the person and hung up.

"That was the charter company," he explained. "The lady who schedules the excursions says she remembers Angela because Angela told her she wasn't going out on the lake to fish. When she chartered the boat, Angela said she didn't want to bring anything back, she was going out on the water to get rid of something."

"The charm string?" The very thought of all those wonderful old buttons lying at the bottom of Lake Michigan made me so queasy, it took me a minute to wrap my head around it.

"It actually makes sense," I concluded, controlling my gut-wrenching reaction to such a loss. "Because Angela really believed the charm string was cursed. She might have figured dumping the buttons in the lake was the only way to get rid of them. But then . . . then she changed her mind." I almost added *thank goodness*, then decided it made me sound like too much of a button nerd. Nev already knew that about me, I didn't need to hit him over the head with it. "And that's when she decided to donate the charm string to the museum."

"The first museum. Then she changed her mind about that—"

"And offered it to the second museum."

Maybe it was too early in the morning. Or maybe I just hadn't had enough coffee. All this speculation was making my head pound. I took another sip of my coffee and I can't say if it was the warmth or the caffeine that jump-started my brain.

"Maybe . . ," Just so I didn't lose the thought, I took another sip. "Maybe Angela's murder wasn't about her dating Larry or about Marci stealing from the museum. Maybe it really was all about that enameled button. Maybe someone knew how valuable it was. And maybe that same someone heard Angela talking about how she was going to get rid of the fish button and all the other buttons by tossing the charm string in Lake Michigan."

"That same someone might have talked her out of the fishing charter and into donating the buttons." Nev liked where this idea was going; his blue eyes gleamed.

"And the reason that someone wanted Angela to donate the buttons was so that person had more time to get his—or her—hands on the enameled button. Obviously, that was never going to happen if the button was in the lake. And that—" Another idea jolted through me and I sat back, my hands clutching the edge of my desk. "That would explain the attempted break-in at her house that Angela told me about. And that fire in her kitchen. Maybe someone was really trying to get her out of the house so she—or he—could get into the house and take the charm string."

Another thought struck and I sucked in a breath. "Oh my gosh, Nev, Angela said there was a small fire at Aunt Evelyn's, too. Angela's the one who put it out. She just assumed it all happened because of the curse, but—"

"The person who was after the button could have engineered the whole thing."

"And . . ." In spite of the coffee, my throat went dry. I grabbed my mug and took another drink, but thanks to the idea that just popped into my head, it didn't exactly help. "Maybe that's why someone tried to steal my purse. To get my keys and get into the shop. The charm string spent the night here. It's the same reason the lights went out here at the shop the day I had the charm string." I would have slapped my forehead if I didn't have both hands wrapped around my coffee mug. "Stan said the fuse wasn't blown. He said it looked as if the breaker had been tripped. Maybe someone thought that if the lights went out, I'd leave the shop for a while. Or maybe that person thought I'd be the one who went into the basement to see what was wrong, and I'd be easy to overpower. He didn't count on Stan being here with me. We didn't leave.

Nev, that could mean the killer was here. In the building."

Even though it had all happened more than a week before, that didn't stop my heart from starting up a rumba rhythm inside my chest. I looked over my shoulder toward the workroom. "If I'd been here by myself . . ."

"We're not going to worry about that." Nev put a hand on my shoulder. "Nothing happened, and we're not sure about any of this, anyway. But if it is true—"

"Then somebody really wanted that button. Enough to kill for it. We need to figure out who that could be."

"You said the cousin—"

I nodded. "Charles. He's pretty up on the value of things. He would have known how much that charm string was worth. Maybe . . ." I didn't like to think about Angela's last moments, but I forced the words out, anyway. "Maybe he meant to steal the entire charm string and never counted on it breaking when he strangled her."

"And the rest of our suspects?" Nev asked.

"Susan and Marci certainly know what's what when it comes to antiques," I said. "They've got museums full of them. Larry, I'm not so sure about. I can't imagine a guy who owns a hardware store knows a whole bunch about buttons."

We both knew what all this meant. For his part, Nev would do the official digging. And me? I'd get on the phone again and make all the calls I'd made the week before to all the button dealers and collectors who might have come across someone trying to unload a particularly pretty button. Maybe the killer had laid low for a bit. But sooner or later, he'd try to sell the button. I was sure of it. It was the only thing that made sense.

I reached for the binder I kept in my top desk drawer that included a listing of all the phone numbers I'd need. "I love buttons," I said. Not that this was news to Nev. "But I can't imagine killing for one."

"And it was worth . . . what? Maybe a thousand bucks or so? It just doesn't seem worth risking life in prison for a thousand bucks." Nev slipped on his coat. I was about to walk him to the front of the shop when something smacked against my front door.

Automatically, we both looked that way.

No customer coming in. No one standing on the sidewalk.

But again, we heard another thump.

Nev got to the door first, and the moment he opened it, he rolled his eyes and smiled. "Friend of yours?" he asked.

LaSalle stood on the stoop, his tail thumping against the door.

The dog had never been inside the Button Box and I wasn't much for setting that kind of precedent, but hey, it was cold and rainy outside, and the poor dog was drenched. I urged him into the back room, closed the door so he couldn't cause any damage to the front of the shop, and looked for a towel to dry him.

Nev had followed us and he pointed at the mutt. "He's got something in his mouth."

I watched the way LaSalle worked over the whatever it was and imagined all sorts of disgusting things. "I'm not sure I want to find out what it is."

"Except that it's crunching." Nev knelt next to the dog. "Come on, good boy." He held out his hand. Yeah, like he actually expected LaSalle to just spit out whatever the tasty prize happened to be.

I had other plans. I'd brought a tuna sandwich for lunch, and I got it out of the fridge and ripped off a piece. "How about this?" I dangled the morsel in front of LaSalle's nose. "I'll trade you, buddy. What you have in your mouth for tuna with mayo, celery, and sweet pickle."

It was, apparently, a deal.

LaSalle spit out whatever he'd had in his mouth and it rolled under my worktable. He was happily munching on tuna before I even had a chance to bend down and retrieve what had almost been his breakfast.

It was a good thing I did.

"Uh, Nev." When I stood up again, I held out my hand so he could see what was in my palm.

Nev's eyes popped open. "Is that—"

"Yup. Gorgeous aqua water. Beautiful underwater greenery. Brilliant red fish. The enameled button." Another thought struck and I dropped the button on the worktable. "One very wet enameled button." I ran to the sink and washed my hands. When I turned around again, Nev was ripping the rest of my sandwich into chunks and feeding it to LaSalle at the same time he was giving the button a close look. "I can't imagine how the crime-scene techs missed it," he said. "It must have rolled under something."

"And LaSalle knew just where to look." In spite of the fact that he was swallowing the last of my lunch, I gave the dog a pat on the head. "No wonder no one's ever tried to sell it. The button's been here all along. That's good, right?" Like I had to ask? I'd just rescued a valuable button from being eaten. In my world, that makes me something of a superhero.

Which meant Nev should have looked a little happier. "There goes our motive," he muttered. "If Angela wasn't killed for the button—"

"But maybe she was. Maybe the killer just didn't find the button."

Nev scraped a hand through his hair. Since it was still damp and as shaggy as ever, it stuck up at funny angles. He didn't have to say a word. I knew exactly what he was thinking. I grabbed a towel and rubbed down LaSalle, and I bet I looked just as miserable as Nev did when I grumbled, "We're right back where we started from."

Chapter Thirteen

THE NEXT DAY WAS SATURDAY, AND I VOWED I WOULD spend it where I belonged—at the Button Box.

I kept that promise, too, arriving early and staying late at the shop, keeping busy with the minutiae of button sales and collecting.

I rearranged one of the display cases, replacing a shelf of tortoiseshell buttons with cute little realistics with a springtime theme, bunnies and flowers and even a couple Easter eggs. I filled an order for military buttons that came in from a group of Civil War reenactors in Philadelphia. I waited on a couple customers, thanked the gods of button dealing for foot traffic, and paid my electric bill and my heating bill and my phone bill. I even balanced my business checking account, going through the motions and fighting to keep my mind on buttons.

And off murder.

I should have known from the beginning that it was a losing cause.

The moment I stopped to sit down and rest, I had the photos of the buttons from Angela's charm string out on the desk in front of me, and I was staring at the one picture of the one still-missing button.

"No way anybody killed Angela to get this button."

It was Nev's day off, and he'd called earlier in the day to say he'd stop by in the evening so we could go out and grab a sandwich. It was a sweet offer, and since I was starving, I was more than ready to take him up on it. But button dealer or not, I apparently still have the heart of a detective—I suspected he had an ulterior motive.

But then, when he showed up at the Button Box, there was a dog biscuit sticking out of the back pocket of his jeans.

That wasn't my only clue. Yesterday's rain had stopped, see, but it was still unseasonably cool. I couldn't help noticing that Nev brought a duffel bag with him (not exactly a necessity for a sandwich date, is it?). And that the duffel bag had what looked like a fleece blanket sticking out of one corner where it wasn't zipped closed.

He'd been looking out the front display window, and when I tossed out that comment about the button, he turned around. "Which button? You mean the missing button?"

I lifted the picture so he could see it. Not that he needed to. Nev has a mind like a steel trap, I knew what he knew, and he knew exactly what that button looked like. "It's small, it's metal, it's worth about a dollar fifty," I said. "Yet it's the only button that's missing."

"The only button we think is missing," he corrected me. "There's always a chance it will turn up. Like that fish button did thanks to LaSalle. Say . . ." I've always said cops are too down-to-earth to be very good at pulling the wool over anybody's eyes. Maybe that's why I thought Nev sounded way too casual when he tried to sound way too casual as he said, "You haven't seen that dog around today, have you?"

"He left here last night when we did, after he spit out the button and finished my tuna sandwich you gave him all of," I reminded Nev, and watched him express not one iota of remorse. "I haven't seen him since."

"But it's cold." Nev was wearing a hoodie with the Chicago Bears logo on it, and he chafed his hands up and down his arms. "How's a dog supposed to live outside when the weather's like this?"

"He's apparently been doing it for a while, and as far as I can see, he's as happy as a clam. As happy as we would be if we figured out who killed Angela." OK, this wasn't exactly subtle, but it was one way to get Nev's mind off LaSalle and back on the case. I liked LaSalle, too, but I'd learned a lesson about him soon after he showed up in the neighborhood: He was a street dog. He liked being a street dog. My fellow merchants and I could feed him all we wanted, but no way did he want to be pampered. Or pestered. LaSalle had a mind of his own.

Kind of like a certain button dealer who didn't like unanswered questions. Or murder. "I was talking about this button." I waved the photo. "You know, the one that isn't valuable enough to steal."

"Which is probably why nobody stole it."

So much for getting a professional opinion.

"I dunno." I took another look at the photo I'd taken the night before Angela was killed. It showed the metal button in question, and the picture in raised relief on it. "Small building, low to the ground," I mumbled, obviously talking to myself since Nev was so busy scanning the neighborhood through the front window, I knew he wasn't listening. Just to be sure of what I was looking at, I grabbed a magnifying glass. "It might be a log cabin," I said.

To which I got no answer.

My mumbling dissolved into something that sounded more like grumbling. "There's a bigger building in the distance, behind the log cabin, a schoolhouse."

I was talking to myself.

"And to the right of the schoolhouse . . ." Whatever was shown in the scene, it was so small, I squinted to try and focus my eyes. It looked like . . . "A cemetery," I said. "Or at least a few headstones and behind them, a little building. Who would want a button with a cemetery on it?"

Even if Nev had been paying attention, this was a question meant only for myself, and I knew the answer even before I asked it. Over the years, button themes went in and out of fashion, just like clothes did. For instance, back in the late nineteenth century, girls wore buttons with photos of their beaus on them. And when celluloid came into common use for making buttons—it was one of the first synthetic plastics and could be made to look like ivory or ebony or other more expensive materials— those were all the rage. Nothing I saw on a button ever came as a surprise so the fact that someone had immortalized this little scene—cemetery and all—really wasn't all that unusual. In fact, I suspected the button commemorated some event in a town's history, like the anniversary of its founding, and as such, would have made a prime souvenir for a young lady looking to add it to her charm string.

As unlikely as it seemed that someone would have swiped this particular button and put it up for sale, I got onto the Internet and checked all the usual auction sites. I'd just clicked off the last one when Nev grabbed the duffel bag, blurted out, "I'll be right back," and headed outside.

Left to my own devices and with my stomach growling for that sandwich he'd promised, I messed around online awhile longer, automatically checking the weather (it was supposed to improve—hurray), my daily horoscope (which unlike Angela, I promptly forgot the moment I closed the page), and the latest listing of antique shows and sales in the area.

Hey, a button collector never knows when something primo might become available.

The newest listing I found was for what was being called a presale showing. That wasn't nearly as interesting as the address of where the preview was being held.

"Angela's house!" I sat up like a shot, remembered I was talking to myself, and didn't much care. Cousin Charles, it seemed, had been one busy little beaver. He was hosting a showing of "Antiques and collectibles of interest to dealers and collectors." Out loud, I read the words written in Old World–looking script. "Including a vast collection of Royal Doulton figurines, exquisite artwork, books, ephemera, and glassware."

It wasn't a sale. The page made that very clear. But if dealers wanted to come have a first look before the items went on sale, they were welcome at Angela's the next day.

The sound of the little brass bell over my front door startled me back to reality and I found Nev looking sheepish and poking one thumb over his shoulder and toward the street. "I just had to go out for a minute," he said. "I thought I saw somebody I knew."

Yeah, and I saw that the blanket was no longer sticking out of his duffel bag and the biscuit was gone from his pocket.

If I wasn't so focused on what Charles was up to, I would have stopped to realize just how incredibly cute this was. Not to worry, I did that later in the evening, and decided that even if he didn't want the world to know— especially because he didn't want the world to know— Nev was a sweetie.

I stood up and turned off the lamp on my desk. "We're going to Ardent Lake," I told him.

"Now?" Nev slipped on his jacket and waited for me to get mine.

"No. Tomorrow. Now . . ." I turned off the rest of the shop lights and locked the front door behind us. "You're taking me to dinner."

COUSIN CHARLES DIDN'T look especially surprised to see me, but then, his preview of the antiques in Angela's house was looking like old home week.

Susan was there. I saw her in the dining room standing next to the wooden Indian.

Marci was there, too. She was avoiding Susan by staying in the living room and pretending to be interested in the statue of that Greek god.

I thought I saw Larry duck into the kitchen.

"Don't look at me that way." Charles closed in on me and Nev in the small space between the front door and the oil paintings he'd strung out for display along the living room wall. I wasn't sure which way was the way we were looking at him, but he blushed from chin to forehead. "I've talked to my attorney. It's all on the up-and-up. He just so happens to be Angela's attorney, too, and he assured me I'm getting the whole kit and kaboodle. All I'm doing is inviting a few friends in. You know, to have a look around. No sales. Not before Angela's estate is settled."

I didn't know if I should congratulate him or tell him I thought he was a greedy creep. Rather than do either, I reintroduced him to Nev, who'd talked to Charles, of course, right after the murder and who was looking around Angela's living room like he'd memorized the contents the first time he'd been there and he was just checking to make sure it was all still there. Knowing Nev, that actually might have been what he was doing.

In the spirit of the moment, I checked that mahogany buffet across the room and breathed a sigh of relief when I saw the Limoges punch bowl was back where it belonged.

I'd just had a pleasant drive from Chicago to Ardent Lake with Nev. The sun was shining. He had a second day off (and two in a row is something of a record for a homicide cop), and we'd stopped on our way out of town for what I'd found out was one of Nev's favorite foods—pancakes.

I knew he was in a good mood.

This did not explain the crease in his forehead.

"The brakes went on Angela's car a couple weeks before she was killed," he said, as casual as can be. Not to me, of course. I already knew this. So did Charles, but that didn't stop his face from going pale. It might also explain why he excused himself and scurried away the moment someone in the kitchen called out a question about a vintage mixer.

"You think . . ." I looked toward where Charles had disappeared. "You think the charm string was just a diversion."

"I think . . ." Nev glanced around again. "I think what I thought the first time I was here," he said. "There's a lot of money tied up in these antiques. And a lot of money always makes for a good motive."

"So Charles didn't want just the charm string." Careful to keep my voice down, I thought this over. "He wanted it all. And the entire time . . ." I swallowed hard. "You don't think he was just trying to steal the charm string with the fire and the break-in. You think all along that he wanted Angela dead."

"Don't you?"

Before I had a chance to answer, there was a commotion on the front porch and I stepped aside to let the newcomer by. Turns out it was Mary Lou Baldwin, the nice Garden Club lady who'd come to Chicago to sell me those buttons.

She smiled when she saw me. "I might have known you'd be here," she said, shaking my hand, then Nev's when I introduced him. "Though I have to say, I'm pretty sure there aren't any buttons around. I remember when Angela first talked about the charm string. She said they were the only buttons Evelyn had left to her." Mary Lou glanced around. "Incredible, isn't it?"

"Not exactly the word I'd use," I said.

She smiled. "We all suspected Evelyn had a stash the likes of which has never been seen in the civilized world. I guess this proves it. But hey . . ." She rubbed her hands together. "I own the Cottage, the B and B over on the edge of town. I'm always looking for furniture and paintings and glassware and such. I can't wait to get my hands on some of this stuff."

"Not until after Angela's estate is settled," I reminded her.

Mary Lou's grin widened. "You've been talking to Charles."

An elderly couple arrived, and as if we'd choreographed our movements, Nev, Mary Lou, and I stepped away from the front door and scooted by the Greek god. Since I was close, I took a look at a stack of old books piled nearby. The top book had a battered brown leather cover. It was a collection of Sherlock Holmes stories, and I reminded myself to put in a good word with Charles for it. It would make a perfect gift for Stan's upcoming birthday. While I was at it, I took a look at the punch bowl on the buffet, too.

I'm not saying Nev's theory about Charles being our murderer wasn't valid, but I had to wonder . . . did Marci give in without a fight and bring back the stolen punch bowl just so we'd think more kindly of her when it came to examining her motives for Angela's murder?

"You are coming, aren't you?"

Mary Lou's question snapped me out of the thought, and I guess she realized it, because she laid a hand on my arm to make sure I paid attention this time. "The festival? You've heard about it, right? I'm sure it sounds like small potatoes to you kids from Chicago, but hey, around here, we take our fun where we can find it. We're having a festival. Next weekend. To celebrate the draining of the reservoir. Oh, and there's a cocktail party at the Big Museum on Saturday night, too." Mary Lou reached into her purse, pulled out two tickets, and handed them to me. "My treat," she said, her smile wide, and added, "I'm on the board at the museum. I had to buy a bunch of tickets or I'd look bad. The whole weekend will be perfect for you, Josie. You like history. You'll get to explore the Big Museum plus we're all going to get a chance to see what's left of Ardent now that the water's been drained."

It sounded like it would be interesting, and I was about to tell her as much when Mary Lou gave me a wink. "I'll reserve a room over at my B and B," she said, glancing from me to Nev and leaping to the mother of all conclusions. "You know, for the two of you."

"We aren't . . . That is, we don't . . ." I am an adult, and a divorced woman. I am mature and responsible and not usually bashful. But the more I tried to find the words to explain a relationship with Nev that even I didn't understand, the dumber I sounded, so I simply clamped my lips shut until I was sure I could talk without sounding like a moron.

"I'll check my schedule," I finally told Mary Lou, firmly refusing to look in Nev's direction. "It does sound like fun."

As soon as Mary Lou walked away, I realized what I'd said. I'm sure my cheeks had been red before, but now I felt them burst into flames. "I was talking about the festival," I stammered, still refusing to look at Nev. "I meant the festival sounded like fun. I wasn't talking about the part about her reserving the room for us together at her B and B, and—"

My words dissolved when he crooked a finger under my chin.

Did I feel better or worse seeing that his cheeks were as red as mine? I can't say. I am absolutely sure, though, that my heart jumped into my throat when Nev said, "I think that part sounds like fun, too."

"Excuse me." That older couple behind us pushed their way past, and Nev dropped his hand. He didn't look at me again until they disappeared behind a stack of quilts, and when he finally did, I think he realized exactly what he'd said, too.

He cleared his throat. "I hope . . . That is, that was out of line. I hope I didn't—"

"You didn't."

"Because I didn't mean—"

"I know."

"Because I wouldn't want you to—"

"I don't."

How's that for being adults and talking about our relationship?

I like to think we actually might have gotten past the awkward stage if Susan didn't pick that exact moment to slip by. "Excuse me. I'm so sorry." She squeezed between me and Nev and we had no choice but to back away from each other. At least as far as we were able.

"I can't believe I left my purse in my office." Susan shook her head, disgusted with herself. "Not that I need a wallet or a credit card or anything, no one's selling anything here today, of course," she added, and I wasn't sure if it was for Nev's benefit or mine. "But I hate being without my cell phone." She glanced over her shoulder. "If you catch up with him, tell Larry I'll be right back. I'm not even going to take my car, I'm just going to run over to the museum and get my phone and run right back."

I promised we would deliver her message to Larry and our closest-we'd-ever-come-to-a-magic moment interrupted, Nev and I made our way over to where Marci was looking at a collection of vintage salt and pepper shakers shaped like everything from lobsters to parrots. The second she laid eyes on us, she clutched her hands together behind her back.

"I returned every last bit of it," she blurted out. "Just like I promised. You didn't bring him . . ." Her gaze slid to Nev. "You're not going to arrest me, are you?" she asked.

"I'm not here to arrest anybody." His words were not technically true, since I practically went into cardiac arrest when he said what he'd said about the night at the B and B. "We're just visiting."

"Visiting. Yes." Grinning, Marci slid around us, her eyes on a stack of Depression glass dessert sets.

Twenty minutes later, Nev and I found ourselves alone in the kitchen. I was checking out a set of juice glasses. He was watching the crowd out in the dining room. It was a perfect opportunity for us to be grown-ups and talk about the delicate topic Mary Lou had broached.

Call me crazy, but I'm pretty sure that's exactly why the subject of murder came up.

"My money's on Charles," Nev said out of nowhere.

I wasn't so sure, and I told him so. "Charles might have wanted the antiques, and the money, but he doesn't have the nerve. Now Marci . . ." She'd just sailed past the doorway, her eye caught by some prize in the far corner of the dining room. "She's plenty bold, she's already proved that. She could just be playing along with us. And Susan's no shrinking violet. I've been to her museum. It's impressive. It takes a lot of brains to keep a place like that afloat, and people with a lot of brains make clever murderers."

My theory was interrupted by a high-pitched shriek from the living room. Crowded house. Lots of people.

I still would have recognized Charles's voice anywhere.

Nev didn't miss a beat; he was out of the kitchen in a second and I was right on his heels, but we had to get through the crowd in the dining room before we could see what was going on. By the time he elbowed his way through the throng gathered in the doorway between the living room and the dining room and I excused myself left and right in his wake, we found Charles backed up against the mahogany buffet, his face as pale as chalk and his mouth hanging open.

There was a large, middle-aged woman standing toe-to-toe with him. She had one meaty hand wrapped around a mantel clock. She was using the other to poke a finger right at Charles's nose.

"How dare you invite us here under false pretenses!" Poke. Poke, poke, poke. "How dare you play us for fools! You haven't heard the last of this, Charles."

"But I didn't . . . I mean, I couldn't . . . I mean, how could I . . . I didn't." He swallowed so hard, I saw Charles's Adam's apple jump all the way from where I stood. "You could be . . ." He pulled in a rough breath. "You might be wrong, you know, Millicent."

"Me? Wrong?" The woman pulled herself up to her full height, which was a whole lot taller than Charles, and gave him a glare that would have frozen him in his tracks if he wasn't already too frightened to move. "You know me better than that, Charles. I'm a certified appraiser. An expert on clocks and other mechanical antiques. You thought you could fool me, did you?"

"But I didn't . . ." Out of the corner of his eye, Charles caught sight of me and Nev and breathed a sigh of relief. "Josie . . ." He gave me a frantic, one-handed wave. "Come over here, Josie. Tell Millicent . . ." He dared another glance at the irate woman and gulped. "Tell her you've looked over the contents of the house, Josie. Tell her how I asked you to value it all."

I stepped through the crowd. "You asked me," I reminded him. "I told you I wasn't qualified."

"There. See." Millicent banged the clock down on the

nearest table. "Besides, whoever she is . . ." Millicent turned a glare in my direction before she swung back toward Charles. "Even if she put a value on this junk, I would tell you she was wrong. These clocks are fakes, Charles. Every single one of them. I wouldn't be surprised if some of these other things aren't, too."

"You got that right." A voice from the dining room behind us made us all spin around to find a man with silvery hair holding up a small wooden drawer. "These tables look like early New England woodworking, but take a look at this. No dovetail joints. No wooden pegs. And the smell . . ." He held the drawer to his nose and drew in a long breath. "No oily odor. In fact, no odor at all, which means that desk over there is finished with a water-based latex acrylic. No way that piece is an antique. And before you try to say it is and that it's been restored . . ." He, too, pointed a finger at Charles. I was beginning to think it was a vintage and antiques collector's gesture that I had somehow failed to learn. "Let me show you the *pièce de résistance.*" He flipped over the drawer and pointed, and a collective gasp went up from the crowd. The man's eyes gleamed with rightful indignation. "It's a Phillips-head screw!"

"Screw is right!" someone screamed from the back of the crowd.

"How dare you try to pass off reproductions as real antiques, Charles," another voice called out.

As one, the crowd moved toward the door. Getting out of it was another thing, but one by one, the gawkers and the collectors filed out of Angela's house.

By the time it was over, Nev, Charles, and I were the

only ones left. Nev stood back, his arms crossed over his chest, looking far more intimidating in jeans and a sweater that matched the color of his eyes than I'd ever seen him look in one of his crumpled suits.

Charles, it should be noted, was so stunned, I'm not sure he realized everyone had left until he shook himself out of his daze and glanced around at the flotsam and jetsam piled around us. "It's phony." He passed a hand over his eyes. "Finally, I've inherited it all, and it's all . . . it's all junk."

"The buttons weren't." I said this more to Nev than to Charles because I figured Charles was in no condition to listen, anyway.

"Aunt Evelyn's collection." Charles pushed himself upright and whirled around, taking it all in. "I wonder. Did she know? I didn't. I swear, I didn't." He looked at Nev, his eyes pleading. "If I did, I never would have asked all those people to come over and have a look. I never would have . . ." His jaw went slack, and his face, already pale, turned the bloodless color of the marble Greek god statue behind him. "Oh my God," Charles wailed, covering his face with his hands. "What have I done?"

There wasn't much room to move, but Nev managed to step forward. "Are you talking about your reputation in Ardent Lake?" he asked. "Or what happened to Angela?"

Charles ran his tongue over his lips. "I didn't want it all. I never said I did. I just thought that she shouldn't hog everything for herself. She'd gotten more than her fair share from Aunt Evelyn. That's why I did what I did. No one can blame me!"

My voice was breathy when I asked, "You killed Angela?"

All the color came back into Charles's face in a rush. His knees knocked. "Killed her? No! I never did. I just wanted . . . I just wanted to scare her. I just wanted to make her think that life is short and it doesn't pay to hoard all the good stuff for yourself." He swallowed hard, and when he looked at Nev, his eyes were wide and filled with tears. "That's why I did it. That's why I cut the brake lines on Angela's car."

Chapter Fourteen

❖ ◉ ❖

By the time I recovered from the surprise of the unexpected confession, we were on the front porch of Angela's house, waiting for the police to come and take Charles's statement. Since he had messed with the brake lines in Angela's garage right there in Ardent Lake, it was a problem for the locals, Nev said. I knew he was right, but since there was a connection to our case—and it might be a pretty darned big one—I had every right to be curious.

"So it wasn't bad luck?" I asked Charles, eager to see if he'd recant now that he'd had time to compose himself. "It wasn't the curse that caused Angela's brake lines to pop?"

With what he'd done, Charles could have caused a serious accident. Or worse. Still, I couldn't help feeling a little sorry for him. He sat on the front steps with his head bowed and tears streaming down his cheeks.

"No, of course not. It was me. Just me," he sobbed. "I never meant to hurt her. You have to believe me. I wanted her to realize that life was short, and she should be generous. And I thought . . . all right, I admit it! She was already talking about that silly curse, and I thought if she figured this was another piece of bad luck thanks to those buttons, she might give the charm string to me. At least then I would have gotten something of value out of this whole mess. Besides, she didn't . . ." The thought struck and Charles lifted his head and actually managed a watery smile. "Angela didn't get hurt, did she? In spite of what I did, nothing happened to her. So it's not like I actually did anything wrong."

If he was hoping for sympathy from Nev, he didn't get it. "We'll let the police decide," he said. "For now, you can help yourself by telling the truth."

Charles raised his chin and tried for a bravado that wasn't quite convincing. "As sure as the sky is blue, it was all I did. I didn't kill her, if that's what you're thinking. Sure, I wanted my share of Aunt Evelyn's fortune." His face fell. "Well, what I thought was Aunt Evelyn's fortune. I wanted a fair cut. But I didn't want it so bad that I would strangle Angela. That's . . ." He jiggled his shoulders. "That's creepy."

"And you never broke into Angela's house?" Nev asked.

Charles shook his head.

It was my turn. "You never started that fire in her kitchen?"

Again, he denied it.

"You never talked Angela into canceling the charter boat so she wouldn't dump the charm string in the lake?"

That was me again, and Charles looked at me in wonder. "Why would she want to dump the silly thing in the lake?" The truth dawned and his jaw dropped. "The curse, of course! She was going to dump the buttons in the lake? The woman was as crazy as a loon. Not that it matters now. Besides, even if she did want to get rid of the buttons, why would I want to talk her out of it? Well . . ." He thought about it for a couple seconds. "I guess I would seeing as how those buttons are the only genuine things in Aunt Evelyn's whole collection." He sniffled.

"Then what about the donation?" Nev had been leaning against the front railing and he pushed off and stalked down the steps. He stood on the front walk, his arms crossed over his chest, and looked up at Charles. "Are you the one who suggested Angela give the buttons to Marci's museum?"

"And then," I put in, sitting down next to Charles, "did you talk her out of that and tell her to give the charm string to Susan instead?"

He was the one who'd just confessed to cutting the brake lines on his cousin's car, so he shouldn't have looked at me as if I was the crazy person. "The first I ever heard about that charm string was when Angela told me about the curse. Of course I ignored her. Who wouldn't? She mentioned it every time I saw her and I was more and more convinced that she'd gone off the deep end. Then the next thing I knew, she called to invite me to a tea the Big Museum was having in her honor. She said it was because she was giving the charm string to them. Before that, I can't tell you what happened or what she did with the silly thing or what her plans were. You say she was going to give it to Marci? Then she actually gave it to Susan?"

"Well, she never got to the point of actually giving it to Susan," I reminded him.

"Susan! Did I hear you talking about Susan?"

Since we hadn't seen Larry come around from the back of the house, I think his question startled us all. I jumped. Charles pulled in a breath. I'm sure Nev was just as surprised, too, but he never moved a muscle, just looked over to where Larry hurried around the rhododendrons.

"We're supposed to be going to lunch," Larry said, dapper that day in dark pants and a purple golf shirt. "And I can't find her."

Instantly, I felt guilty, even though I knew I shouldn't. "I was supposed to tell you, but I never had the opportunity. We didn't run into each other in the house," I said to Larry as if that in itself was enough of an explanation. "Susan forgot her purse, you see. She didn't want to be without her cell phone. She went back to the museum to get it."

He glanced at his watch. "Just now?"

"Well, no." I thought about when we'd run into Susan—it was right after Nev had tossed out that bone-melting comment about us staying at the B and B together—and all that had happened since. "Come to think of it," I said, "it was quite a long while ago."

Larry looked around. There was a late-model blue Ford Focus parked a couple houses down the street. "That's her car," he said. "Which means she hasn't come back. No doubt she got distracted by some project or another. I

swear, that woman lives and breathes for that museum."
Maybe he'd been upstairs when the announcement came
down about the fake antiques and Charles's disgrace. With
a look, Larry included me, Nev, and yes, Charles and I
guess he forgave me for what I'd said to him that day at
his store because he said, "Join us for lunch, why don't
you. We're meeting over at the Bayside. Charming little
place, usually right on the water. Now, we'll get a look at
what's going on at the reservoir."

"We can meet you there," Nev told him. "As soon as
we're done with the local police. Charles has some things
he needs to talk to them about."

"Yes. Of course." Larry got his car keys out of his
pocket. "But just so you know, I heard sirens a little while
ago from over near the Parkway." He waved in some
indeterminate direction. It was, apparently, how Larry
gave directions. "No doubt, there was an accident of some
sort. It's Sunday and I guarantee you that Jimmy Carns
is the only officer on duty. If you're waiting for him,
chances are you're going to be waiting for a long time.
You could go over to the Bayside now—"

"Or we could come with you to pick up Susan, then
we could all leave from there." I stood and marched down
the steps. Yeah, I was being a little pushy, but let's face
it, love of buttons goes right along with love of old things.
The chance to get a peek behind the scenes before the
museum opened was too tempting to pass up.

"All right." Larry put his keys back in his pocket. "We
can all walk over there. Charles, are you coming?"

"Am I?" Charles asked Nev.

Rather than risk having Charles run off, Nev said yes.

The four of us walked the short distance between Angela's house and the museum. Because the Big Museum wasn't scheduled to open for another hour, the front door was locked.

"Not to worry." Larry led us around the side of the building. "On the days Susan is the first one here, she always leaves this door open so the docents don't have to wait for her to unlock the front door."

He opened the door he indicated, and we stepped inside.

As I suspected, the Big Museum was quiet, and after the commotion over at Angela's, it was a welcome relief. I drew in a breath of air faintly scented with the comforting aroma of old things, and followed Larry down a short corridor that led us up three steps, through a door, and into that main entryway just inside the museum's front door.

"Her office is this way," Larry said, heading straight down the hallway. "I'll go get her and tell her you're waiting. That will light a fire under her."

While he was gone, it gave me the perfect chance to wander, and I intended to make the most of it. While Charles and Nev waited in the hallway, I strolled into the room that featured all those wonderful old photographs of Ardent, intending to take another look so I could compare what used to be with what we were going to see down at the reservoir.

I never had the chance.

Just inside the doorway, I stopped cold, and my voice wobbling, I called for Nev.

He is, after all, the professional. With any luck, he

wouldn't be stunned and frightened out of his gourd by the scene that met our eyes. Not like I was.

My heart in my throat, my blood hammering in my temples, I stared at Susan, lying on the floor just inside the doorway. She was on her back in a pool of blood, her arms splayed at her sides, one leg cocked at an unnatural angle. One of the photos of old Ardent had been taken down off the wall and used to batter her over the head and shards of glass glittered in her ashen hair.

I didn't need to wait to see Nev kneel down beside her, feel for a pulse, and shake his head.

One look, and I knew Susan wouldn't be joining us for lunch.

JIMMY CARNS MIGHT have been taking that accident report up on the Parkway, but he hotfooted it right over when Nev called the station and the dispatcher relayed a message that included the word *murder.* Within fifteen minutes, Jimmy's boss and the mayor had arrived at the Big Museum, too, and with the Ardent photo room packed, I'd been asked to step out into the hallway and stay out of the way.

I was only too happy to oblige. Finding two bodies in the space of two weeks does not do good things to a girl.

Of course, I wasn't the only one reeling. Charles had gotten a glimpse of the carnage and that was all it took for his already-shaky composure to dissolve completely. Sobbing, he flopped into a delicate-looking wing chair just inside the front door. When he heard me call for Nev,

Larry had hurried out of Susan's office and had found us bent over her body. Now, pasty and trembling, he paced the hallway.

"It can't be true. It can't be happening. Not again." Larry's voice jumped to the same restless beat as his footsteps. "We just found each other again. To think that Susan's gone, too. Just like . . ." His voice broke. "Just like Angela."

"Yeah, Angela." Since I, too, was too worked up to keep still, Larry and I were at opposite ends of the hallway from each other, and it was just as well. I was trying to make sense of a situation that was messed up to the extreme. First Angela. Now Susan. Angela who'd owned the charm string. Susan who was supposed to be receiving it as a donation. Both murdered.

No way it was a coincidence.

I closed the distance between me and Larry. "When was the last time you saw Susan?" I asked him.

Under any other circumstances, I was sure he wouldn't have had to stop and think about it. But stress does strange things. To our brains and to our bodies. Larry's breaths were coming hard and fast, and when I spotted a water fountain near the entrance, I went over there, took one of the little paper cups from a dispenser on the wall and filled it, and brought it back to him.

He drank down the water in one gulp. "Thank you," he said. "You're very kind."

"I'm very curious." There was no use hiding the fact, especially since—dead girlfriend or no dead girlfriend— I wasn't planning on letting up on the questions. "When did you say you saw Susan last?"

He passed a hand over his eyes. "This morning," Larry said. "When she got to Angela's. I got there a few minutes ahead of her and I waited for her on the front porch. When she arrived, we went into the house together, but . . . well, you can understand how easy it was for us to get separated in that house of horrors. Before we did, though, we talked about what we'd do the rest of the day. We said we'd go to lunch together after the preview."

"And did it seem like anything was wrong?" I asked.

"With Susan?" Larry paused to think about it. "It's hard to say," he admitted. "What I mean is, we'd been apart for a while. You know that. You know I was dating Angela. Susan and I were just finding our way back to some sort of relationship. We were taking small steps. Sometimes . . ." He drew in a trembling breath and let it out slowly. "Sometimes, she seemed distant. Not that I'm saying I blame her. After all, I'm the one who made the mistake of breaking up with her and going to Angela."

"Did Susan feel any resentment?"

Larry shot me a look. "*Resentment* is a strong word."

"It's a strong emotion," I reminded him.

I thought he might argue, but honestly, I don't think Larry had the energy. He drew in a breath and let it out slowly. "I don't think Susan so much resented what happened between me and Angela as much as she was hurt by it. And honestly, I couldn't hold that against her. I was heartless. Not to mention stupid. And now . . ." His voice cracked. "Now I'll never have a chance to prove to her how wrong I was to ever let her go in the first place."

"But you and Angela, you said you were solid that day she died."

Larry's breathing stilled. "Yes, we were. Just like I told you. Angela and I had a little tiff, but we settled things. The last time I saw her, we were in a good place."

"A good place that you've since decided was stupid."

Larry pinned me with a look. "I didn't say it was stupid."

"You said it was stupid to ever break up with Susan in the first place. That must mean it was stupid for you to date Angela. But now you're telling me you were happy with Angela. Which is it, Larry?"

"Are you trying to send me over the edge?" I don't think Larry was actually expecting an answer to this question. One hand on either side of his head, he raked his fingers through his thick hair. "What difference does it make now, anyway?" he asked. "I've lost Angela. And I've lost Susan. Two wonderful women. Gone. Gone, too soon."

"And now all we can do is wonder why. And who did it."

"Yes." Larry bobbed his head. "Yes, we have to do everything we can to bring this monster to justice."

I couldn't have agreed with him more, but I didn't have a chance to tell him. The hallway door—the one we'd come in just a short time before—opened, and Marci stuck her red, spiky head into the museum. "What's going on?" The rest of her followed, wobbling on heels as high as any I'd ever seen. "I was just driving by and I saw the police cars." The cops were all gathered in the room across the hall with the body and a noise from that direction made Marci glance that way. "Something happened? Something bad?"

The worst, and I told her all we knew and watched Marci's face turn a sickly green. One arm out, she braced herself against the wall. "Oh my God, poor Susan. I just saw her. Over at Angela's. She was . . . she was fine."

Who was I to be the voice of cynicism and point out that that's the way murder usually works: fine one minute, dead the next.

Instead, I stuck to facts. "We were all at Angela's," I pointed out. "Larry, I saw you in the kitchen. Did you leave at any time?"

"Me?" He poked a finger at his chest. "I . . . well, yes . . . If you consider going out to Angela's garage leaving. There was a collection of old tools out there that I wanted to take a look at."

"Was anyone out there with you?"

"Are you implying . . ." At his sides, Larry's hands curled into fists. A muscle jumped at the base of his jaw. "As a matter of fact," he said from between clenched teeth, "there were three other fellows out there. No one I knew, so I can't give you their names. Maybe you'd better have your police friends issue an all-points bulletin to find the guys so you can ask them if I'm lying."

I was a theater major back in college; I'm pretty immune to sarcasm.

I turned the other way. "Did you leave Angela's house during the preview, Marci?"

Her shrug was so casual, it was as if we weren't discussing life and death. "I arrived, I left," she said. "But you can be sure I didn't slip out somewhere in between so I could race over here and kill Susan."

"Except you did know about the side door being unlocked."

Her breath caught. Marci's mouth opened and closed. "Everybody . . ." She stammered. "Everybody in town knows that Susan leaves that door open."

"But not everybody in town just happened to show up right after Susan was murdered."

My comment had been as casual as can be, but Marci went up like a Roman candle. "You think I killed her? Why would I? And don't say it's because I want her job. I've got my own museum and it's better . . ." Just for good measure, she kicked the wall with the toe of one pointy shoe. "It's better than this place."

That left Charles.

I strolled over to where he sat, his head in his hands. "You were certainly at Angela's," I said, and I think it was the first he realized I'd drawn near.

His head came up, and Charles sat back. "Of course I was. I was the host. You don't think I could have—"

"Who knows what could have happened?" I made sure my shrug was as casual as Marci's had been. "All that junk. All that commotion. Anybody . . ." I glanced at my companions. "Anybody could have come and gone and come right back before anybody else missed them."

"Well, it certainly wasn't me." Larry stalked to the door. "Tell Chief Barnstable I'll be at home," he said. "I'm sure he'll want to talk to me. Tell him . . ." He looked over his shoulder to the other room and his anger dissolved in a wash of tears. "Do you . . . do you think there really was a curse? That Susan was killed because she's agreed to bring the charm string into the museum?"

I couldn't answer, because honestly, I couldn't say. In fact, at that moment, all I could think was that the real bad luck was that Larry kept losing his girlfriends.

IT WAS HOURS later and Charles had gone home. So had Marci. By then, someone had come and taken Susan's body away, and the room where she'd been killed had been cordoned off with yellow tape.

Too edgy to sit still, I had spent the entire time walking around the Big Museum and thinking.

Both actions resulted in me ending up exactly where I'd begun, in the entryway just inside the front door with no more answers than I had when I started my trek. I could tell from the mumbled conversation going on in the photo room that Nev was wrapping things up with the local cops, and I went into the room with the pirate exhibit to wait. With no one around, I finally had a chance to read that poster about Thunderin' Ben.

"Great Lakes captain . . . pirate . . . gambling, prostitution, thievery." I scanned the poster, reading the important words under my breath. "Buried treasure . . . life of crime . . . Ardent's most colorful son."

Certainly interesting, and in light of everything that had happened at the museum that day, a welcome diversion. While I was at it, I looked again at the exhibit that included Ben's diary and that mini-buoy, thinking—

"Ready?"

When Nev came up behind me and put a hand on my shoulder, I jumped.

"Sorry." He backed away instantly. "I should have known better. The murder has us all on edge."

"It's not that, it's just . . ." I turned and pointed to the exhibit. "I was just absorbed, that's all. And thinking that something here doesn't look quite right."

"Really?" Nev stepped forward for a closer look. "It doesn't look like anything's missing."

It didn't. And it had been a few days since I'd first seen the exhibit. For all I knew, the Big Museum owned lots of Thunderin' Ben memorabilia and rotated what it put out and what it put away. I shrugged off my reaction to the exhibit as inconsequential and suggested we get out of Ardent Lake and Nev agreed.

"It's too bad about Susan," he said once we were back in the car. "And I'm sorry you were the one who had to find her. That's never easy."

"No." As we drove out of town, I stared out the window, wondering what was going on inside each of the houses with their perfect exteriors. "But at least we know one thing. I think we can be pretty sure Susan wasn't our murderer."

Chapter Fifteen

IT WAS NOT A GOOD WEEK, AND I WAS NOT IN A GOOD mood.

For one thing, Nev caught another case and it was a particularly sticky one, what with it having to do with a dead hooker and a prominent businessman. Nev had been busy, and we'd barely had time to talk except to plan a quick trip to the festival in Ardent Lake on Saturday when he was hoping to get away for a few hours. Just for the record, there was no mention of the charming B and B where we'd been invited to share a room, and truth be told, I think that accounted for some of my grumpiness, too. It wasn't like I was ready to commit—to a night with Nev or anything else for that matter. But that didn't mean I wouldn't have liked him to mention it. Just so I'd know he was thinking what I was thinking and that what we were thinking was something that maybe we both wanted to think about.

In fact, if there was any silver lining to the gray cloud that had been hanging over me, it was that buttons did not enter the picture in Nev's new case, so I was not called in to offer my expert advice.

So far, me being an expert was getting us nowhere fast when it came to Angela's murder, or Susan's; I didn't need to be reminded.

Two dead women. One charm string. One thousand buttons.

And one stumped button expert.

"There's Charles, of course," I mumbled, talking to myself about the short list of suspects since it was right before closing time and there was no one in the Button Box except me. "There's Marci. There's even Larry. There's . . ."

In the silence that surrounded me, my sigh echoed.

"There's nobody and nothing, and all I'm doing is wasting my time." I wailed, and dropped my head onto my desk.

It had been that kind of week, and I was getting tired of it.

And then, of course, there was Kaz.

With a groan, I got up to start through my usual closing routine. At least if I kept myself busy, I wouldn't (maybe) be so embarrassed to admit that just a couple days earlier, I finally gave up, gave in, and called Kaz's supervisor down at the Port. Sam Podnowiak remembered me from back in the day when I was Mrs. Kazlowski, and he assumed I was looking for Kaz because . . . well, because I couldn't live without him, I guess.

I did not contradict this theory, mostly because it didn't seem worth the effort. Instead, I told him I was worried, and asked Sam if he knew what was going on.

"Sure." Sam is a big guy with a big voice, and even bigger opinions. When he chuckled and said I must have come to my senses and I was ready to get back together with Kaz, I knew it wouldn't get me anywhere to ask what the heck kinds of rumors my ex had been spreading. Instead, I clenched my teeth around a smile Sam couldn't see since we were talking on the phone, and said, as sweetly as I possibly could, "Of course I want to know, Sam. I wouldn't have called otherwise. Kaz is missing, and I'm worried."

"Missing?" Something about the bray of laughter on the other end of the phone actually helped loosen the knot of tension inside me. "I don't know about that," Sam said. "But I can tell you he took some vacation time."

"This much vacation time?" Kaz hadn't even taken two weeks for our honeymoon in Barbados.

"He had a lot of accumulated overtime hours coming," Sam informed me. "Said he wanted three weeks. What the hell! The guy works hard. I told him, sure."

"And did he say what he was planning on doing with those three weeks?"

Since there was silence on the other end of the phone, I knew Sam was thinking. The way I remembered it, this was not an easy thing for Sam, so I cut him some slack.

"He didn't say," Sam finally answered. "Said he was

going away, but didn't say where. Or for what. Actually, Josie, I figured maybe you and him were . . . you know, going off together somewhere on account of how Kaz, he's been telling us boys around here how you two might be getting back together again and I figured you were, like, you know, hooking up."

I am certain I'm not a rude person. So as not to contradict this opinion of myself, I bit my tongue before I could remind Sam that Kaz has the annoying habit of being something of a liar, and made an excuse about a customer coming into the Button Box.

"Vacation." I'd switched off the lights in the shop and put up the "Closed" sign, and I was in the back room grumbling while I retrieved my jacket and purse. Good thing, otherwise, I never would have heard the scratching on the back door.

A note about logistics here: There is a travel agency upstairs from the Button Box, and while I generally come and go through the front door of the building that leads directly into the shop, Emilie, my upstairs neighbor, always uses the back. The door from my back workroom leads into a postage-stamp-sized hallway, and that's where the stairs are, too, that go up to Emilie's place. From there, the back door opens onto that little courtyard behind the building.

To my knowledge, Emilie was as good as gold when it came to making sure that back door was always locked behind her.

Then again, if my theory was right about Angela's murderer trying to steal the charm string (and at this point, I wasn't sure anything was right), the murderer had gotten in that way—and into the basement—the day Angela was killed.

"Emilie?" I called out, partly because if Emilie was out there and needed help, I didn't want to ignore her, but mostly because whoever it was, that person needed to know I was still around, and the shop wasn't empty. "Did you lock yourself out?"

No answer.

Except for a tiny rap on the door.

"I've already called the police." Yes, it was a lie, but it was all for a good cause. I grabbed the broom that sat in a corner by the back door, and holding the handle like a Samurai sword, yanked the door open and—

"Kaz?"

He hotfooted it into the workroom and slammed the door behind him.

"Boy, am I glad you're here." Kaz was breathing hard. He leaned against my worktable. "I thought I was going to have to break into the place."

"Security system." I pointed toward the unit by the back door.

He fought to catch his breath. "Damn, yeah. I forgot. That would have made things a little tricky. I guess if you weren't here, I would have just had to go over to your place."

"Really?" I crossed my arms over my chest and stepped back, my weight against one foot. "Just like that?"

"Well, sure." Like he actually belonged there, Kaz went over to the fridge, got out a bottle of water, and downed it. "Thanks," he said, tossing the empty into my recycle container. "I owe you one."

"You owe me a lot. An explanation might be a good place to start."

"Oh, you mean for . . ." He glanced at the back door and gave me one of the patented smiles that had attracted me to him in the first place. Sweet as peaches and as hot as an August day. It was a heady combination, and I had succumbed in record time. "I didn't want to come in the front door," he simply said.

"Because the front door is too—"

"Public." He looked in the fridge again. I kept a small stash of yogurt in there, as well as a carton of orange juice, a loaf of bread, and a limited supply of deli meat for those days when I was busy and it was impossible to leave the shop. "You don't mind, do you?" he asked, but since he already had the bread and the turkey out, as well as a pack of cheddar cheese slices and a jar of mayo, there didn't seem to be much point. He slapped together a sandwich and wolfed down half of it before he said anything else.

"There's this guy," Kaz began.

And I knew exactly where the story was going to end.

"And he's looking for you because you owe him money." I threw my hands in the air.

So much for proving to my ex that nothing he did surprised me because he never did anything surprising. "Well, yeah," he said, unfazed and starting in on the second half of the sandwich. "You see, I was up in Wisconsin—"

"Wisconsin?" Call me crazy, but somehow, I'd expected something a little more exotic to explain his long absence. "All this time, I've been looking for you, and you've been in Wisconsin?"

The sandwich partway to his mouth, Kaz stopped. His grin was as bright as the sudden gleam that twinkled in his dark eyes. "You were looking for me, huh?"

I cursed my slip of the tongue and scrambled. "Not exactly looking. I mean, I was, but—"

He set down the sandwich and took a step in my direction. "Because you wondered where I was."

"Yes." That much was true, and there was no use denying it.

Another step and Kaz was close enough for me to see the tiny smear of mayo at the corner of his mouth. "You missed me."

Remember that whole bit about how crabby I'd been? And how tired? I guess it all sort of came to a head, so hey, nobody can fault me for snapping. Then again, if anyone on earth deserved a little comeuppance, it was Kaz. For all the things he was. And all the things he did. For all the times I'd thought I could change him and that one life-altering, heart-wrenching moment when I realized I never would.

My smile was as sweet as I could possibly make it when I said, "You're right, Kaz, I did miss you."

I wasn't imagining it, his shoulders really did shoot back a fraction of an inch. Kaz has great shoulders. Nice abs, too. In fact, Kaz is the total package when it comes to the looks department, and he looked especially delicious that night in butt-hugging jeans and a gray T-shirt with a flannel slipped over it. I almost felt guilty making him feel so darned self-satisfied.

Almost.

I wiped the smile from my face and added, "It's hard

not to miss the most annoying person in my life when he's suddenly not around being annoying anymore."

Kaz took the knock in stride. Then again, that's pretty much how Kaz takes all of life. Grinning, he backed off and grabbed the rest of his sandwich. "Hey," he said before he took another bite, "I'll take what I can get. At least you noticed I wasn't around."

"So?" He left the turkey and cheese out on the counter, and it was the first I remembered I hadn't had lunch. I took one slice of bread and made myself a half a sandwich. While I was at it, I put on a fresh pot of coffee. "What were you doing in Wisconsin? Who's after you? And why?"

I figured it was a long story so I settled myself on one of the high stools next to the worktable and dug into my dinner.

Kaz made another sandwich. "I was playing cards, that's all." He waved away the importance of that part of the story with one hand. "Some guy got bent out of shape. You know, because he won, and—"

"You didn't have the money to pay him what you owed him."

"It's not like that."

It was. I knew it because I'd heard the story a thousand times and seen that same look on Kaz's face. When he lies, his nose twitches just a little bit. It twitched now.

"I have every intention of paying him," he said. Twitch.

A couple bites of sandwich, and I was beginning to feel a little more human. Maybe I wasn't as tired and frustrated by my case as I was simply hungry. "So what was in Wisconsin?" I asked.

"The card game." I never keep things like potato chips around because when they are, I eat them, but Kaz checked the cupboards and I knew that's what he was looking for. He likes crunch with his sandwich, and pickles and celery don't fill the bill. He settled for a box of Triscuits and brought it back to the table with him, fishing out crackers two at a time and popping them into his mouth.

Like I said, I was feeling the teensiest bit mean-spirited so it was only natural for me to wait until his mouth was full before I asked, "The card game in that new tent you bought?"

Kaz stopped chewing. But only for a second. He swallowed and smiled, pointing my way with a cracker. "You went to my apartment."

"Well, what did you expect?" I got a Pepsi out of the fridge for Kaz. It was Diet. He would complain. Too bad, so sad. "I called, Kaz. Plenty of times. You never returned my messages. I figured—"

"You couldn't live without me?"

I was just getting milk out of the fridge for my coffee and it was a good thing the carton was closed, or the look I shot Kaz would have curdled its contents. "If you must know, I figured you were dead. You know, on account of how somebody was sick and tired of your lies." I poured the milk into my mug, put the carton back in the fridge, and slammed the door. "I was worried. At least for a while. I finally felt better when I realized what I was really feeling was disappointment because somebody got the satisfaction of offing you before I could."

"That's a good one." Kaz laughed and ate a few more

crackers. "Say, now that you know where I live and that your key works—"

"Don't." I stopped him with a look that would have flash-frozen any normal human being. "It's been a long week, and I'm not in the mood, and besides, Kaz, all kidding aside, I really was worried. OK, yeah, all right, read whatever you want into that. At least I've got the guts to admit it. I figured something bad had happened to you. Damn, but when it does, I'm the one who's going to be left to plan your funeral, and I'll tell you what, Mitchell Kazlowski, that is not one job I look forward to."

He slipped off his stool and poked his hands into his pockets, the picture of remorse. "I know you're serious when you use my full name. Sorry. I should have told you I was leaving for a while."

"No. That's just the thing. Don't you get it? You shouldn't have told me. You should never have to tell me where you're going, or what you're doing, or anything else. It's just that . . . I don't know, I guess it's just that when you didn't come around, it was a change, and I didn't know what to make of it. I was scared."

"And I was inconsiderate." Words he'd never spoken in the three turbulent years of our marriage. I wondered if Kaz was finally growing up. Or maybe I was just feeling gracious now that I knew his lifeless body wasn't at the bottom of some hole somewhere. "I'm sorry. I mean it. I should have at least called and told you. I just . . ." He rolled back on his heels and glanced away. "I figured, you know, that if I told you what I was up to, you'd tell me I was nuts."

"It wouldn't be the first time."

"You got that right." He patted the stool I'd been sitting on earlier as a way of telling me to take a seat. I did, and he rummaged around in the cupboards again. This time, I knew he was looking for cookies. Kaz likes something sweet after dinner. He settled for a box of cinnamon-covered graham crackers. "I was doing some reading," he said. "And yeah, I know, that sounds a little weird. I'm not exactly a scholar. I mean, not like you. But I saw this article in the paper about this place up in Wisconsin and it kind of caught my interest so I went to the library and—"

"You know where the library is?"

His smile was stiff, but he ignored the question. That was OK, it deserved to be ignored, I just couldn't help getting in the zinger.

"I did a little research. About this town in Wisconsin called Prairie de Chien. It's right on the Mississippi River, a pretty little place. Anyway, there's a legend that says that back in 1832, four soldiers were bringing the payroll to a nearby fort, and they were ambushed by Indians. The soldiers were all killed, but before they were, they managed to bury their saddlebags filled with gold coins. I thought . . ." He scraped a hand over his chin. He obviously hadn't shaved that day; a shadow of stubble accentuated the planes and angles of his face and made him look rugged and weathered.

Kaz looked at me through his so-thick-they're-wasted-on-a-guy lashes. "You're gonna laugh."

"Won't," I promised.

His shoulders dropped. "You should. It was a dumb idea to begin with. I was just thinking . . . you know, sort of about what you said earlier. How I'm always coming around, asking you for help. I was thinking that you . . . well, Jo, you've managed to make something of yourself. You worked on that goofy movie and it paid off. You're getting royalties every month. And you've established yourself with the button crowd as, you know, an expert. And you've got the shop and . . ." He didn't so much shrug as he twitched his shoulders. "You're kind of an inspiration."

Good thing I had just swallowed the last of my turkey sandwich or I might have choked. I took a sip of coffee to wash down the sudden knot of emotion that blocked my breathing. "So you're, what, going to open a button shop in Wisconsin?"

Kaz laughed. That, of course, was what I was hoping for. Kaz's natural state is laid back to the nth degree; seeing him being introspective threw me for a loop.

When Kaz was in the room, I could not afford to lose my sense of equilibrium or my perspective.

"No button shop," he said and raised his eyebrows to let me know he was kidding when he added, "I wouldn't want to give you that kind of competition."

I grabbed my mug and wrapped my hands around it. "So why were you in Wisconsin?" I asked.

"To look for the treasure, of course." Before I could say anything—even though I didn't know what to say— he blurted out, "See, I knew you'd laugh. I knew you'd think it was crazy."

I set my cup on the table. "I'm not laughing. And I didn't say a word about it being crazy, did I?" I thought back to my quick visit to Kaz's apartment and nodded. "That explains the metal detector. But not . . ." I gave him what I hoped was an eagle-eyed look. "But not the card game."

Did I expect more than for him to shrug the whole thing off?

Not really, so I wasn't disappointed when he did and said, "I was camped at this really nice park. I'd look for the treasure during the day, come back to my tent at night. You know, Jo . . ." Thinking, he cocked his head. "I'm a city boy through and through, but I sure liked being out there under the stars."

I did know; I'd thought the same thing about Ardent Lake. Of course, that was before I found out the whole town was a sham. These days, I wouldn't be surprised if I discovered that canopy of stars over the city was as much of a painted backdrop as the Victorian charm.

"So for the first week or so," Kaz went on, "things were pretty quiet. After treasure hunting all day, I'd get something to eat, then go back to the campground and just relax and do some more research about the treasure, you know, check maps and things. Then last weekend, some other campers arrived, and there was this guy who started up a card game."

"And you couldn't resist."

"No, I couldn't." It was as simple as that. At least to Kaz. "The first night, I actually won a few hands. I was in good shape."

"Until you weren't."

"You got that right. And the guy who ran the game was

decent, and chatty, and while we were playing, I mentioned I lived in Chicago and he knew my name, of course."

"So now that you owe him money, and he knows where you live, he's looking for you."

Kaz made a face. "And I didn't even find the treasure."

It was the story of Kaz's life. The story of our marriage. There wasn't much I could say. Instead, I cleaned up the worktable and slipped on my jacket.

I made sure the back door was locked, and Kaz followed me to the front of the shop.

"I can't go home," he said.

"You're not coming with me," I replied.

He tried for slick and, yeah, sexy, too, when he lowered his voice. "I don't take up much room, and I can be pretty well behaved—if you want me to be."

By this time, we were out on the sidewalk and I locked the shop door behind us. "I want you to go away," I said. "Like I've always wanted you to go away."

"Except when I was away—"

"Good-night, Kaz." I turned to walk to the nearest El stop.

And Kaz gave up with his usual equanimity and headed the other way. "See ya, Jo," he called. "Hey, I'll stop in next week. We can get dinner, and I'll tell you all about what it's like to be a treasure hunter."

I would have stopped cold even if I wasn't ready to cross a street and the light was against me. But then, that's because a couple odd things happened at the same time.

For one, LaSalle raced by, hot on a trail of a ginger-striped cat I saw duck into the nearest alley. That in itself wasn't all that unusual. The fact that LaSalle was wearing a bright blue collar was.

And the second thing?

That made me grin from ear to ear. See, I still didn't know who'd killed Angela and Susan. But suddenly, I was pretty sure I knew why.

Chapter Sixteen

Jimmy Carns was just getting ready to pull out of the parking lot of the Ardent Lake police station. He didn't look surprised to see me. Then again, I'd called Nev the night before (it was late and he was still at the station, knee deep in his newest case) and told him what I was up to. No doubt, the police grapevine had done its job.

"Of course we dusted for prints after Susan's murder. All over the Big Museum." It was a warm morning, and it promised to be an even warmer afternoon, and Jimmy had rolled down the windows of the patrol car. His cap was off and lying on the seat next to him. "In a place as big and as busy as that . . ."

The way he refused to say the words spoke volumes. I was afraid this was what was going to happen, and my shoulders drooped. "You didn't find anything out of the ordinary?" I asked. "You're sure?"

"Wish I could say otherwise. Hey . . ." As far as Jimmy was concerned, the subject wasn't so much closed as it was at a dead end. He changed it deftly. "You're staying around for the festival this weekend, aren't you?"

I was. I told him I'd gotten a room at Mary Lou's B and B for the night (and just for the record, it was a single room with a single bed in it) and that Nev would be joining me the next day for the festivities. "Until then . . ." Even from here, I could hear all the hustle and bustle going on over at the park. The festival was scheduled to start that evening with a speech from the mayor and a concert by the Ardent Lake High School marching band, and the sounds of trucks coming and going, of hammering, and of sound systems being checked and rechecked added a staccato rhythm and an air of anticipation to the Friday morning. "You wouldn't mind if I just had a look around, would you?"

"You mean at the Big Museum?" Jimmy laughed in a way that told me he thought I watched too many episodes of *Murder, She Wrote*. Then again, there was that police grapevine. I think he was thinking about that, too, and about what he might have heard from Nev about my skills as a modern-day Jessica Fletcher, because he nodded. "Be my guest," he said. "The Big Museum's expecting a rush of visitors this weekend, so I know it's open now. You know, so they can get everything ready. Go on over there and poke around to your heart's content. I don't think you'll find anything, though."

"I'm sure you're right." I wished he wasn't. I hoped he wasn't. "No one will mind?"

Jimmy punched his patrol car into reverse. "There's an interim head curator in charge. I'll give her a call."

Was I surprised when I told the docent near the front door of the Big Museum that I was there to see that interim curator and she pointed me toward the woman with spiky red hair and high, high heels?

Not really. After all, it made sense. Marci had once applied for Susan's job at the Big Museum, and she knew a thing or two about curating. In fact, she looked perfectly at home click-clacking her way across the marble floors, directing staff where to put up this or that signage, and how to set up the rooms for the cocktail party scheduled after the fireworks in the park the next evening.

"I can't say I'm surprised to see you." Marci zipped past me with barely a glance. "Jimmy Carns called."

I was grateful. It saved me from a lot of explaining.

There was a pile of brochures about the museum on a nearby table, and Marci grabbed them, handed them to the closest docent, and told him to put them into the racks near the door. When she was done, she brushed her hands together and finally gave me her full attention. "He said you wanted to take a look around, but he didn't say what you wanted to see."

"He didn't tell me you were the interim curator."

Her smile was sleek. "Who else would they have asked? Oh, you should have seen their faces. It was positively delicious! As soon as the board of trustees realized the festival was breathing down their necks and there were plenty of people who were going to show up for that, not to mention the cocktail party Susan had scheduled . . . well . . ." She tugged her black suit jacket into place and squared her slim shoulders. "I love that sort of irony, don't you? They came calling, proverbial hat in hand."

"And you jumped at the chance to take Susan's place."

I guess Marci had never thought of it that way. That would explain why she narrowed her eyes and gave me a quick, scathing look. "I wouldn't say that, exactly."

"Really? What would you say, exactly?"

I didn't have a chance to find out. The front doors opened and a couple guys came in carrying huge arrangements of yellow, white, and pink spring flowers in tall white vases. Marci ducked away long enough to show them where to put the flowers, then waved me into the picture room, where less than a week earlier, I'd found Susan lying in a pool of blood.

She propped her fists on what she had of hips. "What are you getting at?" Marci asked.

"Me? Not a thing. I was just thinking. That's all. It's mighty convenient, what with Susan out of the way and you finally getting a chance to step into the job you wanted all along."

Some of the starch went out of Marci's shoulders. "I never thought of it that way. You don't think—" She chewed her lower lip. "I didn't ask for this opportunity. The board of trustees are the ones—"

"You said it yourself. You were the most logical choice."

"Well, yeah." When she tucked a strand of hair behind her ear, I swore I heard her hair gel crack. "But that doesn't mean I'm guilty of anything. You don't think . . ."

Whatever I was thinking, Marci was thinking about Susan. I could tell because her gaze darted from this corner of the room to that, scanning the now pristine floor, no doubt thinking of Susan's lifeless body lying on the cold marble. "I didn't kill her."

"I didn't say you did. But you did want her job. You still do."

She cast another quick look in my direction. This one was far more hesitant than it was challenging. "You're bound to find out sooner or later," she said, and I knew she wasn't happy to admit it because her bowed lips puckered. "I've already told the board, I'll close the Little Museum in a heartbeat. I mean, if they give me this job permanently."

I had to give Marci big points for honesty. Especially when the truth made her look as guilty as sin. Then again, job envy might give her a motive for killing Susan, but it didn't explain Angela's murder.

At least not yet, anyway.

"So . . ." Like most people—guilty or not—Marci wasn't comfortable discussing murder. She waved an arm casually, indicating all of the museum in one gesture. "Jimmy didn't say what you wanted to see."

As far as I remembered, I hadn't told him. Not specifically, anyway. I stepped around Marci and into the pirate room. "Actually, I'd like to get a good look at Thunderin' Ben's exhibit," I told her.

She lifted one shoulder. "Have at it. It's just like any other exhibit. Look all you want."

"No. I mean, I just don't want to look at it like any tourist would look at it. I was hoping to . . ." Now that it was time to explain how I wanted to plunder the pirate exhibit, I found the words hard to come by. I made a little waving gesture, indicating that I'd like the glass case that held Ben's things to be opened.

"Really?" Marci wrinkled her nose, and call me crazy, but I had a feeling she was about to pull out the I-am-interim-curator excuse and cut me off at the knees. It might have been because she was itching to exert a little authority. Or she may have had other reasons. Either way, I couldn't let it happen.

"Jimmy Carns said I've got carte blanche." OK, so it wasn't technically the truth, but hey, we were talking two homicides here, and murder trumps the truth card. "If there's a reason you don't want me to look around—"

"I don't have anything to hide." I actually might have believed her if Marci's shoulders weren't as stiff as her hair. "Look around. All you want. Be my guest."

"IT'S MOONCUSSING, DON'T you see?"

Kind of a bad way to phrase it, since Nev and I were talking on the phone and seeing what I'd seen at the Big Museum that day wasn't something it was possible for him to do.

He reminded me of this with a, "How can I? I'm not there."

I clamped my lips shut before I could snap back and say something I might regret.

The warm morning had transformed into a stuffy afternoon and an even more hot and humid evening. I'd pulled my hair off my neck and back into a ponytail, and I tugged on it. No doubt, Nev was just as uncomfortable in the big city as I was there in Ardent Lake, and dog-tired on top of it, too. He had been busy all afternoon; I'd called him four times before I actually got to talk to him.

Too-early-in-the-spring-for-these-high-temperatures plus multiple phone calls do not a patient person make, and I told myself not to forget it at the same time I imagined he wasn't exactly in the mood for a woman who wasn't making herself clear.

I vowed to make myself clear.

"OK, it's like this," I said, explaining slowly enough (I hoped) to be understood but not so slowly as to make Nev think I assumed he was obtuse. "Mooncussing was something pirates used to do. They'd move buoy markers so that they ended up near rocks and reefs. A ship's captain would see the buoy and assume it was in open water when it was really in a dangerous place instead. The ships would go aground. Or sink. And then the pirates would move in to steal anything they could get their hands on."

I couldn't see Nev, of course, but I could picture him nodding. I knew when he did, a single strand of shaggy hair would end up hanging over his forehead. "And pirates and buoy markers are important to our investigation because . . ."

"Because Thunderin' Ben, the pirate who used to live in these parts and who's something of a folk hero around here . . . Thunderin' Ben used to do mooncussing. And our murderer did, too."

"Uh-huh."

So much for me making myself perfectly clear. Nev didn't sound any more certain now than he had at the beginning of our conversation.

"That's what I found at the museum this afternoon," I said. "The buoy marker in the Thunderin' Ben display . . . it had been moved."

"Uh-huh."

I counted to ten, and when that didn't work, I counted again before I said, "Don't you get it, Nev? There's no reason anyone should have been messing with that display. I talked to one of the docents who's been working at the museum for like forever. She told me that Ben's exhibit has always been the same. Nothing's been changed. Nothing's been added. That's how it's been since the exhibit opened, and that was two years ago."

"Which means . . ." I could practically hear the wheels turning inside Nev's head. I knew he'd catch on sooner rather than later, and I knew exactly when he did because I heard his sharp intake of breath. "There's no reason anyone needed to have the exhibit open and that means there's no reason that little replica buoy should have been moved—"

"From where it was at the southern end of that painted Lake Michigan when I first saw the exhibit, to where it is now, in the northern end of Lake Michigan. Not only that, Nev . . ." I fought to steady my voice. The full impact of what I'd found in that display case still made my blood tingle, and I dropped into the oak rocking chair near the open window in my room at Mary Lou's. "Ben's diary is gone," I said.

There was enough of a pause on the other end of the line to let me know Nev was considering the full implications of this bit of news. Of course, once a cop, always a cop, and he responded in true cop fashion. "No one noticed when a book that's been part of the exhibit for a couple years suddenly wasn't there?"

"Aha!" I hate when people say *Aha!* but if ever there was an occasion for it, this was it. "That's just the thing. Remember when we were at Angela's house that Sunday morning when Charles invited people in to preview what he thought were Evelyn's priceless antiques?"

Of course Nev remembered. I didn't give him a chance to have to say it.

"There was a pile of books in the living room," I reminded him.

"Yeah. You were looking at the one on top. An old volume of Sherlock Holmes stories."

I nodded, then when I realized he couldn't see me, I said, "Exactly. Torn brown cover. Cockeyed binding. And you know what, that's pretty much how I remember Ben's diary looking."

Like I said, cop. Nev had been objective, but now, his voice simmered with sudden interest. "Someone took the diary and replaced it with the old book and figured no one would notice."

"Yes. And that someone—"

"Had to be someone who was at Angela's house with us that morning."

"Just what I was thinking." Now that I'd told him the news that had been eating away at me all day, the knot of excitement in my stomach loosened, and I sat back in the rocker. "And while that someone was stealing the diary," I added, "that same someone didn't realize that he—or she—knocked into that little toy buoy and moved it to the wrong end of the lake. The diary. That's what the murderer wanted. That explains why Susan was killed."

Nev knew this, too. Of course he did. Nev is whip smart and a darned good cop.

"She went back to the Big Museum for her purse," he began.

"And surprised whoever it was who was in there stealing the diary," I finished.

"And whoever it was who was stealing the diary," he added.

"Had to keep her quiet."

"So the diary—"

"Contains something worth killing for." I'd had all afternoon to consider this surprising turn of events, but it still sent my head reeling. I gulped in a calming breath before I dared to add, "Nev, I think that something is—"

I was hoping he'd break in with the final words that would finish my sentence. Partly because it would tell me that we were thinking in sync and that meant my theory was a good one. Mostly because, let's face it, the whole thing still sounded a little too fantastical, even to me.

When I was greeted by silence from the other end of the phone, I gave it another try. "There are legends about Ben," I reminded Nev. "And maybe somebody believes those legends are true. Maybe that same somebody thought there might be proof that they were true. In the diary. Proof about—"

"Buried treasure?"

Yes, I had braced myself for Nev's skepticism. I had even prepared myself for a little gentle teasing. I hadn't actually thought he'd sound so bowled over. And so excited.

I couldn't help myself. I had to ask. I had to be sure. "You believe me?"

I could picture him nodding, slowly at first, then gaining speed as he warmed to the idea. "It makes sense. Lots of sense. A button? That might not be worth killing for. But buried treasure . . ."

"Funny you should mention the button." Those photos I'd taken of Angela's buttons were out on the bed and I got up and went to the other side of the room to get them. "I have a theory about that, too."

The way he laughed told me he wasn't surprised.

I launched into my explanation. "I was down at the reservoir today," I said. "Or at least at what was the reservoir before it was drained. Starting tomorrow, they're going to let people walk the rim and get a look at what's left of the old town of Ardent. I took as good a look around as I was able, and I think . . ." I stared at the picture of the missing button. "I think the metal button shows a picture of Ardent, Nev. You know, before they poured water over the whole town. What that means to me—"

"Is that there were two pieces to the buried treasure puzzle. The diary—"

"And the button. Yes. That's exactly what I was thinking. There's something in the diary that leads to the treasure, and some reason the button figures into the whole thing. The button . . ." I took another good look at the photo. "It shows a log cabin and a schoolhouse and a cemetery. Maybe the treasure is in one of those spots, although why the murderer needed the actual button . . ." Nev couldn't see me shrug, so I felt silly for doing it. "I guess we can't be sure. Not until we do a couple things. One of those things . . . I was hoping you could get here early tomorrow, and that you could get us back into Angela's house."

"Done." It was as easy as that. I thanked the Universe for a friend with the right connections.

"And then there's something else we have to do," I added, while he was still being so agreeable. "We need to get a good look at Ardent."

"You mean from the shores of the reservoir?"

"I mean we actually need to go down into the old town. You can arrange that, can't you? With the local authorities?"

Any other guy might have balked. Or asked about the danger of such a plan. Or the wisdom. Nev? He answered simply, "If you think it's important."

I can't say for sure. I mean, a relationship is one of those things that builds upon itself, incident upon incident. Words and gestures and phrases pile up, and in the end, they either make something that's strong and pleasing, or they're a sort of ramshackle mess and you know it's time to walk away. That means I might not have decided things right then and there. I mean, not completely. But in that one moment, with that one comment . . . I'm pretty sure that's when I knew for sure that I was nuts about Nevin Riley.

Chapter Seventeen

TALL YELLOW RUBBER BOOTS DO NOT MAKE A FASHION statement.

Good thing I'm not all that image conscious, or I would have felt even sillier and more awkward than I already did in my tall yellow rubber boots clumping through the mud that had been churned up by the gully washer of a storm that inundated Ardent Lake right after midnight. Fortunately, the humidity had disappeared along with the lightning and thunder, and that Saturday morning dawned clear and just crisp enough to be comfortable without being too chilly.

At least in Ardent Lake.

Down at the bottom of the reservoir in what was left of Ardent, the air was still and damp, and curls of mist hung over the rotting remains of the town all around us.

It was—

"Eerie." At my side, Nev was obviously thinking just what I was thinking. The night before, he'd promised he'd get to Ardent Lake bright and early, and he'd been as good as his word. Unfortunately, that didn't help my plans for the early morning. It seemed like even fairy-tale towns had their evil villains, and thanks to a break-in at a convenience store, we hadn't been able to hook up with Jimmy Carns until just a few minutes before we were scheduled to come to the reservoir; our trip to Angela's would have to wait, and that meant we'd also have to wait to see if that book of Sherlock Holmes stories was really missing.

We were outside what used to be the Ardent post office and Nev paused to take a picture.

"I know. Geeky." Nev stuck his digital camera back in the pocket of his Windbreaker, though I didn't know why he bothered. He'd only end up taking it out again in another minute, just like he'd been doing ever since we arrived at the lake and descended to the bottom of the reservoir. "I can't help myself. How many people get to visit a city that's been underwater all these years? The whole place is—"

"Unsettling." It was, and as we headed up the street, I moved a step to my right, closer to Nev. Jimmy and two other members of the Ardent Lake Police Department were twenty feet ahead of us, watching for dangerous debris and directing us around potholes, uprooted trees, and a variety of junk that had either been left on the ground when the town was abandoned or had been thrown into the lake since. The mud around us was pocked with beer cans and tackle boxes. I even saw a couple plastic lawn chairs.

It was an apocalyptic scene, a place where the buildings were barely recognizable and the sidewalks and street sucked at our feet as if some muddy deity was just daring us to try and take another step.

"The folks up on the rim . . ." Nev looked up and over his shoulder to where the residents of Ardent Lake were starting to gather to get a glimpse of their old hometown. "They must be as jealous as heck watching us walk around down here. We're getting a whole different view of things."

"And not necessarily a good one." I didn't mean to sound helpless, but my left boot was stuck in the mud and I needed an assist from Nev to brace myself, yank, and retrieve it. As long as I had a hold of his arm, I hung on tight and we continued on, skirting the edges of what was once the center of downtown Ardent and heading down a small but slippery hill.

"This is the spot you were asking about." Jimmy waved toward an expanse of relatively flat land and the pile of rotted timbers and mud in the middle of it. "That's what's left of the old log cabin," he said. "At least . . ." He scanned the area, just making sure. "Yeah. It's got to be. The post office . . ." He pointed. "The library . . ." He turned that way, too, before he spun back around to where he'd started. "The log cabin. They tried to get it moved, you know, before the reservoir was filled. But nobody stepped forward to donate the money to make it happen."

Nev had circled around to the front of what was left

of the building. Fists on hips, he shook his head. "If there is something buried here . . ."

"We'd never find it." I was reluctant to get too close to the heap of rotting wood and oozing mud, but I inched a careful step nearer. "Nobody could find anything in that mess. If Thunderin' Ben buried anything in there—"

"Not a chance." Jimmy dismissed the idea instantly. "It wasn't a real log cabin," he said. "I mean, well, sure, it was a real cabin built from real logs, but it wasn't original. The original one belonged to Ardent's first settlers, and that was torn down years ago because it was falling apart and wasn't safe. This one . . ." Jimmy motioned toward the mountain of muck, where at the top, a small green frog was positioning itself to make the most of the sunshine. "The Boy Scouts built it to replace the old one and commemorate the town's sesquicentennial."

"Which means if the treasure was buried in the original log cabin—"

"Somebody would have found it." Jimmy was so sure of this, I couldn't help believing him. "I was in the Boy Scout troop back then. I remember. They did a thorough job of removing that old cabin so we could put up this one. Shame it's in this shape now." He took off his cap and ran a hand through his hair. "We had a lot of fun building that cabin."

"Then how about the schoolhouse?" I checked the photo of the missing button against the battered landscape around us. "Was that original?"

Jimmy nodded. "Absolutely."

"Then it would have been around in Ben's time."

Another nod. "There's a story around here, you know," Jimmy said, poking a finger at the schoolhouse bell tower in the picture. "They say that when someone's going to die, you can still hear the bell ringing. Even from underneath the water."

Urban legend, and I didn't believe it for a minute, but I could see how stories like that got started. The homes and churches and shops of Ardent had been flooded with something like eight million gallons of water. It was easy to see how spooky stories would naturally follow that kind of planned destruction.

We slipped and slid our way a hundred yards farther on ahead and stopped in front of the schoolhouse. It was built of brick and, except for the mother of all mud facials, had survived the water far better than the log cabin had.

"But why would our killer need the button so badly?" OK, I was obsessing, even as we walked around the perimeter of the schoolhouse and stopped at the front door. "If the picture on the button showed the town as it used to be, and if he needed the picture to figure out where the treasure might be hidden, why wouldn't the picture be enough?"

"You mean why did he need the actual button?" Nev had one hand on the front door of the schoolhouse. "Maybe he didn't need the button. Not really. Maybe—"

"It's just lost. Like our fish button was. Yeah, I know." I was sorry I brought it up, but I couldn't help myself. I felt like we were finally getting close to making sense of all that had happened over the past weeks, and my brain wouldn't stop whirling over the details.

Grumbling, I stepped back so that Nev and Jimmy could pry the schoolhouse door open.

Good thing I did, or like poor Nev and Jimmy, I would have been swamped with the sea of mud that poured out of the school.

"Oh, yuck!" Nev has quick reflexes. The mud flowed up and out, as high as his knees, and he snatched his camera out of his pocket and tossed it to me to be sure it stayed clean and safe.

Good thing I have quick reflexes, too. I caught the camera with one hand and darted back and out of the way of the mudflow that would have easily come up over the tops of my boots.

It wasn't until after I was sure I was out of harm's way that I bent forward and peered into the building. Once upon a time, it had been a one-room schoolhouse, and now, except for what had rolled out the door, that one room was pretty much filled top to bottom with gunk.

"I think it's pretty safe to say we're not going to find any treasure in there," I commented.

Nev didn't answer. But then, he was still pretty busy scraping spatters of mud off his jacket.

That left the cemetery, and in the blasted landscape, it was difficult to tell exactly how far away it was. I tried to stand on tiptoe to see a little better, slipped, and would have gone down if Nev hadn't looped one arm around my waist. Great plan. Or at least it would have been if he wasn't covered with mud.

Cringing, I refused to worry about how I'd ever get my jacket clean, and followed my police escort, and after another couple slip-slidey minutes of walking, we caught a glimpse of the first headstones sticking up through the mud like rotted teeth.

A shiver snaked over my shoulders. "Oh, that's just positively creepy!"

"Not to worry." Jimmy laughed. "The bodies aren't here anymore. They were all removed. You know, before the reservoir was filled. All the dead folks are up at Elm Lawn in town now, and this place is just empty.

"Empty and creepy," I said, hoping Nev would take pity on me and stay close, but it seemed even the mud hadn't soured his opinion of how interesting the drowned town was. He motioned for his camera, I relinquished it, and he darted ahead.

I wiped a dot of mud off the photo of the button and studied the picture again before I realized that what looked like a little building beyond the headstones in the photograph was in reality an elaborate mausoleum.

"Nev." I closed in on him where he was crouched in front of a gravestone that had been completely coated with moss. "Nev, if you were a pirate and eager to hide your treasure, would you take a chance of burying it?"

He got to his feet. "You mean here in the cemetery? I guess no one would notice that the ground had been disturbed, but heck, the whole point of being a pirate is avoiding hard work whenever possible. If I was a pirate, I wouldn't want to put in the sweat equity. Besides, you heard what Jimmy said. This whole place was dug up before the town was flooded so they could retrieve the bodies and bury them in the new town. If there was treasure in any one of these graves—"

"Somebody would have found it."

We finished the thought together.

Rather than allow myself to get discouraged again, I glommed on to an earlier thought and followed it to its logical conclusion. "But what if you were that same pirate and there was a better place to hide something. Like, say in some little building?" I asked Nev. "That would be easier."

"Way easier." He swung his gaze where I was looking, at that mausoleum. "If it's not filled with junk like the schoolhouse was . . ."

He didn't finish the thought. He didn't need to. Moving faster than either of us should have been able to with the ground slipping out from under our feet, we hurried over to the mausoleum.

This close, I could see that the tomb was constructed of gray and pink granite and that it must have been gorgeous—and expensive—in its day. There were carved angels standing guard on either side of the door, and I suspected that what was now a hole in the side wall had once contained a stained glass window. These days, there was greenery sprouting from the gutters and the skeleton of a fish lay on the doorstep. None of that was especially surprising, of course.

The name carved over the doorway . . .

That was another thing altogether.

"Moran." Out loud, Jimmy Carns read the name carved above the door from right behind us, and yes, I squealed and flinched. But then, it was that kind of place. "Family's been around here for years and all of them were buried here. Not Ben, of course. Story has it he died in Chicago and was buried there somewhere. But here, this is where Thunderin' Ben's parents were supposed to spend eternity resting in peace."

I hadn't expected that obvious a connection to Thunderin' Ben, and my spirits soared.

Jimmy didn't look nearly as pleased. In fact, he shook his head, downright disgusted. "All these years, and you think this is where the treasure might be? Hell, when we were kids, we'd listen to the stories about Ben and then we'd grab our shovels and go running around the woods outside of town and dig up place after place. And if all this time, it was really here . . ."

"If."

Nev didn't need to remind me. I was being practical. Honest. I was prepared to be let down—again—by a clue that led nowhere. Of course, that didn't mean I was prepared to give up.

Again, I went over the theory Nev and I had just about talked to death over breakfast that morning. "If the button showed the way to the treasure . . ."

"That would mean that button was worth stealing, and maybe our killer thought it was worth killing for, too," he said. "But I can't help but think about what you said earlier, Josie. Why did the killer need the button? The killer must have known that the button showed old Ardent, the cabin and the school and the cemetery. But for some reason, that wasn't good enough. He needed the actual physical button. Why?"

"Maybe there was something you had to do with the button," I proposed, sounding as unsure of this theory as I felt and like I was coming up with a plot idea for a new Indiana Jones movie. "Like the button is some kind of key or something. And maybe Ben talked about how it worked in his diary. Maybe that's why the killer needed both the button and the diary."

"Maybe." Nev didn't sound any more sure of this than I felt, and before I could convince myself that we were wasting our time, I inched closer to the mausoleum.

I made sure to stay well out of the way of whatever might rush out when Nev pulled open the mausoleum door. "Not a lot of mud," I commented to him, and of course, he was one step ahead of me. He simply nodded and gestured to Jimmy to have a look at a mushy pile of mud just to the right of the front door. I knew where his thoughts were running. "You think that little mud pile looks awfully neat. Like maybe someone shoveled mud out of the mausoleum and threw it over there."

He didn't agree or disagree. "Let's go inside," Nev said, "and find out."

If what was left of Ardent out under the wide, blue sky was creepy, the inside of a mausoleum which had until just very recently been filled with water and left, silent and abandoned, all these years, was off the scale in the scare-me-to-death department.

"Good thing I brought a flashlight."

People had to stop standing right behind me and talk-ing. This time Nev was the guilty party and I was so immersed in the mood of the place that I clapped a hand to my hip-hopping heart and watched as he flicked on the flashlight and arced its light around the inside of the tomb. Apparently, the Moran family's remains had once been laid to rest in niches carved into the granite walls. Those spots were empty now, with decades of accumulated mud and debris on the shelves that had once contained their caskets.

"What do you think?" Nev picked up a stick lying nearby and poked it into the gunk that coated the nearest shelf. "If the treasure was with one of the bodies, it's gone."

"I don't know." I whirled around, taking in the devastation and the grime that showed everywhere Nev's light hit. "For a minute there, my crazy theory about the button being some kind of key or talisman actually made sense to me. But now . . ." His light flashed across the far wall and I pulled in a breath. "Nev?" He was standing next to me, and even though it was coated with mud, I grabbed his sleeve and tugged. "Did you see that?"

"See what?" His light had already moved on, and Nev froze with it trained on the floor. "What did I miss?"

"There. Over there." I pointed straight ahead toward the far wall, but since it was as gloomy in there as the inside of a thundercloud, I was sure Nev had no idea what I was indicating. To help out, I clamped my hand over his—and his flashlight—and slid the light over to the left.

"There," I said, and since Nev is a smart guy, he saw exactly what I saw and stepped forward.

"No mud." Nev knelt down for a better look at an area of the wall that had obviously been recently wiped clean. "There's some kind of carving here." He leaned nearer for a better look, his light aimed at the wall right in front of him. "It's like a little miniature picture of the town, only it doesn't look like that button of yours. It looks like—"

"A perfect mirror image." OK, so button dealers aren't

all that fond of mud, but a little more dirt and grime (OK, a lot of dirt and grime) at this point wasn't going to make any difference, and it wasn't going to keep me from seeing what he was seeing. I knelt down next to Nev and held the photo of the metal button up next to the carving in the mausoleum wall. "If we had the real button . . ." I pretended I did, and held it by its imaginary shank. "It would fit into the wall carving perfectly! So the button was the key!" I said, so pleased and stunned that I'd already sat back on my heels before I realized that now, I could add the seat of my pants to the list of my muddy-beyond-repair clothing. "The killer needed the button in order to fit it into the carving. And once that was done—"

"This little door popped open." Nev had been fiddling at the wall below the carving and found the little door in the wall that had been kept hidden and secret all these years. He bent even closer to the ground to shine his light inside and, just to make sure, stuck his hand into the black hole, too.

"Empty," he grumbled. He called Jimmy over to tell him to get some techs in there to seal off the mausoleum and collect whatever evidence they were likely to find. "The killer had to wait until the reservoir was empty," he said once Jimmy was outside and on the phone. "And once he had the diary and the button and the water was all gone—"

"He came and got the treasure. If there really was a treasure."

Nev held up his hand. It was cleaner than it should have been considering he'd just poked it into that filthy hole. "Oh, there was a treasure, all right," he said. "That would explain the lack of mud in there."

"Because something else was in there, something like a treasure chest. That's why the mud couldn't accumulate." I nodded, following his theory.

And technically, all of this should have made us pretty pleased with ourselves. After all, we'd followed a pirate's clues all the way to X Marks the Spot. Trouble is, the killer had gotten there before us.

I'm sure Nev was just as disappointed as I was, but it didn't keep him from pulling out his camera and snapping a few more pictures.

Pictures.

"Oh, for the love of buttons!" I would have slapped my forehead if I wasn't afraid of getting mud all over my face. "Nev, it's been staring at us all along. From the pictures."

He didn't question this curious statement. But then, like I said, he's that kind of guy.

Chapter Eighteen

Just for the record, the ladies' room at the Ardent Lake police station is not the most comfortable place to get cleaned up, but it served its purpose. Before we headed over to Angela's, I was presentable, if not spic-and-span.

Once there, we found two things. Or should I say we found one thing and found the other missing.

Yes, the Sherlock Holmes book was gone.

And the other thing?

With Nev's blessing, I took that with me, and when I changed for the cocktail party that evening, I made sure I brought along a big enough purse to stash it in.

Call Mary Lou Baldwin a hopeless romantic; even though I'd reserved it for only one night, she'd kept my room for me, and I was grateful. I took a very long, very hot shower, put on black pants, sensible pumps, and a lightweight sweater the color of the darkest grapes on that purloined punch bowl of Marci's, and when I walked out of my room at the B and B, Nev was waiting downstairs. He took one look at me and smiled. "You should wear purple more often. It looks good on you."

He wasn't much for compliments. Not like Kaz, who threw them around like confetti at a ticker-tape parade. I suppose that's what made this one more special.

In fact, he looked pretty darned special, too—in a very Nevin Riley way—and I found out that was thanks to Mary Lou, too, who'd let him use her own private suite in the B and B to get clean and gussied up. Black pants, gray shirt. So far, so good. It was the cantaloupe-colored tie and the khaki jacket that threw Nev's outfit for a loop.

Not to worry. I made a couple gentle suggestions about how warm the evening was and how he might want to carry his jacket rather than wear it.

Feeling as confident as a woman can who's just come out of an abandoned graveyard, I hoisted my purse up on my shoulder and we walked to the Big Museum together.

Just inside the front door, we were greeted by a huge photo of Susan on an easel, along with a book where visitors could write their condolences and a box for donations for those wishing to contribute to the Big Museum in Susan's name. We did both, and we moved out of the hallway and into the room across from the photo room, where a long table had been set up and heaped with appetizers of all shapes and sizes. Nev reached for the clear plastic plates set out near one of those giant flower arrangements I'd seen the day before. He took a dish for himself and handed one to me.

"How can you eat?" I held the plate close to my jumping heart. "I'm so nervous, I don't think I can get a bite down."

"There's another thing you need to learn about police work." He filled his plate with tiny pieces of pizza, stuffed mushrooms, and cheese and crackers. "When you're waiting like this, you've got to keep your strength up," he said, adding two kinds of bruschetta to the top of the pile. "Besides, if you don't eat . . ." He glanced toward the door, where I saw Marci chatting with Larry and beyond them to where Charles had just walked in. "It's going to look weird, and somebody's going to ask you what's wrong. What are you going to tell them?"

"That I'm here to catch a murderer?"

He showed his appreciation for my sense of humor by popping down a stuffed mushroom, and since I knew he was right, I chose a small assortment of finger foods and accepted red wine in a teeny plastic glass from the server stationed at the end of the table. Thus fortified, we chit-chatted our way through the room, biding our time.

"Can't say I'm surprised you're here."

It wasn't the most cordial of greetings from Larry, but then, the way I remember it, the last time we'd been together was the day Susan died, and neither of us was at our best. He sipped his wine. "Any luck?" The question was clearly intended for Nev. "With your investigation?"

"We've uncovered a thing or two." How he did it so quickly, I wasn't sure, but Nev was down to his last bite of bruschetta. He snapped it up. "We should know more soon."

"I hope so." Larry walked away, his words trailing behind him like a shadow. "I certainly hope so."

I had anticipated a long, tense evening, but though the tense part was true, the hours went by remarkably quickly. Then again, we had the run of the museum, and I kept my mind busy—and off the subject of murder—by strolling through the displays, while Nev took care of the rest. I'm not sure how he managed, but by ten when the cocktail party was set to end and I walked into the pirate room, all my suspects were in there, too.

I wasn't planning on this taking long, so we hadn't bothered to ask the staff to bring in chairs. When I set my purse on top of the Thunderin' Ben display case with its displaced toy buoy inside, Larry was standing on my left, Marci was directly in front of me, and Charles was hanging around near the door, looking like he'd rather be anywhere but.

I didn't say a word. But remember, I was once a theater major, and though I'm still not much of an actor, I do appreciate a sense of drama. I held my breath, and waited for my cue.

God bless Jimmy Carns, it came just as the floor clock in the hallway stopped chiming the hour.

The clear, distant sound of a ringing bell.

Marci flinched and red wine slopped over the edge of her tiny glass and dotted her white blouse like blood spatter. "That's not—"

"It can't be." Brave words from Charles, but he ran his tongue over his lips. "The schoolhouse bell. They say you can hear it ring, if there's going to be a . . . you know . . . if someone's going to die."

"Don't be ridiculous." Larry was wearing a navy suit and a blindingly white shirt, and he looked more like a power broker than a hardware store owner. Feet slightly apart, chin high, his top lip rose. "You're imagining it."

"Oh, I don't think so." This was me, of course, sounding as placid as the waters of the reservoir usually are. But then, I'd arranged for the bell to ring so it hadn't taken me by surprise. In fact, it had done exactly what I intended it to do, set the tone for a conversation that was as serious as . . . well, as serious as two homicides.

"Don't worry," I added, because I couldn't bear to watch Charles suffer and the poor man looked like he was going to pass out. "Nobody's going to die. At least I hope not. Of course . . ." I glanced around at the semicircle of faces. "That doesn't mean we're not going to talk about murder."

Charles cast a sidelong glance at Nev, who was standing on the other side of the room, his arms crossed over his chest. "He said you wanted to talk to me, Josie. He didn't say . . ." Charles's gaze slid from Marci to Larry. "He didn't say it was about the murders. What's going on?"

"Good question." Larry finished off his tiny glass of wine and set the empty plastic cup on the display case next to my purse. "I don't know about the rest of you, but I'm ready to call it a night."

"I'm sure we all are." My smile was as bright as if I were one of the docents and welcoming the little group to the museum. "It's been a really busy day. For all of us.

But before we go, I think there are some things we need to clear up."

"Oh, give me a break!" Marci downed the rest of her wine in one chug. Something told me it wasn't her first glass. Marci's cheeks were the same color as her hair, and she swayed just a little on her platform heels. Recovered from the surprise of hearing the bell—or maybe it was the wine that gave her courage—she made a face. "You're not going to start with the interrogations and the accusations again, are you?"

"Absolutely not. Scout's honor." Just like a Scout, I held up one hand as if that would prove it. "In fact, I don't need to. No more questions. No more wondering who did what and why. You see, I've finally got the whole thing figured out."

Charles had been busy picking bruschetta crumbs off the front of his gray sweater, and his hand stilled over his stomach. "You mean . . ." In the reflected light of the spotlight trained on Thunderin' Dan's exhibit, I saw his Adam's apple jump. "You know who killed Angela?"

"And Susan," I told him just in case he'd forgotten we needed to address that problem, too. "And why."

"Impossible." Marci waved away the idea with one hand. "And if you're going to say it was me—" Her slim shoulders shot back. "I didn't have any reason to kill anyone."

"Well, you did, actually." I hated to be the one to remind her, but after all, we were there to find the truth. "You had a motive to kill Susan because you wanted her job. And as for Angela . . . well, if she found out you were taking things from her home and putting them on display at the Little Museum—"

"Stealing from Angela? Really!" Disgusted, Larry stalked away and something told me he actually might have kept right on going if not for the fact that, quickly and quietly, Nev had stationed himself at the door. Apparently, Larry knew a losing cause when he saw one. His jaw tight, he spun around and came back to join our group.

"You've always been a suspect," I told Marci. "For exactly those reasons, and truth be told, my money was on you. At least until yesterday. When we were talking in there . . ." I gestured toward the room that featured the old photos of Ardent. "You mentioned Susan, and you looked all around. Like you didn't know exactly where the body had been found."

"I didn't!"

"Exactly. I've always said you had the smarts and the guts to do it, Marci, but after I saw that, I had to admit it couldn't have been you. Even though you did have one heck of a motive."

Ever since I'd mentioned Marci's pilfering ways, Charles had been opening and closing his mouth, trying to find the words to express his outrage. They finally came out in a sputter. "Angela's things . . . Angela's things are my things now . . . and if you're . . . you're not stealing from Angela. You're stealing from me. How dare you! I'm going to file a police report. Right now."

"Not necessary." I stilled him with a lift of one hand. "Marci returned everything. And besides, now that we know all those priceless antiques are really nothing more than good reproductions . . ."

I let Charles figure out the rest for himself.

By the time he was done, there was a little more color in his cheeks. "So Marci killed Angela and Susan. Good. Now we know. We can leave."

"Not so fast." I was prepared to clamp a hand on his arm if it came to that, but luckily, I didn't need to get physical with Charles. My words were enough to keep him in his place. "We need to talk about your motives, too, Charles."

"Me?" He was back to opening and closing his mouth. "You can't possibly think—"

"You cut her brake lines."

Larry got in Charles's face so fast, I thought Nev was going to have to break up the altercation. Luckily, Larry's fuse was short, but it didn't burn long. He stopped just short of doing something he may have regretted, his arm cocked. "You? You risked my Angela's life. For . . . for . . ."

"For what I thought was a fortune." Charles hung his head. "I've told Josie everything. She knows I couldn't—"

"Actually, Charles, I know you could."

Charles went pasty again.

"Trick is," I comforted him, "while I could find plenty of reasons for you wanting to kill Angela, I couldn't find any for you to want Susan dead. Well . . ." I'd been standing in front of the pirate display and I stepped aside and waved a hand toward the diary. "That is, until we figured out that Ben's diary has been stolen."

"Stolen?"

"Really?"

"Preposterous!"

Their voices overlapped, and as if they'd choreographed the move and practiced it to perfection, all three of them moved forward to peer at the display.

"You see," I said, "we thought the murder could be about love." I glanced at Larry. "Or about envy." I looked at Marci. "Or jealousy." When I looked at him, Charles looked at his shoes. "But what it all comes down to is greed. The murderer was looking for Ben's treasure."

"Treasure." Larry's grumbled word echoed in the gallery. "That's just a lot of nonsense. Nothing more than a story. It's no more real than Angela's silly curse."

"Well, that's just the thing, see. The curse . . ." I looked from Charles to Marci to Larry. "Turns out that curse was real, too."

Again, a chorus of protests and questions went up, and since I knew there was no use trying to talk above it, I waited until the noise died down.

"It took me a while to figure out," I said, when I finally had their attention again. "And that's really too bad. If I'd realized what was going on sooner, Susan might still be alive."

I'd gotten this far on nothing but nerve and adrenaline, but I didn't know how much longer I could maintain the cool facade. I slipped between Marci and Charles and walked to the other side of the room and back, eager to dispel the nervous energy. On the way over, and again on the way back, I glanced Nev's way. There wasn't any hint of emotion in his expression, but his eyes told another story. He was rooting for me. And I was doing a good job. He had my back.

It was time to finish what I'd started.

I stayed where I was, forcing my suspects to turn around when I said, "If it wasn't for the charm string, I guess I never would have figured out what happened."

"First the diary. Now the charm string." Larry expression was sour. "I'm sorry, but you're just not making sense."

"That's because curses don't make sense. And Angela's curse was getting that charm string in the first place. Just like it was Aunt Evelyn's before her. The charm string with two touch buttons."

I was pretty sure none of them knew what this meant, but I let the words fill the silence between us for a little while before I explained.

"A touch button," I told them, "was the button a girl used to start her charm string. It's usually bigger than the other buttons on the string. And Angela's charm string had two. One of them was a rubber button and the other was a button that showed the scene of a town. I didn't know it at first, but I know it now. It was Ardent. How did it get there?"

No one had asked, but hey, I knew they would eventually so I told them the truth. "I don't think we'll ever know. Not for sure. But my guess is that if we did a little snooping, we'd find out that Angela's great-grandmother had some connection with Thunderin' Ben's family. When Ben needed a place to stash the button, he hid it in plain sight. He slipped it onto the end of her charm string. Who would look for a button among all those other buttons? Well, nobody. Not for a very long time. Until our murderer realized he needed the button along with Ben's diary. Without both, he wouldn't have been able to find the treasure."

"You mean there really is a treasure?" Marci peered at me through bleary eyes. "Angela and Susan, they were killed because somebody wanted to get their hands on . . . what?"

I hated admitting I didn't know for sure. "I can't say. Not yet, anyway. Maybe it was coins. Or gold bars. We won't know until the cops get back here. You know, after they've executed their search warrants. The only thing we can be sure of is that it's been hidden in the Moran family mausoleum all these years. That, and that with the reservoir being drained, our murderer saw the perfect opportunity to finally get his hands on it." I had strolled a couple steps nearer and I turned to face Larry.

"Angela suspected, didn't she?" I asked him. "She had an inkling of what you were up to. That explains why she had those books about Ardent town history in her house. And maps of the area, too. She realized you were looking for the treasure, and that for reasons she probably didn't understand, you needed the button to find it. Her button. Did you try to talk her into giving you the Ardent button, Larry? I mean, before you strangled her and stole it?"

"That's . . ." Larry's smile froze in place. "That's crazy."

"Yeah, exactly what I was thinking. But not as crazy as a curse, right? The fire at Angela's, the break-in, all engineered by you so that she'd take the curse seriously and get rid of the charm string. Only you never counted on her wanting to dump it in Lake Michigan. That's when you convinced her to donate it."

"And she said she was going to donate it to me." Leave it to Marci not to miss out on speaking her piece.

Actually, I was grateful. "Exactly," I said, turning her way. "Angela offered you the charm string first. But that wasn't going to work, was it, Larry?" I swung my gaze his way. "Because the Little Museum has a state-of-the-art alarm system, and you knew if the charm string went there, you'd never get your hands on it. You'd read enough about Ben's life to hear rumors about a secret key that would help you find the treasure. You knew Angela had a button with a picture of old Ardent on it. You had to get that button. And she wouldn't give it to you, would she?"

Larry's chin came up a fraction of an inch. "If I'd asked, she would have given me the button. Angela would have done anything for me. But I didn't ask." His eyes snapped to mine. "I couldn't ask for a button when I didn't know anything about the button or the treasure, for that matter."

I figured he'd object, and I was ready for it. "That's what you and Angela fought about the morning she was killed, right? She figured out that you didn't love her, you were just pretending so you could get your hands on the charm string. And you didn't kiss and make up before she came to Chicago. She was still upset when she arrived at the Button Box. And you followed her. You confronted her. You fought and you grabbed for the nearest weapon. Did you rip the Ardent button off the charm string before you strangled her with it? Well, you must have. That would explain how it didn't get lost in the dark. Poor

Angela must have been heartbroken when she realized what you were up to."

Larry crossed his arms over his chest. "And poor Susan? I suppose you have some lame theory about her death, too."

"Well, my guess is your feelings for her were just as phony as your feelings for Angela. You dated Susan originally because you wanted to get your hands on Ben's diary. Then when you realized you'd never get the button unless you were close to Angela, you switched your affections. Once Angela was out of the way, you were free to start wooing Susan again. And it almost worked, didn't it? You would have gotten away with it if she didn't walk in here that Sunday morning looking for her purse. Once she found you with your hand in the Thunderin' Ben exhibit switching one of the old books you found at Angela's for the real diary . . ." I looked at the display case, picturing the horrible scene. "You had no choice but to kill her, too."

"Absolutely not!" Larry stomped one foot. "None of it is true, and I won't let you repeat a word of it. Not to anyone. There are laws about slander, you know, and if word of this gets around in Ardent Lake, my business will be ruined. You can't prove it." He stalked toward the door. "You can't prove any of it."

Nev stopped him with one simple phrase. "We will," he said, "once the police are done searching your house and we find the treasure. And the diary. And the button."

"And even if we didn't have that . . ." I walked over to

where I'd set my purse. "There is the whole thing about Aunt Evelyn."

Larry went as still as if he'd been flash frozen. "How dare you bring up the memory of that nice, old lady? Evelyn was a dear."

"And you were a dear to humor Angela and take Evelyn along on so many of your outings." I opened my purse and pulled out the photograph of Larry and Evelyn in the park that I'd originally seen in Angela's bedroom. "You were kind to Evelyn."

"Of course I was."

"And you did it just to humor Angela. Not because you wanted to get the button from the string when Evelyn owned it?"

"I told you that's not true!" At the same time Larry took a step toward me, Nev moved in my direction, too. Even that wasn't enough to get Larry to back off. His hands curled into fists and his arms tight at his sides, Larry bent to look me in the eye. "You're lying."

"Pictures don't lie." I showed the photo to Larry and, since they were leaning forward to try and get a glimpse, I held it out so Marci and Charles could see it, too. "This picture shows you with Evelyn," I said, though Larry certainly didn't need a reminder. "I found it in Angela's room along with the other pictures of you she'd taken down from her wall."

Larry sniffed. "She was repainting."

"She was as mad as hell. Because I'll bet anything that Angela found this picture when she cleaned out Evelyn's house, and when she cleaned out Evelyn's house . . ." I gave Larry another chance to fess up, and when he didn't, I had no choice but to go on. "Angela realized you were romancing Aunt Evelyn two years ago."

"I . . ." Larry's jaw went slack and he blinked rapidly. "I wasn't . . . I didn't . . . I . . ."

"You can explain it all down at the station. If there's any way to explain." Jimmy Carns stepped in from the hallway and slapped handcuffs on Larry.

THE NEXT MONDAY, I was back at the Button Box and grateful for it. I was back where I belonged, lost in a world of buttons, and as happy as any button-a-holic can be.

I was just finishing switching out a display of calico buttons for one of clear glass (mostly because I hadn't played with my clear glass buttons for a while and I was itching to get a look at them) when the bell over the front door chinked and Nev stuck his head into the shop.

"Just got a call from Jimmy Carns," Nev said. "Larry confessed."

"Poor Susan, and poor, poor Angela. She had the charm string with one thousand buttons on it, and her Prince Charming finally came along. Too bad he wasn't the man of anyone's dreams." I'd been on my knees, checking the lower shelves of the display case to make sure everything was perfect, and I got up and walked to the front of the shop. "But at least a confession saves a long, drawn-out trial."

"Well, it's not like Larry could do much else. He didn't hide the diary very well, or that missing button. As for the treasure . . ."

Nev's voice drifted off, and I knew exactly how he felt. It still took my breath away to think that the Ardent Lake police had found a jewel case filled with old gold coins hidden in Larry's attic.

"Maybe they'll put the treasure on display at the Big Museum," I suggested.

Nev grinned. "I wouldn't be surprised."

He was still positioned half in, and half out of the shop, and I was just going to ask what was going on when he jerked to the side, as if his arm had been pulled.

"What . . ." I got as far as the door, and when LaSalle saw me, he let out a bark. He was still wearing that bright blue collar and he was tethered to a blue leash. Need I say that the other end of that leash was in Nev's hand?

"What?" He acted like this wasn't any big deal.

"Bring him in." I waved cop and dog into the shop and LaSalle ran over to greet me, paws on my knees and ears flapping. "So, you've got a new best friend, huh?" I asked the dog. He didn't answer. He didn't need to.

"He'd only get in trouble out on the street," Nev said, rubbing the dog's head. "And when I suggested he might want a permanent home—"

I laughed. "You don't need to explain. LaSalle's had plenty of opportunities to go home with the merchants and the workers from the neighborhood. He was never interested. I guess he was just waiting for the right person to come along."

Nev dropped the leash and LaSalle wandered over to stick his nose in the trash can near my desk. With the dog busy, Nev propped his hands on my hips. "I think that's what we're all looking for, don't you?"

I couldn't have agreed more. I slipped my hands around Nev's waist.

"Except, I hope you understand . . ." he said. "You know . . ." I looked up just in time to see the tips of his ears turn pink. "I mean, about the B and B."

I wiped the smile from my face. I wasn't actually mad about what had happened in Ardent Lake on Saturday night. In fact, I was actually pretty relieved. But it didn't hurt to tease a guy, just a little. "You mean about how Mary Lou offered us that room for Saturday night and we turned her down?"

"Yeah." A look of regret crossed his face. "I just . . . well, we'd just caught a murderer, and let's face it, murder isn't exactly romantic."

"No, it is definitely not."

"And I . . ." Nev tightened his hold. "When it happens, Josie, I want it to be perfect."

This time, I didn't even try to control my smile.

See, that was the moment I knew for sure. Perfect? Oh yeah, it would be.

I find the whole notion of charm strings (also called friendship strings or memory strings) terribly romantic. Imagine all those girls way back in the late nineteenth and early twentieth centuries, trading and saving buttons, giving and getting them as gifts, then stringing them in the hopes that once button number one thousand arrived, so would Prince Charming.

In fact, there were a number of superstitions associated with charm strings, and a number of them were variations on the Prince Charming story. One said that the prince was the one who had to string that one thousandth button. Another turned the romantic notion on its head and said that if a girl got button number 1000, she would die an old maid.

Whatever the legend, old charm strings are extremely rare these days. That doesn't mean the hobby couldn't be renewed. Save up old buttons, and string them with the princes and princesses in your life! Who knows, someday, those charm strings, too, might be precious, old and valuable.

For more information about vintage and antique buttons and button collecting, go to: www.nationalbuttonsociety.org.

Turn the page for a preview of Kylie Logan's
new League of Literary Ladies Mysteries . . .

Mayhem at
the Orient Express

Coming soon from Berkley Prime Crime!

IF IT WASN'T FOR JERRY GARCIA PEEING ON MY PANSIES, I never would have joined the League of Literary Ladies.

No, not that Jerry Garcia! Jerry Garcia, Chandra Morrisey's cat. In fact, it was that peeing incident, and the one before it, and the one before that . . .

Well, suffice it to say that if it wasn't for Jerry's less-than-stellar bathroom habits, there never would have been a League at all.

Jerry, see, was the reason I was in mayor's court that Thursday morning.

Again.

"That damned cat . . ." I bit my lower lip to hold in my temper and the long list of Jerry's sins I was tempted to recite. After all, Alvin Littlejohn, the court magistrate, had heard it all before.

Then again, so had Chandra Morrisey, and her cat was still peeing on my pansies.

Chandra was standing to my right, and I swung her way. "He needs to be kept in the house. That's all I'm asking."

It was all I'd asked the week previously, too, and just like that time (and the time before and the time before that), Chandra rolled her eyes, which were the color of the gray clouds that blanketed the sky outside the town hall building. "Cats are free spirits," she said, her voice as soft as the rolls of flesh that rippled beneath a tie-dyed T-shirt that fit her like a second, Easter-egg-swirl-of-color skin. "They are the embodiment of nature spirits. If we don't allow them to roam free, we impede their mission in this world. They can commune with the Other Side, you know." Like it would help the information sink into this nonbeliever's skull, Chandra looked at me hard.

If I was still back in New York City, I would have given her a one-finger salute and been done with it. But we were, in fact, on an island twelve miles from the southern shore of Lake Erie, and as I'd come to learn in the six weeks I'd lived on South Bass, residents here were a different breed. They moved slower than folks back in the Big Apple. They were friendlier. Considerate. More civilized.

Well, except for Jerry.

And, obviously, his owner.

"This is ridiculous!" I threw my hands in the air. Not as dramatic a gesture as I would have liked, but hey, like I said, people here were considerate, and my goal in coming to the island in the first place was to blend in. "You're wasting my time, Chandra. And the court's time, too. All you need to do is—"

"All Chandra needs to do?"

Honestly, I was so fixated on Jerry's loony owner, I'd forgotten Kate Wilder was even in the room. She stood on my left, tapping one sensible pump against the black-and-white linoleum. "It's not like I have time for this, Alvin, and you know it," she grumbled, her arms crossed over the jacket of a neat navy suit that looked particularly puritanical against flaming orange hair that was as long as my coal black tresses, but not nearly as curly. "We could settle this whole thing quickly, if you'd tell her . . ." Kate was a petite, pretty woman who looked to be about thirty-five, the same age as me. Her emerald green eyes snapped to mine. "Tell Ms. Cartwright here to cut down on the traffic at that B and B of hers and there won't be anything left for us to discuss."

"Oh, we'll still have plenty to talk about," I shot back. "Especially if your constant nagging about traffic means my renovations don't get done by the time I'm scheduled to open. Come on, it's not like it's any big deal. It's just a few trucks coming down the street now and then."

"A few?" Kate ticked the list off on her fingers (which is actually a pretty pithy way of putting it since while she was at it, she was ticking me off, too). "There was the truck that brought the new windows, and one that took care of the heating and air conditioning, and one from the painters and one from—"

"I thought you said you were busy and had better things to do?" Ah yes, me at my sarcastic best! Not one to be intimidated (see the above comment about New

York), I, too, crossed my arms over my black turtleneck and adjusted the dark-rimmed glasses on the bridge of my nose, the better to give Kate the kind of glare anybody with that much time on her hands—not to mention nerve—deserved. "Apparently, you don't have anything better to do than spend your time looking across the street at my place. Once the renovations are complete—"

"At least those trucks won't be spewing fossil-fuel exhaust fumes near my herb garden." Chandra tugged at her left earlobe and the three golden hoops in it. "Once *she* gets rid of those—"

"And *she* cuts down on the traffic jams—"

"And *she* takes care of that damned cat—"

"All right! That's it. Quiet down!" In the weeks I'd been appearing before Alvin in the basement courtroom, I had never seen him so red in the face. He fished a white cotton handkerchief from his pocket and mopped his forehead. "This has gotten . . ." There was a plastic bottle of water on his desk and he opened it and took a gulp. "This situation has gotten out of control. You're out of control."

I would have been willing to second this last comment if he'd kept his gaze on Chandra. When it moved to Kate . . . well, that was understandable, too. But when it slid my way and stayed there, I couldn't help myself. My chin came up and my shoulders went back.

Alvin scraped a hand through what was left of his mousy-colored hair and pointed a finger at Kate. "You're mad at . . ." He arced his finger in my direction. "Her because of the traffic. And you're . . ." His slightly trembling finger remained aimed at me. "Mad at her . . ." The accusatory gesture moved to Chandra. "Because her cat—"

"Pees on my flowers. All the time. What's going to happen in the summer when I have guests and they want to sit out on the front porch and—"

"I get the picture." A muscle jumped at the base of Alvin's jaw, but he kept his gaze on Chandra. "And you, Chandra, you're mad at Kate. Do I have that right? Because . . ." He flipped open a manila file on his desk and consulted the topmost piece of paper in it. "Because Kate plays opera too loud on Sunday mornings."

Chandra nodded, and her bleached blond, blunt-cut hair bobbed to the beat. "I do my meditating in the morning." She said this in a way that made it sound like public knowledge. For all I knew, it was. From what I'd heard, Chandra Morrisey had lived in Put-in-Bay (the little town that was the center of life on South Bass) nearly all of her nearly fifty years. "She's messing with the vibrations in the neighborhood and that affects my aura."

"Oh, for pity sake!" Kate's screech fell flat against the pocked tiles of the drop ceiling. "She hates opera? Well, I hate that creepy sitar music that's always coming from her place. And I don't have time for this. Any of it. I need to get to the winery."

"Oh, the Wilder Winery!" If we hadn't been enmeshed in our own little version of a smackdown, I might have laughed at Chandra's attempt at a la-di-da accent. "Play your screechy opera at the winery, then, why don't you," she suggested to Kate. "And leave the rest of us in peace."

"Which actually might be possible," Kate snapped back, "if it wasn't for you, Chandra, and those stupid full moon bonfires you're always building." She fanned her face with one perfectly manicured hand. "The smoke alone is bound to kill somebody one of these days. Add your singing to it—"

"It isn't singing." Chandra was so sure of this, she stomped one Ugg-shod foot. "It's chanting."

"It's annoying," Kate countered.

"And it's getting us nowhere." Me, the voice of reason. "It all comes down to the stupid cat. If you'd just make Jerry Garcia—"

"In the animal kingdom, cats are among the highest beings, intelligence-wise." Need I say that this was Chandra talking? The heat kicked on and blew my way and it was the first I realized she was wearing perfume that smelled like the herbal tea they sold in the head shops around Washington Square Park back in New York.

I wrinkled my nose.

And ruffled Chandra's feathers.

Her eyes narrowed and her voice hardened. "In fact," she said, "the ancient Egyptians—"

"Are dead, mummified, and poohed to dust. Every single one of them," I reminded her and added, just for the sake of a little drama, "they died from the germs because they let their cats pee anywhere they wanted. Like on their neighbor's flowers."

"Oh, yeah?" It was the ultimate in bad comebacks, and yes, I knew better. I swear, I did. I just couldn't help myself. I answered Chandra with a "yeah," of my own.

It should be noted that at this point, Alvin dropped his head on his desk.

I'm convinced he would have kept it right there in the

hopes that when he finally looked up, we'd all be gone, but at that moment, the door to the courtroom opened.

"Oh. I'm sorry. I didn't know you were busy." The woman who poked her head in, then stepped back, looked familiar. Short. Round. Dark hair dusted with silver. I'd been introduced to Marianne Littlejohn, the town librarian and Alvin's better half, at a recent potluck.

Only the evening of the gathering, her eyes weren't puffy and her nose wasn't red. Not like they were now.

"Marianne! What's wrong?" Yes, this would have been a perfect thing for Alvin to say, but it wasn't the magistrate who raced to the door and grabbed Marianne's hands. It was Chandra. She drew Marianne into the room. "Your aura is all messed up."

"It's . . . it's . . ." Now that it was time to explain, Marianne hiccuped over the words. "I've had such terrible news."

Kate checked the time on her phone. "And that's a shame, really, but we need to finish up here. I've got to get over to the winery—"

"And I've got someone coming to repair the stained glass window in my front stairway," I piped in, refusing to be outdone by Miss I'm-So-Important. "So if I could just pay a fine or something, I'll be heading home. And by the way . . ." I hoped Kate could see the wide-eyed, innocent look I shot her from behind my glasses. "I hear the stained glass artist is going to be driving a really big truck."

A head toss from Kate.

A click of the tongue from Chandra.

A whimper from Marianne.

And Alvin was on his feet.

His teeth clenched and his palms flat against his desk, he turned to his wife. "Marianne, honestly, this isn't a good time. We're kind of in the middle of something and—"

"I know. I said I was sorry." She sniffled. "It's just—"

"That we need to finish up," Kate said.

"And get out of here and back to the B and B," I put in.

"Nobody's going anywhere. Not until you women learn to get along!"

In all the weeks I'd been appearing in court thanks to my neighbors' not-so-neighborly complaints, I'd never heard Alvin raise his voice. Now, it ricocheted against the walls like buckshot on a barn door.

We pulled in a collective gasp and as one, took a step back and away from his desk.

Alvin, apparently, was as surprised by his outburst as the rest of us.

"Look what you've reduced me to!" he said, suddenly ashen and shaking like a hoochie-coochie dancer. "I've been doing this job for nearly thirty years and in thirty years of weekend drunks and fighting fishermen and vandals tearing up the mini-golf course . . . in thirty years I've never lost my temper. Now you three . . ."

Since Marianne was standing next to me and sobbing, I can't say for certain, but I think Alvin growled to emphasize his point.

That was right before he pulled in a long breath and let it out slowly. "Maybe what we all need," he said, "is a time-out."

"Great." Kate reached for her Coach bag and slung it over one slim shoulder. "I'm out of here."

"No. That's not what I meant. You're not going anywhere, Kate. Not yet. None of you are." Alvin sat back down and folded his trembling hands together on the desk in front of him, his suddenly flint-hard gaze hopping over each of us before it came to rest on his wife. "You have the floor, honey. Tell us what's going on. That will give us all a chance to take a few deep breaths and get our collective heads back where they belong before we figure out what we're going to do about the problems in Ms. Cartwright, Ms. Wilder, and Ms. Morrisey's neighborhood."

"Okay. Sure." In a perfect mirror image of her husband, Marianne clutched her hands together at her waist. "It's the library. Our funding. We're . . ." A single tear slipped down her cheek. "Oh, Alvin. What are we going to do? We're going to lose Lucy Atwater's grant!"

It goes without saying that this meant something (and apparently something important, from the looks on the faces around me) to everyone but me. Newcomer, remember, and I leaned forward, to remind Marianne that I was there. And I was lost.

"Lucy Atwater," she said, her voice clogged with tears. "She died . . . oh, it must be twenty years ago now. Don't you think, Chandra? Wasn't it the winter Bill Smith over at the hatchery fell into the fish tank and drowned? It must have been right after that, because I remember Lucy telling me how much she missed Bill. They used to date, you know. Well, I'm not exactly sure it could be called dating. But they'd step out together and—"

Alvin cleared his throat.

Marianne gulped and collected herself and the quickly

untangling ends of her story. "When Lucy died, she left the library a chunk of money. It funds most of our programs, but there's a catch. We can only get our yearly payment if we have an ongoing book discussion group. And . . ." Marianne's shoulders rose and fell in a slow-motion shrug. "These days no one's signing up."

"People are too busy," Kate said.

"Yes, of course, that's part of the problem." Marianne dug a tissue out of her purse and touched it to her nose. "There are so many other distractions these days, books aren't high on enough people's lists. The other part of our problem is that there are so many summer visitors here to the island. They don't sign up for programs because they know they're not going to be around long enough to participate more than once or twice. I don't know what to do. I'd hate for kids to come to the island in the summer and stop at the library and . . ." A fresh cascade of tears started and Alvin handed Marianne his handkerchief. She blew her nose. "Wouldn't it just be awful for some poor, sweet child to show up at the library and find it closed?" she wailed.

"It's really too bad," Kate agreed. "Now can we leave?"

In the hope that she was actually right about something, I grabbed my purse.

Chandra didn't move a muscle. That is, until she slipped an arm around Marianne's shoulders. "Of course you're upset. Who wouldn't be!" With her other hand, she grabbed for the denim hobo bag she'd plunked on a nearby chair when she entered the courtroom. She opened it, dug around inside, and came up holding a small glass bottle.

"It's neroli oil," Chandra said, pressing the bottle into Marianne's hand. "Rub it on your solar plexus. You know, right here." She pressed a hand to a spot just under her own stomach. "That's your Manipuri chakra, and remember what we talked about when you came for your last crystal healing, that's the chakra that corresponds to feelings of fear and anxiety, and that's what we need to contend with first before we look for an answer to your problem. No worries," she added, when Marianne gave the bottle a questioning look. "Neroli smells really nice, zesty and spicy with a little flowery note. Go on, Marianne, just pull up your sweater and—"

"Not in my courtroom!" Alvin was on his feet again and one look from him and Marianne blanched and handed the bottle back to Chandra.

With a sigh of epic proportions, Kate dropped into the nearest chair and checked her text messages. "This is a perfect example of everything I've been telling you, Alvin," she said, her fingers flying over the keyboard. "I told you, the woman plays sitar music. Loud. Day in and day out. Chandra's nuts. Do you get what I'm talking about now that you see her in action? Someone needs to do something about the music and the bonfires and the chanting."

"Actually . . ." I stepped back, my weight against one foot, lest Alvin get lost in the moment and forget the real reason we were there. "What someone needs to do something about is Jerry Garcia. That stupid cat—"

"Is nicer than a lot of people I know," Chandra grumbled.

Since she really didn't know me, I didn't take this personally.

Kate dropped her phone back in her purse. "Can we leave now? It's obvious nothing's going to get done. And I don't have time for this nonsense. Just tell Bea here . . ." she cast an icy green glance in my direction, "to cool it with Grand Central Station, and the Good Witch of the North over there . . ." She looked toward Chandra. "To put a sock in it, and—"

"And the cat!" I butted in before Kate could get even more carried away. "Don't forget the freakin' cat!"

Honestly, I hadn't even noticed that there was a thick legal book on Alvin's desk until he picked it up and slammed it back down.

That got our attention. So did his voice. He spoke in what was nearly a whisper, each word so clipped and so precise, there was no doubt that he meant what he said.

"I've had enough. We're going to solve this problem once and for all. And we're going to do it right now."

"Make Bea close her B and B?" Kate asked.

"Make Chandra keep her cat inside?" I countered.

"Make Kate turn off that horrible music?" Chandra retorted.

Alvin banged a fist down on top of the book. "No. None of those things. What you women need to do . . ." His gaze moved from one to the other of us. "What all of you need to do is learn to get along. You're neighbors. Start acting like it. You have to stop talking *at* each other and start talking *to* each other. And I'll tell you what, I'm going to go down in South Bass history, because I'm the one who's going to make sure you do it."

Yeah, I sounded as skeptical as I was feeling when I asked, "You're going to sentence us to talk to each other?"

Alvin's smile was sleek. "I'm going to do you one better than that," he said. "I'm going to make each of you report to the library at seven o'clock, this Monday, and every Monday for the next year. I'm sentencing you three to be a book discussion group."

Marianne's miserable expression morphed into a smile.

Chandra's mouth dropped open.

Kate (do I even need to say it?) rolled her eyes.

Good thing one of us didn't lose her head. "You can't do that," I said. "It's not legal."

"Well, it's not illegal," he told me. "And believe me, it beats all the other things I could do to you. You don't want to find out what those things are."

I had to agree with Alvin there.

But just for the record, that didn't mean I had to like it.

From the looks on their faces, I'm pretty sure Kate and Chandra didn't either, and I left the town hall with a cynical smile on my face, thinking it was the first thing we'd ever agreed on

No, at that point, we didn't think of ourselves as the League of Literary Ladies. Not yet, anyway. I'm pretty sure we didn't think of ourselves as anything but royally pissed, not to mention inconvenienced.

But then, that was before the murder. And the murder? Well, that changed everything.

A new Needlecraft Mystery from *USA Today* bestselling author

MONICA FERRIS

Buttons and Bones

❖ ❖ ❖

Owner of the Crewel World needlework shop and part-time sleuth Betsy Devonshire heads with friends for the Minnesota north woods to renovate an old cabin. But beneath the awful linoleum is something even uglier—a human skeleton. Betsy's investigation leads her to the site of a former German POW camp, a mysterious cro-cheted rug, and an intricately designed pattern of clues to a decades-old crime.

penguin.com

M708T0510

WELL-CRAFTED MYSTERIES
FROM BERKLEY PRIME CRIME

- **Earlene Fowler** Don't miss these Agatha Award–winning quilting mysteries featuring Benni Harper.

- **Monica Ferris** These *USA Today* bestselling Needlecraft Mysteries include free knitting patterns.

- **Laura Childs** Her Scrapbooking Mysteries offer tips to satisfy the most die-hard crafters.

- **Maggie Sefton** These popular Knitting Mysteries come with knitting patterns and recipes.

- **Lucy Lawrence** These brilliant Decoupage Mysteries involve cutouts, glue, and varnish.

- **Elizabeth Lynn Casey** The Southern Sewing Circle Mysteries are filled with friends, southern charm—and murder.

31901051855502

M5G0610